WE ARE THE
SONG

WE ARE THE SONG

CATHERINE BAKEWELL

HOLIDAY HOUSE · NEW YORK

HOLIDAY HOUSE is registered in the U.S. Patent and Trademark Office.

Printed and bound in February 2022 at Maple Press, York, PA, USA.

www.holidayhouse.com

First Edition

1 3 5 7 9 10 8 6 4 2

Library of Congress Cataloging-in-Publication Data

Names: Bakewell, Catherine, author.

Title: We are the song / Catherine Bakewell.

Description: First edition. | New York : Holiday House, [2022] |

Audience: Ages 8-12. | Audience: Grades 4-6. | Summary: In Cadenza
music is power, and twelve-year-old Elissa is one of twelve singers, voices
of the Goddess, who can sing miracles into being and bring healing and
hope to the world—but in the war-torn kingdoms of the world there are
rulers who would like to use her and her song to gain power instead, and
Elissa struggles to understand what the Goddess wants her to do, and
how to protect herself, her composer, Lucio, and Cadenza itself.

Identifiers: LCCN 2021036017 | ISBN 9780823448890 (hardcover)

Subjects: LCSH: Singers—Juvenile fiction. | Songs—Juvenile fiction. |
Magic—Juvenile fiction. | Composers—Juvenile fiction. |
Goddesses—Juvenile fiction. | CYAC: Singers—Fiction. | Songs—Fiction. |
Magic—Fiction. | Composers—Fiction. | Goddesses—Fiction. | Fantasy.

Classification: LCC PZ7.1.B354 We 2022 | DDC [Fic]—dc23

LC record available at https://lccn.loc.gov/2021036017

ISBN: 978-0-8234-4889-0 (hardcover)

To Becca,
who spent her birthday, dandelion, and Point Zéro
wishes to make this book come true

Author's Note

Dear reader,

Growing up, I always clung fast to my love for art. For music. For languages. For story.

Some people may make fun of you for how fast you speak when you get to talk about your favorite book. When you can name the favorite foods of your favorite historical figure. When you smile as you sing.

Never be ashamed of that spark of excitement that burns in you.

Kindle that flame and let it push you forward. Let it light up the dark times of your life.

Whatever your passion is, love it with all you've got.

Someday you may even get to write a book about it.

Love,
Catherine

PS If you think you'd like to listen to some of the music that inspired this story, check out *Atys* by Jean-Baptiste Lully, *Le Nozze de Figaro* and *Così Fan Tutte* by Wolfgang Amadeus Mozart, *La Cenerentola* by Gioachino Rossini, and anything by Eric Whitacre.

Movement One

VERSE ONE

In Cadenza, my homeland, everything is flat and calm, covered in grass and clover.

I used to run through open fields, and Mother and Father would chase after me. We skipped rocks on a lake said to have been made from Caé's joyful tears when She created the world. Cadenza is full of stories like that; stories my parents told me with vigor.

Cadenza got its name from the Goddess, after all—the Place Where Caé Fell. And there were whispers, always, that Caé Herself had been seen there again.

But Lucio and I had been traveling through the kingdom of Basso for two years now, and day by day, we journeyed farther from home. The soft beauty of Cadenza's fields was almost forgotten to me. We were in the Bassan mountains, where the air was thin and crisp and cold. The lakes were frozen over. The grass was gray and trampled.

Worse still, for two years now, war had left scars upon this land as well as my homeland.

Mountains had great chunks missing. Houses had been turned into piles of brick and wood. The forests had been felled, leaving only mangled roots. Debris, broken cannons, and beams from houses dammed up rivers. Wagons were tipped over, wheels missing, wooden panels torn away.

I saw it all from the warped window of our little carriage. So much destruction—but new beauty to be found as well. The sparkling snow that I'd never seen before two years ago; the tall, dark pine trees; the winter birds. Out the window, out beyond the road ahead of us, day faded into lavender evening, with the blue and black of the mountains around us as shards of stained glass.

In the front seat, as always, was my Composer, Maestro Lucio, his white-blond hair pulled into a tight queue with a black ribbon. Most of his face was obscured by a large, bloodred scarf, its loose threads frizzy. My heart always swelled when I saw him wear that scarf—I'd knitted it for him years ago, when we'd first begun to work together at the monastery. It wasn't that long ago, truly, but in my memory we were such little children then.

His gloved fists trembled slightly as they clung tight to the reins of our horse, Melody. Little strands of hair broke free from his queue and whipped in the biting wind, from which I was protected, safe and warm in the carriage.

Lucio sometimes said that the Goddess was proud of us when we endured suffering. But I wasn't certain. When I watched him tremble in the cold, when I watched the destruction outside my window, when I sang for people starving for hope, I didn't feel proud. Just sad.

Out of the corner of my eye, I saw the basket full of provisions we kept hanging on a hook on the wall. The people we sang for donated money and food and clothing to us in return for our miracles. When I pulled back the cover from the basket, though, I realized that even the gifts we'd been given were becoming fewer and fewer. A day-old baguette. A quarter of a wheel of cheese. Three apples. Some cured ham, wrapped tight in paper. It would only last us a day or two, at most. The war was everywhere, touching everything.

With a frown, I chose a big red apple, then darted across the carriage on socked feet. I clambered atop my bed and rapped on the window as a warning before I opened it. Lucio scooted a little more to the left on his bench, and I stuck my arm out to offer him the snack.

"I thought you might be getting hungry," I said above the percussion of Melody's hooves.

He held the reins in one hand and accepted the apple, placing it in his lap. When he pulled the edge of his scarf below his chin, my heart lifted to see his smile. "Thank you, Elissa." His eyes, bright green as the meadows of Cadenza, met mine. A line formed between his eyebrows. "You look troubled. Is something wrong?"

I rested my arm against the windowsill and pressed my cheek against the crook of my arm as if it were a pillow. To our right, bricks were scattered across an empty field, along with the husk of three walls of a house. What little family had called that cottage home? And where were they now?

All of this chaos, simply because the Queen of Acuto and the King of Basso each wanted to claim the lush, beautiful, Goddess-blessed land of Cadenza for themselves.

"I thought the war would end by now," I murmured. "But there seems to be more and more of it, no matter how many miracles we work."

He watched the jagged horizon, his shoulders softening with a sigh. "I feel that way, too, sometimes. Our miracles help people, yes...but surely there is more power in our music than little healing spells."

Those spells didn't feel "little" to me. They still left me weeping as the last bits of Caé's golden magic flowed through me after I sang a holy composition. But I understood Lucio. If Caé wanted the war to end, She could have done so. She could have done so through us. He didn't say this exactly; it would be blasphemous—but I knew what he meant.

"I wish I could see Her," I said. "I wish I could speak to Her, face-to-face."

He laughed, and it cut at me. I was perfectly serious.

"They say if we were to look at Her directly, we'd go blind," he said.

That didn't sound like the Caé I knew, motherly and warm and beautiful. But if anyone knew Her best, it was Lucio. He had come to the monastery in the capital, Cadenza Citadel, when he was just six years old; he'd read all of the literature about the Goddess; he'd studied music theory and learned all the holy songs before I'd ever arrived at the monastery myself. He was the youngest Composer the monastery had ever seen. The other members of Caé's Choir reminded me often how lucky I was to have such a gifted teacher.

But I did sometimes wonder if he was wrong about Caé. Once in a while.

"Couldn't She change Her shape if She wanted?" I asked. "If She wanted to visit the people She loved, surely She would know not to go about blinding people."

Lucio grinned at me over his shoulder. "You could have been a scholar, if you'd been born under a different star."

"Why not a scholar *and* a singer?"

His smile faded away. "You've been given a very special gift. One only twelve people in the whole world have. You must dedicate yourself to being the best at singing that you can be. You have to be obedient to Caé's plan for you."

Caé's plan. It made my stomach sink into my toes.

I was only twelve, Lucio just seventeen. We seemed so young to bear the weight of Her plans for us, never deviating, never questioning. But here we were. Spreading Her miracles. Just like that, the small, shiny idea, *Could I be a scholar, too?* was dismissed. But Lucio knew better. He was right. I was born to sing. My parents had nearly sacrificed everything because of my voice. Nothing else could distract me.

Lucio lifted the apple from his lap, holding it toward me. "Have you eaten yet?"

"No, Maestro, not yet," I murmured. "But it's all right; I'm not hungry just now."

He pointed to the horizon with the apple. At the end of this cold mountain pass, a gray splotch was growing bigger and bigger, clearer and clearer. "How about this—if there's a bakery in town, I'll buy you a pastry."

I sprang from my slouching, sleepy posture so fast I almost hit my head on the top of the carriage's window. "Really?"

He bit into the apple, a sharp sound. "That last composition was complicated, and you sight-read that final arpeggio perfectly on your very first try. I think you deserve a reward."

My mouth began to water as I imagined a treat. I'd practically memorized every pastry there was. Little tarts filled with fruits of every color. Thick slices of pie, topped with clouds of cream. Puff pastries bursting with chocolate, stacked atop one another like the spires of the monastery.

Back in Cadenza, if I was a good girl and did not sing with the others during festivals, Father bought me a roll filled with chocolate.

One day, I sang, and others heard me. I didn't get a pastry that day. It was the day that tore me away from Mother and Father.

I slipped back through the window so only my fingertips clung to the sill. "Thank you," I mumbled, my appetite gone. "Maybe another time."

His voice drifted soft as a breeze through the window, "As you like," and I latched the little door.

}

We steadily approached the gray stone wall surrounding the tiny town.

Lucio drove the carriage to the stables near the town's gate. From the window, I could see a thin horse and another wagon hitched outside, but not much else.

I pulled a deep-brown hood over my blond curls and tied it under my chin. We wore our hair loose in Cadenza, but women in Basso tended to keep their heads covered. Back in the monastery, my fellow Singers and I wore sapphire-blue robes decorated with silver thread: delicate stars and musical notes stitched across a night sky. But when my journey began, I'd traded my fine things for plain clothing that would be unremarkable among the common folk.

On the road, I couldn't dress in the proud blue mantle of a Singer. It was not safe. Lucio said we must be discreet in a world hungry for miracles. We revealed our power only sparingly.

Before I exited the carriage, I took a thin wooden box off Lucio's desk, holding it close as if it were delicate as porcelain and precious as gold. I kept it close to my heart under the folds of my cloak as if it needed to be kept warm, too.

As I stepped outside onto gray stone, the bitter chill that cut at my cheeks made me even more grateful for my woolen cloak and knitted mitts, given to me by worshippers at the border of Basso. We didn't have weather like this in Cadenza. The world was always temperate and green.

Maestro Lucio stood beside the carriage with his arms folded, looking very severe and like a Bassan native in his dark coat and broad-brimmed hat. He even let his hair hang down in soft waves, as was the fashion, instead of tying it back, as he preferred. He handed some coins to a thin man with a thick black beard.

"What brings you to Passaggio?" asked the stableman.

Lucio's bottle-green eyes flitted to me. He took a small, sideways step closer. "We're traveling to the governor's."

The bearded man shook his head. "I'm afraid you won't be able to." He pointed to his left, to the road that led through the town. "The only road onward goes through a tunnel, but not a month ago the Acutians came and bombed it. It's all closed up now."

I looked at Lucio with wide eyes, pressing the hard wooden side of the compositions box tighter to my ribs. We had studied the maps together. There wasn't another way up to the governor's. There wasn't another way *onward*, not one that didn't carve through wild, freezing forests or jagged mountainsides.

Lucio pressed his gloved fingers to his lips, his brows lowered as he thought. He glanced back at the emerald-green carriage, which was achingly bright against the white and gray of snow and stone. "Could you take us to the tunnel?"

The bearded man narrowed his eyes. "Why?"

"We'd like to have a look at it."

The stableman scoffed. "I don't know you, sir." He pointed at our carriage. "I don't know that you aren't an Acutian, loaded up with more gunpowder!"

Lucio sighed. Though the only passersby were several paces away in the town square, he lowered his voice. "I'm a Composer. From Cadenza."

The stableman folded his wiry arms and shot me a glance, one eyebrow raised. "And the girl?"

I waited for Maestro Lucio to speak for me. Sometimes, he said I was a Singer. Other times, I was a servant girl, or his sister, or a lute player. Whichever was safest.

Reaching into the folds of my heavy cloak, I held tight to the little Goddess Eye bead against my heart, offering up a soft prayer to Caé. Mother and Father had asked me never to speak, never to sing. I'd broken that rule, and we all had to pay for it.

Caé, teach me to obey.

"She's a Singer," Lucio said, careful and quiet. He glanced my way, and his mouth curved into a reassuring smile, a smile for *me*, spreading warmth from my head to my toes. *One of twelve in the whole world,* he'd said. *You are special.*

The stableman scoffed. "We've had players come through town before. Asking coin in exchange for their merriment—"

"We aren't performers," said Lucio firmly. "We are mouthpieces of the Goddess."

The man's face grew pale and his arms dropped to his sides. His shoulders slackened.

"I...I will fetch the mayor. She will accompany us to the tunnel. If you are what you say you are...well, Caé knows we need you now." He waved his hand, saying *Come with me.* "Leave your carriage and horse for now."

≀

A crowd had gathered to follow us to the tunnel. They looked much like other Bassans: gray clothes, gray faces, gray eyes. Their hands shook. Their cheeks were sunken in.

"We've been entirely cut off," explained the mayor, a tall woman with orange curls peeking out from under her hood. "Our crops were destroyed by the Acutians, and any aid we once got from the king we can no longer receive, with the road sealed off. All the food we had stockpiled for emergencies...it's dwindling fast."

I followed close at Lucio's heels and kept my fists balled tight. This morning, I had felt the food we had was not enough. But looking at the children carried in their parents' arms along the mountain path, at the old women hobbling onward with tears spilling down their cheeks, I felt an immense pang of regret. I'd easily give up my supper forevermore if I could help feed these people.

I wished I'd put my Goddess Eye in my shoe, so that it could hurt me and remind me of my sins. Instead, I slipped my hand within my cloak again, fishing the long string of my necklace from underneath my itchy woolen scarf. Under the soft fabric of my gloves, I could scarcely feel the shape of the little bead.

"We have seen much destruction in our travels," Lucio told the mayor as we walked.

"I imagine things are worse in Cadenza," she replied, the snow crunching beneath her boots.

My stomach twisted sharply at the thought. I wouldn't know. We had been away so long. Even if I wished it to remain the same, untouched and pristine, I knew it was not.

Years ago, the King of Cadenza had died suddenly—childless. He had a great many cousins and relatives who could have taken his place, but among those, unfortunately, were the royal families of both Basso and Acuto. The two nations tore each other—and Cadenza—apart, each claiming it was *they* who deserved the throne.

"Elissa?"

At the sound of my name, I whipped my head up, my heart galloping.

Lucio tipped his head toward the woman at his side. "Mayor Corde asked you a question."

The woman dipped her head as if she'd been caught doing something shameful. "Oh, I don't want to disturb her. Her voice isn't made for idle chatter, anyhow."

Lucio often warned me of that himself, so that I'd not lose my voice from overuse, but I had so *few* conversations outside the carriage. And I most certainly didn't want to be rude. I moved closer to the two of them, careful to balance the thin wooden box against my left hip. Within were the tools Lucio would use to perform our miracle.

"Please, I don't mind," I said. "What was your question?"

Her eyes crinkled at the corners. "I understand you come from Cadenza."

"Yes, my lady mayor."

"What's it like there?" She smiled wistfully. "I had always wanted to visit. 'The Place Where the Goddess Fell.' Is it true that the birds sing entire arias to Her?"

I nodded eagerly. "That's where our oldest hymns come from." The tunes were ancient and familiar. Mother and Father would take me into the woods, sit beside me on a blanket, and teach me the words to the birds' songs.

"It's beautiful there," I continued, the joy and enthusiasm in my voice decrescendoing little by little as the pain of the memories picked at me. I tried to turn away from the darkness at the back of my mind. "But Cadenza doesn't have snow. I'd never even seen it before I came to Basso. It's beautiful, too."

The mayor laughed gently. "Yes, it's quite pretty. But it can also be a bother. We've had a few roofs cave in from the blizzards. Many families are housed together now." She sighed, her eyes narrowing at the stony side of the mountain. "Sometimes I wonder if Caé is punishing our kingdom."

My brows pinched together. "But why?"

"'Man fathoms not the compositions of the Goddess,'"

said Lucio, the words of a droning, croaking song that I'd never really liked. It was good for setting a broken bone but didn't do much for the spirit.

"Too true, Maestro," the mayor replied.

The gaggle of townspeople pressed closer. There was a massive arch carved into the mountain stone ahead, as a gaping mouth, but debris and boulders filled it from top to bottom.

"Curse the Acutians," growled the stableman a few paces away.

Lucio strode toward the mess, his hand over his mouth as he thought. He glanced back at the mayor.

"If you please," he said, "my Singer and I need a little time. And peace."

Mayor Corde bowed. "Of course." She shepherded the group a minute's walk away from us down the road. All still craned their necks to watch us. A father lifted his son up on his shoulders.

I stood at Lucio's side, unlatching the wooden case. A little wooden desk unfolded itself, along with a tray including parchment, a quill, and ink. I held it steady in my arms for him to write on.

He dipped the quill in the ink, working his lip under his teeth. "A spell to clear the path," he muttered.

"Something *sforzando* to open," I suggested, excitement quickening my words, "and accented notes, as a sudden blow through the rocks."

His eyes met with mine. "Shh, Elissa. I need to concentrate."

I bit my lip. I was a Singer, not a scholar; not a Composer. To ignore Caé's role for me was blasphemous. Mother and Father were in a cell for their blasphemy, held for a steep ransom worth more than I'd ever make from meager donations—and it was all my fault. All because I couldn't shut my mouth.

If I wanted to earn their freedom, I needed to be better. Holier. Like Lucio. I pinched my teeth harder against the inside of my cheek.

Lucio squiggled the clef on the left side of the page. Watching upside down, I marveled as he dotted notes across the staff. Then he paused, thinking again. He scratched out the work he'd done.

Not wanting to distract him with my staring, I looked toward the mountain, the snow coating the rocks like sugar, and toward the woods around us. The still, piercing beauty that Caé had made with a song. What kind of song had it been? Loud and fast? Powerful, earth-shaking? Or quiet, subdued, and coaxing, like a lullaby?

When I turned back to the tunnel, a song started in my head, as clear as if Maestro Lucio had been playing the lute right beside my ear. I could even feel it reverberating in my chest. Bright, loud, rapid, with trills and cadenzas, successions of falling notes, winding like a river. I could almost tap my foot to the song. My throat ached, *yearning* to sing it, to feel that song upon my tongue—

Lucio lifted the paper and shut the lid of the box. He

passed the sheet to me. "Here you are," he said. "Do you have any questions?"

The melody scrawled on the page was efficient, controlled, and did not stray far from its starting point. It was five notes, really—but Caé had created the world with only eight.

I breathed out, expelling the silly, made-up song from my head. *A Singer, not a Composer.* "I'm ready," I told him.

He smiled and lifted the desk from my grasp, folding it closed again. He glanced back at the crowd, still maintaining a respectful distance. "Should we have an audience for our miracle, do you think?"

I nodded eagerly. Some people went a lifetime without seeing Caé's magic. To keep this wonder of the Goddess from them was unthinkable.

My stomach soured at the thought. Hadn't Mother and Father done the same thing when they kept me to themselves?

Lucio fetched the crowd, the crunch of his footsteps waking me from my swirling thoughts. I returned my focus to the music marked on the page and made comments to myself as I read. *Sing this part loudly. Crescendo the phrase here; delicately. Be mindful of that trill.*

The crowd gathered close at my back. Lucio came to stand before me, separating me from the mouth of the tunnel. He lifted his gloved hand and kept his eyes on me. On my inhale, I thought of the first time I'd learned to sing. Longing and happiness intermingled in me; sour and sweet. Mother and Father sang lullabies over me every night. They said I had been fitful one night and that I'd reached for them; reached for their voices. I could barely speak, but I wanted to sing. They sang for me to repeat, call and response, the ancient words that birthed the world, the ancient words I sang now. So simple. Little bricks that could build up a mighty fortress.

Maestro Lucio kept time with the graceful sweeping of his hand through the air, *One, two, three, four.*

When I sang the melody, it was noble, grand; powerful. There was something royal and marchlike about it. The swelling phrases. The steady, authoritative meter. And as I sang, I could feel the presence of the Goddess around me, as sharp and real as the wintry air. My skin prickled like She was standing at my right side. When I took a breath, it felt as if She were breathing, too.

She was why I loved music. When I sang, I was never alone.

Yet as all songs did, this one came to an end. The final note, clear, piercing, resounding, and without vibrato, was long and cold and pointed as a blade.

A deep, low rumbling sounded, like mallets hammering in a steady roll against a drum. Lucio grabbed my arm, and with a crash, the boulders in the cavern fizzled into a fine dust, filling the air and stinging my eyes. As quick as a snap, the feeling of Caé at my shoulder disappeared, just in time for Lucio to pull me close and shield me from the debris in the air. I hid my face against his shoulder and coughed.

The sound of cheering stirred me. I wiped at my eyes and lifted my head.

The pathway was entirely clear—bright daylight streamed through the open tunnel.

A large woman swept me up in a hug. A child kissed my hands. Men clapped Lucio on the back; bowed to him; kissed his knuckles.

The mayor approached the two of us, bending low with her folded hands pressed to her lips. "May the Goddess smile upon you both," she said, her voice soft and strangled with tears. She beamed and touched my shoulder. "We do not have much to give, but please, rest here for the night before you continue on your journey. Anything we have, we will gladly share with you."

They did not have flowers or gold to give—but I knew that every scrap of food they offered was just as precious.

Their praise and their offerings weren't the thing that made my heart quiver. Lucio's gloved hands squeezed against mine.

"Wonderfully done," he whispered, his smile as brilliant as the snow around us. "Caé would be proud of you. I am."

Happiness glowed like an ember in my heart.

VERSE TWO

That night, we left the town hall with our bellies full of stew made from scraps. The Passaggians played music for us; plain music, nothing holy, in the Bassan dialect. Some of their songs weren't even about Caé. Still, something in my spirit lightened as I heard them singing in one voice alongside the strumming of Lucio's lute. Cheerful, swooping songs, some sharp and accompanied by stomps and claps, got men and women dancing and twirling. I spun and spun until I laughed from dizziness.

As we walked back to our carriage, the destruction left by the Acutians glistened in the white moonlight. Toppled buildings. A well that had been dismantled. The bakery windows, shattered and hollow. There were no treats Lucio could have bought me here.

The smile on my face faded away as I gazed upon the brokenness. I trailed after Lucio, faster and faster, a chill sweeping up my back, like something was chasing us.

I'd once cherished being able to see the world. Being able to escape some of the guilt I felt for my parents' fate when I was in my homeland. But gloom was everywhere now.

As we walked across the dirt-paved square in the white darkness, the only thing that brought me a bit of comfort was Lucio humming a song to himself. Hearing his voice kindled a warm hearth-glow in my chest. It was as familiar as the perfume of Cadenzan flowers, or the feel of my blankets swaddling me.

Long ago, it was his singing that first gave me peace when I thought I had none. On my first night at the monastery, I wept and wept and could scarcely sleep. I wandered the halls, restless, and sat in a window, wondering if I could jump out and run far, far away, run until I'd be back in my cottage where I belonged.

A boy appeared, looking almost like an icon with his candle making a golden halo around him.

Why are you crying? he'd asked.

My voice, this thing that was so venerated, trembled and caught. *I fear I'll never see my family again.*

He set down his candle on the floor, brought his lute—the same one he had still—and sat beside me on the sill. I watched in confused, sleepy silence as he plucked out a little tune.

It was an old hymn. The one the birds sang.

Do you remember the words? he'd asked.

I did. I sang them with him as he played again,

**"Mother Caé, e'er enfolding us within Her loving arms,
She protects us, She will bless us, She'll shield us from every harm.**

*Dry our tears, hold us close, keep our loved ones safe and
sound,
Blessed be the kindly Goddess, by the stars forever
crowned."*

That night, his voice had been as calming as any lullaby.
It dried my tears, as the song had said, even with no magic
in the voice that sang it. Those words still rang in my heart
when I grew fitful. They were always in his tones.

He was as dear as a brother might be, and his singing had
always, always comforted me, but now he hated his voice. It
was said that Caé didn't want sacrifice of us, just our songs—
that even songs without magic were precious to Her. But he
felt his voice was simply too poor to please her.

Only the twelve singers in the Holy Choir had the power
to perform miracles with song. I could not understand it;
Caé choosing me over him to have the power that I did. A girl
from a village in the valley, not a boy from Cadenza Citadel?
A girl who wanted to collect flowers, chase birds, roll down
hills, not the boy who'd been raised in the Church, who'd
been raised in music, who'd studied it before he learned his
alphabet?

I skittered closer to Lucio—he always walked too fast for
me—and hummed along with him in harmony. As soon as I
did, he stopped. He bowed his head, striding forward into
the stable. From the key ring on his hip, he unlocked the
large brass lock of the carriage door.

"I'm sorry," I said softly. "I didn't want you to stop."

"Stop what?" The wooden door creaked on its hinges as he held it open for me.

I climbed up the small set of unfolding stairs. "Singing. I like it when you sing. It makes me think of the monastery."

The blush on Lucio's cheeks spread to his ears. He smiled, but it was forced. "That's kind of you." He scuffed one boot against the snow-covered cobblestone. "It's better that I concentrate on my compositions. I'm not meant to be a singer."

My heart fell. He loved music, he studied it day and night, and he smiled so brightly when a composition of his came to life. But even so, Caé had not given him the magic She'd given me. *Why?*

"The mayor invited us to visit her at her town house," he said from the bottom of the steps. "But I think you should rest. You've done so much today."

Relief washed over me. The day had been so loud, so beautiful, so much. To sit by myself and wrap up in a warm blanket seemed better than a dream now.

"But you're still going?" I asked. He was always mindful to be proper, to be correct: accepting an invitation like this was good etiquette.

He nodded. "I'll lock the door and come back in an hour or two. Can you manage on your own? Will you sing a protective spell?"

The lightness in my chest dissipated. "Oh," I said. "Well...

I suppose." I took a match from the little box near the door and lit candles throughout the carriage so that I could see my way and look at Lucio before he left.

In the golden light, the shadows beneath his brows and cheekbones were all the darker. In Cadenza, he would paint his lips gold and his eyelids purple; he wore flowers in his hair; he favored coats of violet and emerald. The style was so severe here. *He* looked so severe; pale and dressed in dark furs. Over time, his warm face had sharpened and grown colder. The soft pink blush on his cheeks from the chill was all the color he had.

I took hold of my Goddess Eye between both hands and pressed it against my heart.

"May Caé guard you on your path," I sang, soft and sweet, despite the commanding, marchlike rhythm of the song. *"May Caé spare you mankind's wrath. May Caé watch you as you sleep. May Caé hush you as you weep. Let it be so."*

The final words, the benediction, were always my favorite part of Her hymns. Descending, landing in a minor key, and then resolving in one last final, peace-giving note. The melody *itself* restored—as Caé Herself would do in fulfilling my prayer.

As the song finished, Lucio smiled, his gloved hand taking mine. "I meant a spell for *you*," he said with a laugh.

My fingers, tingling with cold, squeezed his tight through the thick wool of my mitt. "I'll be all right."

He touched his lips to the back of my mitt.

"Get some rest. I'll be back soon." His eyes glimmered in the lamplight as he shut the door between us.

My body uncoiled as I let out a deep sigh. Something had been bunched up and tense inside me, and being alone—it freed me, somehow.

I untied the hood I wore and tossed it aside, shaking out my curls. Feeling like myself again, I plopped into the blue-painted chair in front of his desk, hunching over and massaging my eyes as he did.

We were never apart, the two of us. Lunches in the sunlit courtyard of the monastery. Studying music theory by candlelight. The time he took me to a shrine in Dal Segno, the spring where Caé had bathed. He'd tutored me day and night. Even without him, whenever I found myself wondering what to do next, I heard answers in his voice:

Say your prayers, Elissa.

Practice your scales.

Rest your voice.

Listen to the Goddess.

When I opened my eyes, I gazed at the blank music sheet on his desk: jet-black lines on white paper like carriage tracks in the snow.

I remembered Lucio's brow furrowing as he composed his spell today. Bombastic, crushing, powerful enough to clear the blocked path.

But I'd had a song, too. A song that still rang in my ears,

falling and sighing and sweeping at the end, a hopeful curve to it, like a question mark.

That song clung to my brain, and I knew it wouldn't let go.

I watched the sheet music on the table. And then my gaze shifted to the little icon of Caé that Lucio kept over his desk. I didn't care for this depiction of Her—Caé the Just. She had a spear in one hand and a set of balanced scales in the other. Her eyes, one all blue, the other brown, were wide and watchful. It was said that She gave one of Her eyes to serve as the moon, always watching over us, protecting us. Her halo of five staves jutted out in spikes behind Her head, more like horns than lines on which music was written.

I unwound my scarf from my throat and pulled on the string of the Goddess Eye, the blue bead tucked safe inside the collar of my gown.

With this little bead, she watched over us.

I held it in front of my face, frowning.

Had she ever looked at me before from this little neck-lace? Had she ever seen me face-to-face—or from the inside of my shoe? Could she really see me now?

"Caé?" I asked her, gazing into the bead. Tiny. Blue. Unembellished. Plain.

Could a goddess, the one powerful enough to create uni-verses, to heal the sick, to tear open mountains, really be hidden in something so small?

That song continued to ring in my head, reverberating as if my skull were a stone cathedral. Along with it came a smaller, atonal voice, Lucio's voice, saying, *Remember your place, remember your place, remember your place.*

He was right. Caé had given me a unique gift—singing—and I should not let myself be distracted by anything else. Our roles in this life were defined for us.

But the song in my head was louder than the voice of his logic. Music was aching to come out of me. My fingers twitched as they pinched the Goddess Eye.

"Just one song," I murmured. "Caé, why would you give me a song if you *didn't* want me to write it down?"

She didn't answer, of course.

I took the Goddess Eye and draped it over the nail that hung the icon of Caé the Just. If I was disobeying Her by writing down this song, at least I'd be doing it out in the open. If this was a sin, I wouldn't hide it.

From Her, anyway. Lucio…maybe.

I dipped the white quill in ink, and within moments, my hand had flown across the page, dotting note after note. It wasn't my own voice that was singing the song in my ear, guiding me, but someone else's, someone I didn't know. The voice was a woman's. Raw, broken at the edges, sliding the notes, but singing them so tenderly, like a lullaby.

Like my mother's voice.

I stopped. Ink blotted against the page. I squeezed my eyes shut and breathed.

Thinking of Mother and Father too long made me horribly sad, but they were always in my mind. Always. So many times, when my eyes started to fill with tears, Lucio would notice, and give my chin a little nudge.

"That's no way for the Voice of the Goddess to be," he'd say. "You're supposed to be joyful."

Somehow, though, that female voice—rising and falling, singing to me—made me write even more. My hand moved faster, more harshly, and it took great effort not to break the nib of the quill, given the intensity with which I punctuated notes upon the page.

Then, my chest heaving, tears sticking to my cheeks, I blinked, and found that the song was done. It ended with the *Let it be so* that I loved, and with that, somehow, everything felt right again. I knew what this song was to be called.

Song of Restoration.

I looked over the page slowly, my eyes following the melody. It was perfect, peaceful, hopeful, simple. So simple. It was so clearly written by a child. But it was lovely, and somehow, it had come from my own mind. I hadn't even studied for years and years as Lucio had. This song, stubborn and small, simply *wanted* to exist. And I was proud of it.

There was a clicking sound and the creaking of the carriage's steps. I gasped, hopped to my feet, and hid the composition behind a stack of books. I stood between the desk and the door, watching and waiting with my heart thrumming at an unhealthy tempo.

The door ticked as it unlocked, and then it drew back.

A woman was standing at the top of the little steps. She

wore a faded brown dress and a fawn-colored cloak and had a gray scarf wrapped around her throat and over her head like a veil. Her face was gray and thin, with round, curious brown eyes. Despite her frailty, she smiled at me, her hand still upon the doorknob.

"Hello, friend," she said, her voice like a sugared cake, warm and light and sweet.

I kept my hands braced against the desk, a chill running over me as the icy wind slipped through the door. Lucio had locked the door—hadn't he?

"Are—are you a friend of Lucio's?"

She nodded, smiling. "I am on a pilgrimage to Cadenza," she said. "I've been traveling for a while and need something to eat. Do you have anything to spare?"

Hanging from the hook near the door was our basket of food—the apples, the cheese, the meat, and the bread.

"Yes," I said, then, thinking of my own belly, full and warm, added, "But there is a party going on in the town hall, down the road that way. They have food and hot cider... the townsfolk have been very generous to us."

The pilgrim's smile faded somewhat. "Oh," she said. She stumbled another step into the carriage, clinging to the door for support. One of her feet was missing a shoe, and was bound in old, bloody bandages over her stocking.

I gasped, clutching at my chest. "You poor thing! You shouldn't walk another step. Shut the door and come, sit here. Rest that foot for a while."

The woman hobbled to the blue chair as I scampered to our basket of food. I gathered it all up and placed it before her on the table. Her dark eyes sparkled as she smiled up at me.

"Thank you," she said.

One of the fingers of her gloves was missing, exposing a pale, shivering finger. Her cheeks, too, were dark pink, and even inside the warmth of the carriage, the pilgrim wrapped her arms around herself.

"It'll only take a minute," I said, "but can I make you some tea?"

She nodded, cradling an apple in her hands. "Only if you'll join me."

"Yes, madam." I carefully held out my hand. "I'm Elissa, by the way. Though I'm sure Lucio's told you before."

She gave my hand a little shake, her eyes crinkling at the corners. "But that's not your first name."

I blinked. She was right, of course—almost every Cadenzan girl was, like me, given our first name in honor of the Goddess. "That's true," I said. "I'm Caé Elissa."

Her smile deepened. When she smiled like this, true and unhindered and warm, her cheeks dimpled on both sides. "Elissa. It means 'friend of the Goddess.' "

My forehead furrowed, and something in my middle twinged. "My parents told me it meant 'promise of the Goddess.' "

"A good friend keeps her promises, doesn't she?" She

batted a hand at the air and took a bite from her apple. "I always get languages mixed up, though."

"And what's your name, madam?"

"Madam," she repeated, her laugh tired and dry as a dusty road. "Few people treat me so formally these days. I'm Caé Veronica. Just Veronica will do."

"It's nice to meet you, Veronica." I turned from her, lifting the kettle off the small table a foot away from her. We kept it filled with snow or water as often as we could, and to my relief, I found it still to be full. As I filled up the tiny metal infuser with our gathered leaves and flowers from the mountains, I said, "What does your name mean, then?"

"'Image of Caé.'" The bread crackled as she ripped off a piece, scattering fine white dust across her lap.

I lifted the little teapot with both hands, cupping the bottom. Then, in a soft voice, like I was murmuring to myself, I sang a spell of warmth.

As with every song, if used too much, it would grow less and less powerful. We'd used this spell many times, and Lucio would soon have to write another. For now, though, I just had to sing it a few times through to feel the smooth ceramic of the teapot start to warm beneath my palms. It was fast, in triple time, in a minor key, scaling up and down and up and down. In my mind, I liked to imagine a couple dancing together, dressed in flame red, twirling, spinning closer and closer to the fast beat of the music.

The heat in my palms stung, making me gasp and nearly

drop the tea. I'd been caught up in the music again. I blushed and took the handle of the pot, pouring the tea into two cups. When I turned to her, a cup in each hand, Veronica was grinning at me, her eyes shimmering.

"You have the gift of the Goddess," she whispered. Her voice was laced with pride.

A shiver rolled down my back. Mother and Father used to say it the same way.

"Yes," I said meekly, setting the cup before her on the table and sitting on the edge of Lucio's bed. "Lucio prefers that I rest my voice unless I'm on the stage, but really, there mustn't be any harm in warming up some tea." Unprompted, I could hear him lecturing in my head. I hid behind the curtain of my hair. "Perhaps it is wrong of me to use a miracle for such a trivial thing."

The warm, excited smile had quickly left the woman's face, replaced by a thin notch between her dark brows. "I have been wandering in the cold for a very long time," she said. "A cup of tea is no trivial thing."

My face burned as hot as the cup in my hands. "I—I didn't mean—"

She hushed me, a soft, lulling sound, like the hiss of the waterfall we'd passed in Allegretto weeks ago.

The light had returned to her eyes. "So," she said, "Caé Elissa, how long have you been out in the world, serving the Goddess with your songs?"

"I came to the monastery at Cadenza Citadel five years

ago, when I'd just turned seven. I studied for three years, and then, when the war began, our teachers sent Lucio and me out to help others. Bassans and Acutians and Cadenzans alike."

Veronica drank her tea and gazed into it. Her long lashes were suddenly decorated with little beads of tears. "You must have seen a great deal of hardship."

We had. Bassan soldiers mutilated by battle. Crops burned to the ground. Forests scored by fire. The houses in this little town, blasted to dust, and the people, thin-faced and empty-bellied. And yet they'd shared so much with us. They'd shown us such generosity and kindness, even after all they'd lost.

Another one of Caé's miracles.

Veronica sighed. "It breaks my heart, this war."

I nodded and then sipped at the tea. "I wish I could do more."

From behind the pale blue of the teacup, Veronica's lips curled in a smirk. "Be careful, saying such things. When you tell the Goddess you'd like more responsibility, She'll give it to you."

"I do, though," I said, leaning forward on the white sheets of the bed. A memory flooded my mind, making my nose sting with the odd, far-off smell of the beeswax candles and orange peels of my childhood home. Mother braiding my hair. Father singing prayers over my life. "The Goddess gave me a gift. And I want to use it. I want to make Her happy.

I want to help people. I want to give them hope again, like today—"

"Why, then, are you ignoring your gift?"

I paused, her words shocking me like a fist striking my breastbone. "I—I'm not. If she wants me to sing, I'll sing—"

"Not your singing, Caé Elissa." She set down the cup of tea, pivoted in her chair, and lifted up the stack of books on the table. Then she pulled out the sheet of music I'd written.

My stomach fell like she'd thrown it through a trapdoor. "Oh, no—I'm not a composer."

"You composed this, though, didn't you?" She winked. "Can't imagine Maestro Lucio would feel the need to hide his music."

"Yes," I admitted, my fingers itching to grab hold of that piece of paper and crumple it into a ball. Forget it existed at all. "I wrote it."

"Then you *are* a composer."

"But it's not—it's not my gift. My *voice* is; you said so." I bowed my head, my heart hammering in my throat. "Please don't tell Maestro Lucio that I wrote that song. I won't do it again. I don't mean to act outside the role Caé gave me—"

"Child," she said, firm but kind, "that song in your head, the song you wrote down—where did it come from?"

I bit my lip. "From Caé, I suppose."

Veronica nodded eagerly, tapping her forehead. "Every song, every work of art, everything beautiful, was first born in the mind of the Goddess Herself." She pointed to me. "If She sees fit to share one of Her songs with you, who are you—and who is Lucio—to say that you cannot write it down?"

I thought of Lucio, of how he carefully scratched each note upon the page. Of the hours he used to spend in the library of the monastery, learning about music theory, sketching out a new song only to throw it away.

Every song he wrote was laborious, painful, purposeful. For me to write one so flippantly and for it to be considered equal... it made my stomach turn.

"I haven't trained like Lucio has," I whispered. "That song, it—it's just a collection of notes."

She flicked the paper, making it crack like a whip, and then brought it to her eyes. "*Song of Restoration.*" Veronica held the music to me. "Sing it for me. Perhaps it will not just be a 'collection of notes.'"

Cautiously, I took the paper in my grasp, glancing from it to her. Did she truly mean to imply that there was *power* in this music, in *my* music?

"I shouldn't," I whispered.

But looking at the woman before me, her bleeding foot, her tired eyes, her hungry, exhausted face, I considered which was more brazen—to sing a song I'd composed, or to possibly withhold a miracle from a woman in need.

"I—I could sing you a different song," I offered, rising from the bed to step toward the trunk of compositions. But Veronica held up a hand.

"I want you to sing this one," she said. There was authority in her voice, unshakable as the teachers' in the monastery.

I wilted back onto the bed. The sheet of music trembled in my hands like the wings of butterflies that flew so freely in Cadenza. I squeezed my eyes shut and swallowed a lump in my throat.

Sing, whispered a voice in my head, a comforting, ageless voice. *It's what you were made to do.*

I squared my shoulders and stared down the piece of paper—such a silly thing to find so fearsome!—and treated it as any other assignment. I pretended it was not my music. That it was not even Lucio's. But that Caé Herself had written it somehow, and had handed it to me, and had asked for a private concert.

My voice came out shaky, soft, pathetic, but it slowly built, as the song did. Gentle, lulling tones, rising and falling, growing and growing, my voice changing from a piercing silver needle to a flood of liquid gold.

Then that gold spilled into the room. A warm, honeylike ray of light poured from my lips. It enveloped the woman's foot, snaked up her body, filled her chest. She sighed and smiled.

"Let it be so," I sang as the final benediction, the only words of the song; and the gold sparkling in the air faded, leaving behind only wisps of dust in the dim candlelight.

Veronica opened her eyes, rimmed with tears. She stood

tall, rolling her foot back and forth, now able to place all her weight upon it. She no longer hunched, no longer hobbled, no longer seemed cold or weary. She held herself as a queen.

"It worked," I whispered, my heart pattering. "*My* song!"

The woman beamed down at me, her soft hands resting against my cheeks. "Remember this day. Remember the power of your song." She looked me in the eyes, hers warm and attentive and watchful. "There is only one voice you must listen to, Caé Elissa. And that is your own."

Without another word, she strode toward the door.

"Wait!" I said. "You are going to Cadenza, you said?"

She turned back to me and nodded.

"If you go there," I said, "my mother and father are in the capital's prison. Giacomo and Iole Marcia. Could you... could you tell them that I am well? And that I miss them?"

It was a foolish, desperate request; my heart ached just making it, and even more so at the sadness in her eyes. It was like she could hear the poisonous, cynical voice in my head, saying, *After five years in jail, are they even still alive?*

"If I see them," Veronica replied, "I will tell them what a marvel their daughter is."

With that, she slipped out the door. When I dashed after her, I took hold of the doorknob, only to find it locked again.

I pressed my back against the door and touched a hand to my forehead.

Lucio *had* locked the carriage. I was sure he had.

He had the only key. How had Veronica entered? How had she locked it again?

Perhaps I was imagining things. Perhaps she was like me, with some sort of magic to her—but no; why couldn't she have healed herself? Why did she need my song?

My song.

Amid the fearsome, troubled haze of my mind, I laughed, clapping a hand over my mouth.

I had made a miracle, not just with my voice, but with notes written by my own hand.

I'd always loved music; I'd always known about its power, siphoned straight from the Goddess. And now? Now I'd *created* it.

I was confused, and afraid, but equally overcome with a rush of excitement, building inside my chest, a crescendo-ing hum. Along with that rhythm, more music began to play in my mind. Descending, gentle bells; a *new* song of healing.

I raced to Lucio's desk.

VERSE THREE

I awoke to the sound of a door creaking open and whistling wind.

The dim candlelight of the carriage burned against my eyes. I glared toward the door through the fog of sleep. Lucio shut and locked the door behind him, carefully unwinding the crimson scarf from around his neck.

"What time is it?" I mumbled.

"Midnight," he whispered. "Go back to sleep."

I closed my eyes, just for a blink. When I opened them again, Lucio had softly padded toward his desk. He frowned at something on the tabletop. A page. He held it before his long nose, his brow scrunching up. "What's this?"

My mind was muddled from sleep; I couldn't remember what was on the paper he held.

And then, memory hit me as fast and bright as lightning. Music. *My* music. A new song, just as powerful as the one that healed Veronica.

"Oh!" I burst out, springing up on my bed. "I wrote some music! And not just silly songs or notes thrown together; it's magical, just as powerful as any of the litanies we sing or any of your compositions!"

He let out a breath, harsh and low, "This is *wrong,* Elissa. Composing is a holy art, reserved only for those who've dedicated their lives studying it. Not singers. Not children."

My face burned and my heart fell. I remembered the light spilling from my lips, the smile upon Veronica's face, the power that was coursing through me just a few hours ago. That was holiness. I knew it well.

"But my song *was* holy," I said, pushing back. "I saw it heal someone."

He looked at the paper and then at me, his eyes widening. "What?"

I held out a hand as if I could grab hold of his attention and keep it. "A friend of yours came to visit a few hours ago. A woman, Caé Veronica? She didn't tell me her last name, but she said she knew you."

Lucio turned pale as snow. The hand holding up the sheet music dropped to his side. "A woman came into the carriage?"

"Yes," I said, my words gaining tempo as I spoke, "she is on a pilgrimage to Cadenza and needed some tea and some food and I gave it to her—"

Lucio turned around, finding the cup of tea leaves on his desk, the crumbs, and our basket of food now empty. He tossed aside my music, ran to the door, and jiggled the locked handle. Then he checked each of the windows, which were all latched shut.

"Lucio, what's wrong?" My voice came out thin and reedy.

He stood before my bed, his hands against my shoulders, his face cold and white as the moon. "Did she hurt you, Elissa? Did she force you to sing for her?"

I had never seen him so afraid before. Not even on the coldest, loneliest nights out here in the mountains. He was always so brave. He always knew what he was doing.

"No, she didn't hurt me, she didn't force me, she—" I stopped myself as I realized something. As the fear in his eyes began to make sense.

And I felt incredibly foolish.

I swallowed down the guilt sitting hard in my throat. "You don't know her, do you? She was a stranger?"

Lucio leaned against the wall of the carriage, pulling his blond hair from his forehead with a deep sigh. "Thank Caé you're safe." He rubbed his fingers against his eyelids. "I'm sorry, I never should have left you alone. It won't happen again. Caé's eye, I'm such a fool."

I curled my arms around my middle. Had she really been a stranger? That glittering moment when I'd done something kind—had it been for someone who could have harmed us?

"She was so gentle," I murmured. "What would she have wanted from me?"

He gasped and dove beneath his desk, pulling out the

round-top lockbox. Using the key on the chain at his hip, he tremulously started to unlock it. Pushing back the lid, he plucked out the gold and silver and copper coins and nestled them in his palm.

It didn't take very long to count them.

The war had taken from everyone. Worshippers were as generous as they could be with their donations of food, of shelter, of coin—but it was still a meager amount.

He tossed the money back in and locked the box with a heavy sigh.

"It's all there," he muttered. He curled his hand around the Goddess Eye hanging from his ear and said a grateful little prayer.

"See?" I whispered. "She didn't steal anything. She was just looking for some warmth. Some kindness. And her foot was injured. I sang her the song I wrote, and it healed her. After that, she went on her way."

He crouched on the floor, sweeping up the discarded sheet music that had been scattered about. His eyes were pale as thin spring leaves as he looked over my music. I couldn't help but lean forward a bit, my heart plucking the strings of my ribs, desperate with hope that he'd perhaps find goodness in my songs.

"Veronica told me that the Goddess gives music to whoever She chooses," I offered quietly. "That She is happy when we create, no matter who we are...?"

"She's wrong, Elissa. You know what we've been taught.

Every person, every note, is precisely placed." He pulled himself to his feet—clad in the nicest, shiniest black boots— and set the sheet music upon his desk. He kept his back to me and lifted the Goddess Eye I'd hung upon the nail. "Are you feeling distant from the Goddess, Elissa?"

I sprang from the bed, swiping the bead from his hand and pressing it to my heart. "No, no. I just put aside the Eye for a while. I'm faithful; all I want to do is serve Her!"

"Then you must listen to me." His voice was cool and soft, but it trembled slightly. "When we left the monastery, I promised Maestro Tenuto that I would protect you. There are so few Singers in this world. And people are hungry for miracles. They will lie to you. They will try to hurt you. They will do whatever they can to have your power in their hands."

His hand rested soft upon my shoulder. "There are twelve recorded Singers in this world," he whispered to me. "Eleven, but then we found you. Hidden away by your parents as a jewel."

I lowered my gaze. Guilt sat like a stone in my chest.

"I worked for years and years to learn to compose. That's the duty Caé gave me, and I want to obey it. You need to obey, too. She asked you to be a Singer, not a Composer. She gave you such an important job." His thumb nudged my chin, making me tip up my head. "She would want you to make your parents proud."

He was right.

It echoed in my head, a discordant refrain: *He is right.*

My parents had ignored Caé's call for my life, had tried to keep me and my voice to themselves. And now I was imitating their selfishness by trying to take on some other role. As if my voice alone weren't good enough! As if I were arrogant enough to claim *I* could compose the songs of the Goddess!

My head pulsed. My heart fluttered. Tears stuck to my cheeks as raindrops on a windowpane.

Lucio placed his hand upon my hair. With the other, he brushed away the tears.

"I know you have a repentant heart," he murmured. "But the Church would be unhappy if they heard you were taking on the role of a composer. They'd see it as prideful. The next time I find you've been composing, I'll have to reduce your wages."

My throat pinched tight. I needed every cent to save Mother and Father—to pay their bond. Risking such a loss, just for putting notes upon a page...it was foolish.

"Maestro," I whispered, my lips trembling, "I meant no evil in that song. And it—it really *did* heal that woman—"

"Caé is merciful," he said. "But She is also wrathful. She likes order. That is why our every song resolves, isn't it? Every note has its role, has its place in Her music. So do you. A very important role."

I bowed my head and pressed my damp eyes against the fur of his coat. "I'm sorry," I said, mostly to Caé. I touched the Goddess Eye to my lips.

"I'll let you prepare for bed. Let us forget about all of this tomorrow." He lightly patted my cheek. "You'll be the Voice of the Goddess. Joyful. Hopeful. You'll show your best face to the governor, won't you?"

The Voice of the Goddess. Joyful. Hopeful. I tried, but it was so hard. My voice was not always happy—it broke with tears, it shook with rage; it showed a whole spectrum of emotion. I knew very well that a goddess was not the same as a mortal, but surely She was like me in that Her voice was not always pleasant and happy—wasn't She?

Still, I nodded, and Lucio smiled, satisfied. He slipped out of the carriage, the door thudding shut behind him, so that I might change for bed.

But unbidden—and almost like an echo—Veronica's words rang through my head. *There is only one voice you should listen to, Caé Elissa—and that is your own.*

And Mother—what had she always said?

When you were born, when you cried, I knew you had been given the gift of the Goddess. That you had a promise put over your life. And that is why we call you Promise of Caé.

Was being a Singer that promise? Was it being a Composer? Was it both? Neither? Why could I write music?

A part of me knew that Lucio was right—that I was prideful; that when I composed, I was playing with the power of a goddess. But another part of me...a new part, faint and fresh...wondered if perhaps tonight's mysterious stranger had spoken wisdom.

Lucio had studied Caé; knew Her teachings; knew Her rules.

I knew less, but I called Her my friend. And Veronica; she'd called me *friend of the Goddess.*

I looked from the icon on his wall—stern, severe, able to spill fire from Her mouth—and then to the icon over my own bed. The icon my family had owned, once.

Caé the Beautiful. She had rich brown skin and dark hair that flowed unbound, in the Cadenzan fashion, adorned in ribbons and flowers. With one hand, she touched the temple of Her own head, and with the other, She touched the ear of a woman. Her holy notes flooded down Caé's arm and into the mind of the woman in the painting. And all the while, Caé was smiling.

I'd barely known Veronica, a stranger, a liar, but somewhere inside, I could hear her voice, see her confident smile as she told me, *If She sees fit to share one of Her songs with you, who are you—and who is Lucio—to say that you cannot write it down?*

There was nothing in that icon to indicate that the woman receiving Caé's song was a scholar, or a queen, or a pauper—she very well could have been a small, wild-haired girl from Cadenza.

With the few minutes I'd been given, I reached into Maestro Lucio's desk, removing a few sheets of paper. I slipped them inside one of my prayer books, and then tucked that book under my thin mattress. When I looked up, all the pictures of Caé nailed to the wall watched me, as well as the eyes of the small, feeble sketch I'd drawn of my parents.

I wondered how much they had changed in these long five years. In my drawings and in my memory, they were frozen in time. I could picture them, sitting at the dinner table, with soup cooking in the hearth and warm bread set on our blue plates, my place empty, waiting for me to return.

When I thought of them, they were alive. I could not allow myself to imagine the alternative.

I wondered, too, if they thought of me, and if I was still seven years old in their imaginations. If they knew that I was alive. That I was in Basso now.

Did they remember me at all?

I brushed my fingertips against their sketched faces, careful not to smudge the charcoal.

If they could see me now, with my own compositions tucked within my mattress, if they knew what I was doing, they would encourage me. I knew they would. They always had, in everything.

They had hidden my music from Caé. Now I would hide my music *for* Caé.

VERSE FOUR

As we drove out of town, the path to the tunnel was lined with Passaggians calling out to us in thanks. They cheered and banged pots and pans as if it were a parade. Despite the cold, I leaned my head out the window and waved farewell to the people. I dearly wished I was an artist, so I could properly draw their faces and remember them, too.

Then I wondered if such a wish was also selfish of me—I already had Caé's gift of singing and *now* this power to compose. Art, too? I drew my hand back and removed my mitt. Clinging to the sharp, cold wood of the windowsill felt like acceptable penance.

After we had driven through the tunnel and on into snowy woods, the road narrowed, guiding us to the governor's mansion. It was made of gray stone, the exact color of the mountains, and had a pointed, jutting roof like the snow-covered peaks, too.

Outside the tall manor—which reminded me a bit of a grave marker in its shape—stood a line of people, the majority of whom shivered in the frigid air. Only one person wore furs: a broad-shouldered man with a gold eight-pointed star pinned to his chest, connected to a strand of Goddess Eyes.

"Come, come! Step down, Maestro—let my stableman take the carriage for you!" boomed the man in a loud, deep voice.

Lucio pulled into the drive and opened the carriage door, holding out his gloved hand to me.

"Are you ready?" he asked with a smile.

Excitement made my stomach do a little flip. A new place. A new host. A *governor,* wanting to see us! Wanting to hear my voice! And the thought of the miracles he'd ask us to do in Caé's name—I could scarcely wait. How many we could help!

With Lucio's help, I descended the small carriage stairs. I kept my hand clenched against the sleeve of his black brocade coat. Standing on my toes, I whispered, "If the governor's taking the carriage to the stables, where will we sleep tonight?"

"Governor Mosso has very generously offered private chambers to both of us," he said. "Don't forget to thank him."

My eyes widened. On our journeys, we very rarely stayed with the wealthy, or even visited with them—if we were not so much in need of food, we would not be at the governor's manor now. Our miracles were for the common, the poor, the sick, and the old. If we didn't sleep in our carriage, we would stay in the meager houses of faithful, generous townspeople, or in the cold, ascetic dormitories of local monasteries.

To have a room to myself! My imagination began to wander. A large, warm bed and perhaps even a hot bath!

I'd only been able to sponge myself down over a washbasin for months and months. I wore a pomander filled with cloves and dried mountain flowers, but more and more, I missed the sweet smells of Cadenzan fields. It never grew cold there: people could bathe and wash their clothes in the brooks, and adorn themselves in all the fresh flowers they liked. Here, with the world bitterly cold, and us unable to wash our clothes in frozen rivers, I feared I'd never smell sweet again.

I did not feel the need to express this to Lucio, who already had to suffer through the less delicate parts of living with me. The trouble of finding a place to use the privy, given the cold. When I woke up and found my sheets bloodied. When I discovered a large red dot on my nose, which he hastily covered up with the powder he used to wear in Cadenza.

Standing before the governor, Lucio looked nothing like the boy I'd always known. Tall and confident and grown-up. Nearly a man. Sometimes in the mornings I'd peek through my curtain and watch him shave his face with a straight razor, a long knife that looked mightily dangerous to me. He never spilled a drop of blood.

Lucio bowed to the governor, and I followed suit with a

curtsy. "Governor Mosso, I am Maestro Lucio Arioso, and this is Caé Elissa, the Voice of the Goddess."

He never introduced me by Marcia, my surname. Perhaps it was because I did not belong to my family anymore, but to Caé. Perhaps it was another way to punish my family for having hidden me from the Church.

The governor, strange in form, like a wooden doll carved to be perilously top-heavy, stooped down, kissing the back of my glove. His hair was long, black, and curly, draping over his shoulders and down his back—some brushed against my hand as he bowed over it. When he stood tall again, he kept his gloved hands around mine.

"It is a great honor to host you both," he said, his gray eyes fixed only on me. "Come in from the cold." The governor turned toward the house, still holding my hand, pulling me forward with unbridled enthusiasm. I smiled back at Lucio, who bit hard on his lip like he was holding back a laugh.

Two men in brocade coats pulled open the set of large double doors, as tall and as broad as our carriage.

The hall within was just as grand, with a rack laden with long-furred coats, and oil-paint portraits of governors past on the blue-gray paneled walls. I stopped in front of one large, square painting, depicting someone familiar to me.

Caé.

She was different, though. She was not wearing any clothes; nothing but Her sheer blue veil from the top of Her head down to Her feet. I'd never seen Her like this before. She played a harp. Her long brown hair tumbled down, covering one of Her exposed, pale-white breasts. Her blue eye and the eight-pointed star on Her forehead were clear indicators of who She was, but it was Her face that seemed so familiar to me. Soft, round features, a rose-pink mouth, a sloping nose like other Cadenzans—like mine. I used to think my nose too big for my face until I saw Caé painted like this; like me.

"Do you like it?" asked the governor.

I wasn't sure. I hadn't seen a woman like this before. I hadn't seen anyone naked before, except for myself. I wondered if Caé was embarrassed to have Herself shown this way—and in the entryway of the governor, no less.

I pointed to the blue Bassan mountains hovering in the background of the painting. "She must be cold," I murmured.

The governor laughed once and took my coat himself, hanging it upon the coatrack.

Lucio joined us in the hall, at my right side. When he saw the painting, his cheeks flushed, and he turned his eyes to the plush, patterned rug.

"I tell you," said the governor in a light, bubbly voice, "I never thought I would be blessed enough to host a Voice of the Goddess!" He turned his silvery eyes from me to Lucio, but they dimmed somewhat. "And one of her Composers, too, of course."

With an open palm pointing down the hall, he said, "I

long to hound the two of you with questions, but it would be quite rude of me to do so without offering you a hot meal. Please, come dine with me."

Following him, I could already smell the foretastes of a good, full lunch—warm meats with rosemary, the sweet sting of spicy apple cider, the saltiness of fresh bread...I could almost feel the crust crackling under my fingers.

Lucio bumped me with his elbow, his eyes squinted with a smile. "Don't eat yourself sick."

I grinned at him. "I've seen how you behave with a plateful of cake, Maestro!"

He winked, and I laughed. Sometimes, if I isolated moments such as these, just a phrase of the song of our lives, one could believe we were truly brother and sister. He was only five years older than I was, though he liked to act as if he were much, much older and wiser. I liked both of us this way. Happy. Teasing. Children. That was what we were, after all—only children, with far too much responsibility draped over our shoulders like a cloak made of lead.

The governor's dining room was small and cozy, but the table bore enough food to feed a dozen. My mouth hung open in a very unseemly way just at the sight of all the food.

A dish full of red sausages, sitting alongside beets and roasted carrots and slices of apples, sprinkled with cinnamon. A roasted duck with glossy, golden skin, adorned with orange slices and herbs like honorific medals and garlands. Bowls of gravy and dishes with stuffing, sprinkled with little dried fruits; several warm baguettes and dishes of butter. Potatoes, whipped and roasted and served a dozen different ways. A massive silver bowl of amber-colored cider, filled with citrus and spices. And lastly, sitting in the center of the table as noble as a crown, was a chocolate cake, decorated with cream, cherries, and—in more chocolate—the curved symbol of the kingdom of Basso.

The governor sat at the far end of the table; Lucio took his place at the opposite end, and I sat in the middle of one of the long sides, looking squarely at the cake. My stomach twisted, and my mouth tingled and watered as if I hadn't eaten in days.

I thought of the people I'd met in Passaggio. Tired-eyed, sunken-cheeked. They'd shared their every scrap with us to give us that final warm meal last night.

It didn't feel quite fair, having such abundance before me.

"It is beautiful, what you artists do," said the governor with a wide, surprisingly white smile. "Going through the world, spreading good."

"It is what the Goddess wants from us," replied Lucio.

Governor Mosso rested his head against the palm of his hand. "Even so, you must miss your homeland. And you're so young! What are your parents doing with you gone?"

"My family work as tailors in the Cadenzan capital. I suspect they've been busier sewing uniforms than court gowns, these days."

Governor Mosso raised an eyebrow at Lucio. "And how

does the son of tailors come to be a Holy Composer? Why not go into the business?"

Lucio meekly bowed his head. "I'm the second son. Mother and Father wanted to honor the Goddess by dedicating me to the Church. Fortunately, I took to music lessons quite well."

"He's the youngest Composer they've ever seen at the monastery!" I chirped.

Lucio blushed the same deep red as his cloth napkin. But the smallest smile crossed his lips. They used to praise him for his youth and his talent back in the monastery. Nowadays I rarely got the chance to boast about him.

"It's no wonder you two were placed together, then," said the governor. "Two prodigies!" He grinned at me. "Are you from Cadenza as well, my dear?"

"Yes, sir. From the countryside." Thinking about home hurt as much as my pangs of hunger.

Eagerness made his eyes glow like little candle flames. "Everyone in the world wants to see Cadenza's fields, especially in this icicle of a kingdom. Won't you tell me about your homeland? Help me imagine it! Is it as holy as they say?"

Lucio spoke up before I could. "Caé's magic is visible in every flower and birdsong. It is a wretched thing to see people tear it apart with their fire and their cannons." He sighed and dragged his finger around the rim of his glass. "There is some purpose in all of this, I suppose. Our lives are simply verses in the great song Caé is writing. She will choose a new ruler in Her own time."

He often spoke like this to me when I had a moment of doubt, of fear. The way he spoke now, though, was less like a comforting friend and more like one of the lecturers in the monastery.

"Yes. Quite." Governor Mosso turned back to me, leaning his head against his fist with an almost dreamy look. "You know, I've met a holy Singer before. Years and years ago, when I was just a boy, another Singer visited my father and sang for us. She went to the rooftop and blessed the whole house, our whole family." He smiled with pride. "She was an alto, I believe. Musetta was her name?"

I lifted my head, my heart twingeing with a memory.

On the first day of the week, the day we honored Caé for creating the world, all twelve Singers gathered in the sanctuary and sang litanies to Her. We were perfect, all of us, when our voices combined. Three basses, three tenors, three altos, three sopranos. It was like we were twelve broken pieces, and when we were together, we'd been fixed back into one.

"She's a dear friend of mine," I said. She was an older woman, beautiful, with deep-brown skin, silver hair, and thoughtful eyes. She didn't speak very much, to save her voice, as we were all instructed to do, but she used to slip me a pastry at the end of rehearsals. "I believe she and her Composer started their journey in southern Cadenza."

"So all of you, all twelve of you—you were scattered to the winds to work marvels?"

Lucio nodded. "In our absence, the Choirmaster spends

her time overseeing Caé's land. And it wasn't safe to keep Caé's treasures in one place, threatened by the war. The decision was to have them go throughout the world spreading miracles."

"Good. Basso has gone without Singers for far too many years." He waved his fork at the two of us. "The king has a court composer, but without the Goddess's voice, it's just light, profane art. The man is monastically trained, but without Singers, his work is nothing."

Something cracked in Lucio's mouth, like he'd found a bone in the piece of meat he'd eaten. He cast his gaze down and brought his napkin to his mouth, likely to spit it out.

"But the king's composer is now on his deathbed," continued the governor. He lifted his glass toward Lucio. "I don't suppose you've considered the position?"

Lucio drew the red napkin from his lips, his face pale and gaunt. "I serve the Church."

"So did Court Composer Spinto. He used the Goddess's gift to bring joy to the King of Basso and his court, even if his songs had no real magic to them. It is a magnificent and noble task nonetheless, isn't it? To please and comfort royal blood? It brought him fame, certainly."

Lucio rested his hand delicately upon the ivory tablecloth, his fingers fluttering as they did upon harpsichord keys. Perhaps he had a song in his head. "It is noble indeed, sir. But as for where we go next, that decision belongs to the Goddess alone."

I swirled my fork through the deep-yellow fluff of potatoes on my plate, my thoughts ebbing and flowing, focus-
ing and refocusing on the men and their conversation.
They spoke on and on of the war and duty and politics—but
staring down at the food on my plate, I could only think of
Veronica, of the mayor of Passaggio, of a girl at the banquet
who gave me a bowl full of berries.

The governor's voice startled me into attention. "Is the
food not to your liking?"

I set down my fork and twisted the cloth napkin in my
fingers. "Oh, no, sir! It's beautiful, all of it."

Governor Mosso pouted. "Why, then, do you look so
unhappy?"

Lucio turned pale as fresh parchment as he looked at me.

"We passed through a town on our travels," I told the
governor. "Passaggio. The people there were starving. The
tunnel that led to your home and to the palace was completely cut off, thanks to an Acutian barrage. Maestro Lucio
and I were able to clear the path, but as I look at all this
abundance, I cannot help but think of the people we met—
the hungry people."

Lucio stammered and said, "S-sir, I—"

The governor cut him off with his hand held aloft. "Maestro, you wanted the Goddess to decide for you. Here She
has!" He turned back to me, his eyes crinkled in the corners. "My dear, I could write to the king asking him urgently
to send provisions to the people of Passaggio and sign it

with my seal. And you and your composer could take it to the palace yourselves."

Hope lifted in my chest, the light, soaring feeling erasing any heaviness hunger had left inside me. "That would be wonderful, Governor Mosso!"

He smiled at me. "In return," he said, "I'd like you to sing for me."

I nodded. "Certainly, sir. We know plenty of Bassan folk songs."

"No, no." Governor Mosso's eyes gleamed with interest as he leaned forward. "I want you to sing me a spell."

It was a strange request. This man wanted for nothing. When we sang, when we wielded the power of the Goddess, it was to help the helpless. To bring them hope, or heal their wounds, or repair what had been broken by war. But Governor Mosso seemed completely undisturbed by war. His table overflowed with food; his house stood tall and proud. He smiled, even now.

"Our—our music is not to entertain," said Lucio softly. His fingers twisted the red fabric of his napkin.

The smile faded fast from Governor Mosso's face. "I'm certain the Goddess would want to bless me with a performance. Why, I'm housing Her servants right now. I am in Her favor. You mustn't withhold holiness from your host!"

Lucio's gaze flitted to me. He pressed his lips tightly together, as he always did when thinking deeply.

"We mean no disrespect, sir," I said, in a small effort to

help Lucio. "It's simply that we only perform when there is a great need for it."

The man touched a hand to his chest. "Why, there *is* a great need—I do not speak for myself! Forgive me, for I was not clear. I speak on behalf of the *Passaggians*! Your magic is powerful; I have read stories of it. If the music of the Goddess can cure wounds and ease a restless spirit, surely by Her music, you can ease the pain of their hunger! After all, it will take another week at the soonest for provisions to be delivered to Passaggio."

"Forgive me," I said, "but—but you intend for us to perform a spell to take away the hunger of all of the people of Passaggio? All the way from here? The pass…"

"You sing for vast crowds of people, surely," he said. He gestured to the two of us, grinning. "You can project. The east side of my house overlooks the lower slopes; you can see the town from my balconies. Sing over it! You have come here for a reason, and who are we to challenge the power of the Goddess?"

His words hung strangely in the air, sharp and unsatisfying; a discordant note.

"W-well said, Governor," Lucio replied gently. "Unfortunately, I do not know of a spell to stave off hunger, so I'm afraid we cannot—"

"You're a Composer, aren't you?" The governor's voice had an icy edge to it. He folded his begemmed fingers and cocked his head. "The Goddess gave you that special gift of

composition, and trained you up in it, and you cannot think
of a way to create a new spell?"

Lucio's face flushed. "No, sir, I could write a new spell, if
it was needed—"

"The people need it," said the governor, jabbing a finger
toward the window, in the direction of the mountain road
and the town beyond. "Caé's eye, why would you withhold
miracles when you have Her very power at your fingertips?
Why would you keep all that glory for yourself?" He raised a
dark brow at Lucio. "Perhaps I was wrong to have welcomed
you here, if you will not act to help my people."

"No!"

Lucio's voice was so loud I flinched. He cleared his throat,
settling back into his chair with the tall posture fit for a Holy
Composer.

"We...we do not wish to displease our generous host,"
said Lucio, looking to me. I nodded furiously.

"Very good," said the governor. He reached his hand
toward Lucio. "If you write that song against hunger, I'll
write a petition to the king."

Something like fear shimmered in Lucio's green eyes. But
he quickly bowed his head and shook the man's hand. "I will
begin writing it immediately, sir."

The governor clapped, his cheeks bright pink from smiling. "Wonderful. After we've dined, I'll let you compose.
How much time would you need?"

"I...I can write the spell within the hour."

I had never seen Lucio so afraid before. He hid it as best he could, with his calm expression and his head held high—but I noticed his fingers trembling as he picked up a golden fork.

Something was wrong about this spell. He felt it, too.

I gazed at the plate before me: the cooling potatoes; the meat that was far too much for me to eat; the large grapes, full to bursting with juice. And my body betrayed me, *ached* to eat.

Alidoro, a baritone in the Goddess's Choir, had once said to me that everything—even unexpected things—was a gift of Hers.

Without this pain of hunger inside me, I'd never know that I needed to eat. Was that a blessing, too? Was this pain a gift?

What would become of Passaggio if I took that away from them?

Verse Five

Lucio had shut the door to his private chamber in an effort to compose in peace. Doors were not something we had the luxury of in the carriage. Nor in the monastery: we were always surrounded by people—students hard at work studying music theory, teachers instructing us in our singing, people coming to listen to our music and pay homage to Caé.

We were apart, only separated by a door, but the distance felt monumental, nonetheless.

I paced back and forth along the carpeted hallway, my hand pressed to my stomach, which twisted beneath the hard boning of my stays. I walked along the staves stitched onto the carpet and thought of music, thought of Caé, thought of the pain in my stomach.

Lucio's spells didn't *always* work. Sometimes he had to rewrite a phrase or two to properly convey the intent of the spell. And as he'd told me before, some things could not be performed with magic. Determining the limits of music had been the study of scholars for generations; Composers wrote songs, gave them to Singers, and if they succeeded, they were written down.

I'd never heard of a spell such as this, a song that would affect a *townful* of people. But the impossibility of it wasn't what concerned me the most. My toes curled inside my slippers, covered in emerald silk—we had dressed in our best packed clothes for the governor. I leaned against the wall, feeling my lungs strain against my stays as I gasped for air.

Why was this different?

With songs, we had dried people's tears and lifted people's sorrows. Alleviating hunger; that was, in a way, the same sort of thing, wasn't it?

But it was taking *away* something. It was like when tears rose up inside me and Lucio said, *"You are not sad, you are the Voice of the Goddess"*—except his words alone didn't make me happy. Even if I smiled for him, I could still be sad underneath.

I imagined speaking to the crowd, saying to them, "You are not hungry," and them *believing* it so—and all the while, their bellies would be just as empty.

Leaning against the wall, I faced dozens of paintings of Caé. Unlike the one in the entryway, She was clothed in these paintings, but in different attire—the dress of a peasant girl from Cadenza; the bright, full-sleeved gown of a Bassan noble; even the dark, wide gowns I'd heard were fashionable in Acuto. In each, She seemed content. Distracted. Too happy to think about listening to prayers.

Still, I took the Goddess Eye from where it dangled against my heart and squeezed it tight in my palm.

"I don't feel right about this," I whispered to the Eye, to the paintings, to Her.

I waited to hear a voice, maybe sounding like Mother, or like myself, or even like a woman I didn't know. A voice that comforted or chastised or advised or *something*—but my mind was quiet. The only sound was the soft whining of Lucio's lute, muffled by the door between us.

I squared my shoulders and turned, pulling at the double doors. They were locked fast. I huffed, a curl fluttering against my forehead. Frowning, I sorted through the repertoire of songs in my head. Something to unlock a door. A melody that was the same forward and backward, like two sides of a keyhole.

There.

Squeezing my eyes shut, I softly sang the melody, not entirely sure if it was made for unlocking doors, or locking them, or simply for opening up a service of worship of Caé. As I sang the final notes, the *Let it be so,* I heard a little click.

My eyes flew open. I pressed my hands against the door handles and shoved my weight against the doors. They fell open with ease.

Lucio sat at a yellow desk, his lute in his lap. His right hand was on the desktop, scratching notes onto paper. His eyes narrowed at the sight of me.

"I swear I locked those doors," he muttered. He tossed back his head, flicking white-blond hair from his forehead.

The Goddess Eye hung from his ear and glowed sapphire blue in the candlelight. "Are you all right?"

I shut the doors behind me and pressed myself against them. "Are you still composing the song for erasing hunger?"

"Yes." He bowed his head over his lute, plucking a note. "And you ought to be warming up your voice."

"This song doesn't sit right with me," I said, twirling my Goddess Eye back and forth between my forefinger and thumb. "I—I don't think I should sing a song like that for the Passaggians. I don't think you should write it. I don't think anyone should."

I closed my hand so tight around the Goddess Eye my knuckles bulged white beneath my skin. I felt like I was in a courtroom. In the portrait gallery of my mind, I could see Mother and Father hand in hand before the tribunal, trying in vain to speak their case before a jury who'd already made up their minds.

"People need hunger to survive," I said softly. "It is a horrible, painful thing, yes, but the Goddess gave it to us. If we did not know hunger, we would not know we'd need to eat. If we never grew tired, we'd never know we needed to sleep. Do you understand?"

Lucio stared back at me, his fingers gently picking at the strings of the lute. "Elissa, it isn't our place to decide something like that. Governor Mosso is...well, a *governor.* He knows better than we do. And he's right: Caé favors him by delivering us to his door. She must be using us through this visit."

My grip on my argument was slipping. It felt less and less to me like I was being the reasonable one. My voice was shrinking. "But what if a person ordered us to do something evil on the Goddess's behalf?"

His fingers gently pressed against the sheet music; the same light touch with which my father would brush curls from my brow.

"We must have faith," Lucio murmured. "It is the Goddess who has brought us this far. And She chose the governor for power and authority. She is good—I don't think She would lead us into wickedness. I believe in Her."

His eyes softened sympathetically. "I know how it feels to doubt," he added gently.

Perhaps that was what this feeling was. Guilt made my blood run hot. It was not my place to question the Goddess. I did not know better than Her. I should not be suspicious of this, if it was Her plan for us.

Do penance, said a small voice inside me. *Sing a song of forgiveness until your voice goes hoarse.*

He reached for me; touched my hand with a small, unconvincing smile. "Who brought us safely through war-torn lands? Who helped clear the tunnel? Who gave us the favor of the governor? Who gave you the breath in your lungs and the ability to sing?"

I knew. Her kind eyes, Her sweet lullabies creating stars above us. I could almost feel the warmth of Her chest against my cheek, and I said to myself, *Caé is too gentle for a spell that could harm people.*

"The Blessed Goddess," I answered.

Lucio nodded. "The two of us, we've been given a very important duty. The governor is right—it's not our place to decide when to make music or when to keep silent. We are servants. Of Caé and Her people. In this case, that's Governor Mosso."

He was right. I looked at the Goddess Eye hanging from his ear, his reminder to listen to Caé.

I was disobedient once. I sang in a crowded square, and my parents were punished for it. They had been disobedient, too. They had strayed from Caé's plan to share me and my gift with the world. It had been good and just that they had been punished; that was what the Choirmaster herself had told me.

Why, then, did that memory feel so *horrible*? And why did this song, this blessing, feel just as wrong? Perhaps there was something wrong with me—with my heart.

Lucio nodded toward the door. "Go warm up your voice," he said. "The song will be ready soon. We'll perform it and make Her proud. I know it."

I nodded, turned, and ducked out of the room and into the corridor, shutting the doors behind me.

My skirts swished as I slumped onto the floor, a pile of

stiff black satin. I closed my eyes and pressed the Goddess Eye hard against my forehead.

"I'm being silly," I whispered. "The spell will do great good. You'll make sure of it."

My stomach turned, my heart leapt, and sweat gathered under my arms. Why was I so *frightened*? Was Lucio right— was I just desperate for prideful control over my own voice?

It's not your own voice, he'd say. *We must not act like we control Caé Herself.*

I didn't *think* I wanted to control Her. But did I? Deep down? Lucio was so smart, so wise, and he often warned against arrogance.

I brushed tears from my cheeks. The portraits of Caé on the wall before me blended and swayed through the film of tears. Caé's familiar face twisted in my vision.

I turned from Her and cried.

{

The mansion's easternmost balcony was a small, flat space like a stage, surrounded by an iron fence. It was lit by orange lanterns, and by their light one could see the faint, jagged line of the mountains around us, including the greatest one, Mount Brio, and its twin over in Acuto, Mount Maestoso.

I thought of how Caé had created the mountains—the peaks grew out of the rising of Her voice and softened into plains and valleys as Her song grew lower and gentler. Cadenza, all meadows and valleys and fields, was assumed to have been sung from a lullaby—and if this was the case, Basso must have been sung as a war hymn: loud, sharp, high notes, accented, accented, accented.

Little flakes of snow twirled through the air and tangled themselves in my curls and my eyelashes. I stood at the edge of the balcony, watching the snowflakes drift down, down below. My belly swooped. It was so far down I couldn't even see the grounds of the manor. I couldn't see the road through the pine forest.

And then, a glowing ember amid the black-and-blue horizon, I spotted a village.

Passaggio.

Lucio's heels tapped against the slate of the balcony as he joined me at the iron fence. He stood at my side, cradling his music, and then held it out for me.

"Tell me if you have any questions," he murmured.

A knot tied itself in my throat. I touched the sore spot and looked upon the yellowed page of sheet music. Instead of *solfège*, the words of the song were written again and again: *To the people of Passaggio, to the people of Passaggio.* The melody played itself in my mind: slow, but growing; swelling; a gentle trickle of notes that eventually built to three notes repeated *fortissimo*, three notes over and over, like a bird's call.

C-A-E.

Her name, again and again. Asking for Her help.

Even the *Let it be so* was *fortissimo*. Conviction was written in every note; I could see the last note spattered with drops of ink as if Lucio had stabbed at the page with his quill.

"Do you have it?" he asked.

He wanted me to sing this. The governor did. Perhaps Caé did, too.

Why was my heart, my voice, my whole *body* revolting against this?

"Are you sure about this?" I whispered to him.

Lucio pressed his lips together. He inched closer, his hand lighting on my shoulder. "We must have faith," he whispered back.

He was right. My heart was foolish and rebellious. It always was. I couldn't trust myself—I needed to trust *Her*.

I nodded and took the songbook from him, as gently as if it were an infant.

Lucio tossed his hair over his shoulder and looked at the governor. "It's time, sir."

The governor, dressed in furs and in a shimmering smile, pressed his gloved hands tight against his breast, his eyes wide and glowing as orbs in the lamplight.

Lucio pointed over my shoulder. "Elissa, I want you to direct yourself toward them and think solely of them. Remember their faces. The food we ate with them. The sounds of their voices."

It all made my stomach roil even more.

My legs wobbled as I stepped forward, so that Lucio stood off-center between Passaggio and me. I stared at the village beyond, with him in my peripheral vision. He held out one hand and used the other to keep time.

I sang.

All of Lucio's songs were lovely and majestic; this one was no different. But my mind was so muddled. One voice in my head was reminding me about vocal technique, to lift the soft palate, to raise my brows to sharpen that note, to breathe from my stomach and not to be so nervous. Another marveled at the piercing, arcing sound of my own voice, this gift of Caé. And a third still continued to war over whether this spell could do harm, and whether it was even possible for a goddess, pure and perfect, to do something wicked, even tangentially.

When I sang, I always felt Caé with me. Her presence was always so palpable and marvelous and arresting that it took great strength to keep from crying. Singing was holding tight to a thin thread, and when I lost my breath, I could lose my grip on the song altogether.

Now, as I sang notes infused with Caé's holy power, Her presence felt less pronounced. She was not at my side, Her hand upon the space between my shoulder blades, the flowery smell of Her breath filling the air. As I sang this song, my eyes on Passaggio, the hairs on the back of my neck prickled. She was farther away from me, standing, doing nothing, saying nothing. Watching the performance as the governor had.

I waited for Her. I carried the melody, the filling, growing notes, over the sloping mountains and into the village, and I *waited*. I waited for a bolt of lightning—Her telling us *No, don't do this!* Or for the song to break out from under me, for the *roof* to break from underneath us.

She was all-powerful, and yet as I stood, doing something I was sure would cause ruin, I felt her standing silently mere paces away from me.

Say something!

Out of the corner of my eye, Lucio directed. The final *fermata*, and then carefully dropping his hand. I sang the *Let it be so*, four loud, accented notes, like tolling bells.

My voice bounced through the cold night and through the Bassan mountains. Lucio's hands fell delicately to his sides.

"*Brava!*" bellowed the governor, clapping his hands *pizzicato*. Tears beaded in his eyes, and he grinned so broadly it nearly took up his whole face.

No one else stood on the balcony, apart from the three of us.

Movement Two

VERSE SIX

The dawn was gray and stiflingly quiet as we left the governor's mansion. Lucio expertly performed the dance of acting as a courtly gentleman: bowing and complimenting our host and thanking him profusely. But there was no light in his eyes, not like there should be after we made music together. After a song, the joy of Caé's music should linger with us even to the next day.

Not this time. There was only silence around us now, clinging to us even as we drove from the governor's mansion. Neither of us wanted to speak of what had happened. Neither of us could.

As we drove closer and closer to the palace of Basso, carrying the governor's petition to supply the people of Passaggio with food, my stomach kept sinking within me as if I were falling down a dark, dark pit.

The day passed slowly. The soft thump and crunch of Melody's hooves on gravel and snow changed to a loud, rhythmic clopping. The sound of cobblestone, like the sound of the horses in Cadenza Citadel.

We had reached the edge of the king's estate.

Out the window, the Bassan palace was vast: white, with windows one after another in neat little rows, three stories' worth, the building stretching from one end of the horizon to the other. Our carriage was small and meager and *pianissimo* compared to this palace, as majestic and mighty as the rare, fond moments when the voices of the Choir sang in unison.

My mouth fell open as I watched it grow closer—I felt a strange blend of awe and fear. I longed to poke my head out the window and tell Lucio about this, to ask him everything he knew about this place—but we had not spoken much. Not today.

I turned my head away from the bright light bouncing off the windows, off the sparkling snow on the hipped roof. The notes of Lucio's song against hunger ricocheted through my brain, off-key and sharp like screams. I pulled my knees tight to my chest and wrapped myself in my blanket, trying to smother dread as it rose in me like nausea.

My hair still smelled sweet from the oils and perfumes the maids had given me for my bath in the governor's mansion. Lavender soap, oils from lilies, rose petals: all of that must have been imported from afar—from Cadenza. The sweet scents did not help the curdling in my stomach.

To my left was my wall of drawings. Mother, with her gentle smile. Father, with his laughing eyes. Caé the Beautiful, so serene, so at ease, as if nothing in the world could trouble Her.

But *I* was so troubled. The thought that my actions, my voice, could have harmed anyone...my blood became icy water.

I could not say any of this to Lucio, even though he was tense and silent. He'd only insist I was being anxious over nothing. That Caé was faithful and just and that She gave him good songs to do good things.

From underneath my swaddling of blankets, I withdrew the Goddess Eye from where it hung around my neck. I pressed the cold glass against my lips.

Is it me? I prayed. *Am I not trusting enough?*

But I *did* trust the Goddess, down to my marrow. She'd given us shelter time after time as we traveled. We never were far from a kind and hospitable person, even in the most barren, unforgiving lands. Cobblers and weavers and candlemakers would open their doors to us, sometimes even before learning who we served. Caé was good; abundantly so.

This song Lucio and I had made together, this spell we had cast...I knew just as deeply that it was wrong.

The carriage slowed to a stop. Voices sounded around the walls of the carriage, deep and gruff.

"What brings you here, sir?" a man asked Lucio.

"I am sent here by Governor Mosso to petition the king. We have two letters for His Majesty."

The message rolled off his tongue so cleanly, like he was some ruler giving a speech to a crowd of thousands. I wished I could do that. I could sing in front of anyone, but if I was asked to speak confidently—I'd faint from fright.

"Here," said Lucio. "He also gave me this notice so that we could enter."

There was a pause. Then something loud and metallic clattered against the cobblestones.

"This—this says that you are a Holy Composer? And that one of Her Voices is with you as well?"

"Yes."

I turned around, kneeling on my bed and cautiously peering out the window. Over Lucio's shoulder was a clean-shaven man with long dark curls, his eyes wide—the unmistakable look of awe and surprise that I'd seen over and over. The man wore a deep-blue uniform with gold epaulettes and a tricorne hat with feathers—a soldier. And even so, he was flustered to be in *our* presence.

"Open the way!" cried the soldier, and with that, other soldiers in blue drew back the doors of the long, golden gates, brilliant and shimmering as rays of sunlight.

In my life as a Singer, I'd met many people. But never a king.

Men in matching silver furs took the carriage and Melody to the stables. All of my possessions—my clothes, my portraits of Caé and my parents, even the pieces of parchment I'd stolen from Lucio—were locked in a trunk and carried to a guest chamber. Lucio and I were left waiting in a long antechamber to be received by the King of Basso.

The inside of the castle reminded me in many ways of the monastery: curved, soaring ceilings, made mostly of stone (although I doubted this was for acoustic reasons, as it had been in Cadenza). Here, though, every ceiling was painted with a marvelous scene. The brilliant oranges and golds of sunrises. The soft blue of Bassan mountains. The magnificent night-sky robes of Caé Herself, Her hand stretched out over the mountains, over the fields and the little villages. In the paintings, the world was so green. It was summertime there. I wished to jump inside—to feel that warm sunshine, to smell fresh grass again.

Lucio's elbow nudged me in the ribs. "Careful," he said with a grin. "You'll hurt your neck if you gawk like that all day."

It didn't feel right to tease or to smile. Not after our last song. How could he still find lightness? How could he think I could laugh as easily as I did before?

"Lucio," I murmured. "About…about the governor's song…"

A shadow seemed to pass over his face. He gave my shoulder a firm squeeze. "It's done now," he said. "We shouldn't dwell on it."

"But I feel so—"

"Have faith in the Goddess, Elissa." His voice was so fervent, so desperate. Like he wanted to believe in his words as much as I did. "Let us leave it in the past."

But my insides still twisted themselves in knots. Not

because of him, but because of the notes of that song. Because of the governor. Because of the thought of the kind people of Passaggio crying out in pain.

I dug my fingernails into my palms, trying to leave it behind, as he said. Dwelling on it was keeping us from the present, from our mission. More importantly, it was making me doubt Caé. I held fast to Lucio's arm and marched forward with him to the end of the corridor.

Don't look back, I thought. *Obey. Obey. Obey.*

We stopped a few paces from a set of menacing, ceiling-high double doors. Lucio patted my hand. I hadn't noticed how much I was shaking until he gripped my fingers, steadying me.

When the world spun, he was there to anchor me. But things still felt crooked.

"Why are you nervous?" he whispered, his smile reassuring and familiar.

Because I *couldn't* put the song behind me. But this pain, this fear inside me, it was a note too low for him to comprehend, to hear. I kept silent.

"Is it the thought of meeting a king?" Lucio asked. His hand squeezed mine. "You are very important. Don't you realize that? People tremble in their boots thinking of meeting *you*. Why, I'm certain when the king meets us, he'll faint from sheer veneration."

A few days ago, I would have laughed. My chest felt so cold, so hollow.

Lucio nudged me. "Remember: there is *nothing* to fear here. This journey of ours, it's practically *impossible*—who would have thought two children from Cadenza would reach the throne of the King of Basso, whole and unharmed? It is only by Caé's blessing that we are here. Everything to come, it is all as She ordained it to be. We need only trust Her." He smiled, and then, in a low, almost timid voice, sang a verse of that old song he used to sing for me, *"She protects us, She will bless us, She'll shield us from every harm…"*

That used to comfort me so. Now, I wondered if Caé *would* shield the people of Passaggio from harm. If Her very music was capable of harming, then…?

"We have nothing to fear," Lucio repeated.

I wasn't so certain. My stomach cramped even tighter, as if an iron glove were gripping it.

A guard at the door, a young man wearing black from his tricorne hat to his stockings, stepped forward.

"Whom do I have the pleasure of announcing?" he asked.

"Maestro Lucio Arioso, a Composer from Cadenza Citadel—and this is Caé Elissa, the Voice of the Blessed Goddess."

The boy's mouth popped open. He threw himself into a bow, his hat flying off his head, exposing bright-orange hair. My brows rose. Lucio was right. People *were* intimidated by me, even those in the king's household.

"Forgive me," the young guard peeped, sweeping up his hat. "It is an honor."

"What's your name?" I asked.

The boy paused, wide-eyed. He looked from one of us to the other, as if we held the answer. "Rodolfo," he finally murmured. He bowed to me again, his hand trembling as he clung to the hat. "My lady."

My lady. I was only a girl; the title fit as a pair of shoes that were too big for me.

Rodolfo knocked his knuckles upon the deep-brown wood of the door ten times his height. It was swung open by unseen attendants on the other side. He turned on his heel and took us into the next chamber.

My heart galloped in my chest. The walls of the room were of brown marble, capped in golden trim, leading up to another painted ceiling, this one of Caé in the sky, her robe made of shimmering stars, gold and silver, a glimmering white moon held in her right hand. The eye she'd given to watch over us.

Below, before a gilded hearth with a roaring fire, two golden thrones sat side by side. One was empty. But in the other sat a man with long reddish curls spiraling over his shoulders. His coat was the deep green of emeralds, with frills of perfectly white lace at his sleeves and cravat. He furrowed his brow as he listened to another man in a deep-red coat read aloud from a scroll. With my simple brown hood and my gown the color of ash, I felt horribly plain before them.

As we walked across the long red carpet toward the

throne, Rodolfo halted us with a hand. He didn't move until the man on the throne—the king—lifted his head.

My heart didn't thump so furiously as it had before. The king was *so* young. His eyes were wide, watchful, his face clean-shaven, unlike the men in rural Basso with their thick beards. He was no more fearsome than I was.

The king held up a finger to silence the man reading from the scroll. The man bowed and scuttled backward into a gaggle of other colorfully dressed men, who whispered and peered at us as a flock of bright birds.

"Maestro Lucio Arioso, Composer of Cadenza Citadel, and the Voice of the Goddess, Caé Elissa," announced Rodolfo.

"Blessed be the Goddess," murmured the king. This was often said as a reflex; you said it when you greeted someone, or when it rained after a long drought, but when the king said it now, his voice quavered. He wobbled to his feet, clad in golden shoes with frills and bows and heels as red as blood.

I wanted to know why a king should look so sad.

Rodolfo swooped into a bow. Lucio gracefully mimicked the gesture, and I dipped into a curtsy, doing my best to keep my head lowered.

"Rise," said the king breathlessly.

The king strode across the chamber until he stood before us. He swept up Lucio's hands, kissing them, and then repeated the gesture with me. When he looked into my eyes, his were full of tears.

"My prayers have been answered," he said.

"Sire?" asked Lucio.

The king touched his neck—no, he had a chain of Goddess Eyes there, and clenched them in his fist. "The Goddess's servant, the court composer, passed away in the night. And worse, there's—" The king paused, took a slow breath, stood taller. "Composer, you will prepare a blessing for the health of the entire palace. But first, you are both asked to perform a song of healing for Her Majesty." The king flicked his blue eyes toward Rodolfo. "Fetch her chief lady-in-waiting at once." With his chin held high, I could see now why he made a perfect king. There was fire in his eyes, and surety in every inch of him.

Rodolfo bowed and exited through the door by which we'd entered.

"Your Majesty," said Lucio in a soft, courtly voice, sweeping his arm in a second bow, "we will attend to your wishes immediately."

The king's brow smoothed out somewhat and his shoulders did not sit so squarely anymore.

"Is it your mother who is ill?" I asked, for he'd said only *Her Majesty*.

The king smiled halfheartedly. "No, it is my wife who needs Caé's help today. She is in poor health. What's more, she's with child. You understand the fragility of her situation."

The young man before me was, for a moment, not a

king, but just a boy, just a person about to become a father. Someone who held unimaginable power, but in the face of an unknown and dangerous event, the birth of his child, was rendered frightened and helpless. My heart twinged with pity.

"Yes, Sire," I said. "We understand."

He exhaled and shook his head, setting his shoulders straight once more. "Caé brought you here to us. She cares for us in all things, and in hunger and in sadness and in pain."

The word *hunger* reminded me of the song I'd sung on the governor's roof. Of the envelope tucked into the satchel on my hip. I gasped in realization and pulled out the letter.

"Here, Your Majesty! Please. A letter from Governor Mosso."

The king accepted the letter, quirking an eyebrow as he held it. "Concerning?"

"There is a town called Passaggio that greatly suffered from an Acutian bombardment," I said. "They are in dire need of provisions. They're...they're starving." My heart fell at this. Because of Caé's spell—my spell—they were not actively suffering, or so I prayed. But I could not vouch for their current state. I did not wish to tell the king of what I'd done, even if all turned out to be well; even if my magic, Her magic, somehow saved them all.

The king nodded, tapping the envelope against his heart. "I will have supplies sent to Passaggio at once."

To think that hunger could be so easily relieved—that with a wave of his hand, the king could procure enough food to provide for a whole town, even in the midst of war. It was like its own kind of magic. I sighed with relief and bowed my head. "Thank you, Sire."

Glancing at Lucio, I found him with his lips pursed, as if he'd tasted something sour.

"Maestro Lucio has a letter for you as well," I told the king. I had seen the governor give it to him that morning, after he had handed me the petition for Passaggio. I did not know what it was, but I knew it was for the king—it was addressed to him, and sealed with the finest red wax.

Lucio's eyes widened and his jaw tightened. Caé did not grant me the power to read thoughts, but sometimes, I felt as though I could: Lucio had a lecture for me on the tip of his tongue.

"Is that so?" asked the king. He pressed his lips together, amused. "I did not realize the servants of the Goddess also served as couriers."

Lucio bent over, long strands of white-blond hair falling out of his queue as he bowed. "I did not want to impose upon His Majesty so soon after our arrival," he said, his voice clipped, the tone aimed straight at me. A lump formed in my throat. Had I been rude?

His Majesty held out a free hand. My maestro sighed, reached into the breast pocket of his coat, and handed an envelope to the king.

The king rubbed his begemmed finger across the deep-red seal on the envelope. "Do you know what this note concerns? Is there more trouble in my kingdom that I've not yet heard of?"

Lucio kept his head low and his gaze to the floor. "No, Sire. Governor Mosso only instructed me to deliver it to you."

The king waved his hand back toward the clutch of murmuring courtiers beside the empty thrones. A boy dressed in black, like Rodolfo, approached with a silver tray, upon which was a letter opener with rubies on the handle. The king flicked his wrist and sliced open the envelope, muttering, "Why, now you've got me curious."

He read. Lucio and I shared a quick, confused look.

The king's forehead creased as he read, and he emitted a low, thoughtful hum.

"What is it?" I asked.

Lucio hissed my name, and I demurred, holding my hand against my mouth to silence myself. I imagined living inside the little box of a whole rest on a sheet of music, beat after beat of silence.

The king dropped the two notes on the silver tray. "The governor made a recommendation to me. Whether I will agree with him on his suggestion remains to be seen."

He clapped his hands together as if he'd been working hard and had gotten dust all over himself. Raising his eyebrows, he nodded once.

Then he looked past us. Turning, I saw an older woman with her hair unbound, curled, and adorned with pearls. Her gown was yellow as a buttercup, and cut low, showing off her bare shoulders. Her satin skirts puddled around her as she curtsied.

"I'm here to escort you to the queen," said the woman.

Lucio bowed to the king yet again. "Thank you for your audience, Sire."

The king held up a hand. "You need not thank me just yet, Maestro. I'm coming with you."

VERSE SEVEN

The queen's bedchamber was filled with light. Her gossamer curtains were parted, letting sunshine stream through the flawless panes of glass. The air was thick with the perfume of flowers, great clouds of blossoms in bouquets covering every surface. And they weren't just the petite alpine flowers that dotted the cold, barren mountains, but also the large, colorful plants that grew in Cadenza. Red poppies; wild orchids; crown vetch; many, many others. I stood beside a glass vase and ran my fingers along the petals of a fluffy pink flower.

They were called Giacomo flowers. My father's name. Mother used to make crowns of them and drape them across his brow or hide them in his beard. He looked at her with such love. I didn't even mind when they kissed in front of me.

Giacomo flowers. Mother and Father holding hands. And then, the two of them before the tribunal, still looking at each other as if they were the source of all the light in the world.

Heretics, the Church had called them. They'd kept me, my voice, Caé's gift, from the world.

I couldn't do the same. If the queen needed help, I must help her.

I followed the king, Lucio, and the lady-in-waiting to a massive white bed, crowned in gauzy white bedcurtains and boughs of more fresh flowers.

A beautiful dark-skinned woman lay there, and though she only wore a shift to sleep in, I could tell she was a queen just by the look of her. Her lips were plump and unpainted, as perfect as a portrait of Caé. Her long lashes brushed against her cheekbones, prominent and the color of onyx. Her raven-colored hair cascaded in ordered waves down her shoulders and splayed across her pillow. There was even something refined about the swell of her belly underneath the white sheets.

The king approached the bed, kneeling beside it. He looked at his queen as if she were divine. He looked at her as Father and Mother looked at each other.

Are Father and Mother together still? I wondered. *Do they share a prison cell?*

The king clutched his wife's hand. "My darling, I've brought you a gift."

The queen's eyelids fluttered open. Her cheek dimpled with a smile. "I do hope it's flowers," she said, her voice soft and lovely as the sheer fabric fluttering around her bed.

"Not quite." He brushed his thumb against her cheek and then pointed to Lucio and me, standing at the foot of her bed. We each bowed to her. "I've brought you a Singer."

Her eyes crinkled in a sleepy smile at Maestro Lucio. "What will you sing for me, sir? A folk song? Something from Acuto, I pray?"

With a start, I remembered that the queen herself was Acutian. I had heard the talk, hadn't I? Before the Cadenzan king died, she had been married to King Massimo in an effort to unite Basso and Acuto. But still the war came. Still they tore each other—and Cadenza—apart. Still none could agree on who held the right to claim Cadenza: *this* king, *that* queen, *this* nobleman, *that* nobleman, Bassans, Acutians...

I wonder if she yearned for her home as much as I did for mine.

The king brushed little hairs from her forehead. "The boy isn't a Singer—he's a Composer from the monastery in the Cadenzan capital." He gestured to me with an open palm. "And this girl is not just a traveling player. She is one of the Voices of the Goddess."

The queen sat up against the massive stack of goose feather pillows behind her. "But you're just a child!"

I blushed—she was right, of course, but it was a flaw I could not control. Sometimes my youth was seen as something marvelous, other times as an annoyance. The queen seemed more astounded than frustrated.

"I don't know any songs from Acuto, my lady," I told her softly.

The queen's black eyes shimmered as sunlit water. "I can teach you some. I had prayed that someone would sing the lullabies of my people over my baby, when she is born. Now that you're here, you're proof to us of the goodness of the Goddess, even in hardship. You can be here to sing blessings over our baby every day of her life."

I winced, sharing an unsure glance with Lucio. "We—we are only here for a short time," I began, bowing my head as if the respectful gesture would take away the sting of the words. "The monastery wishes for us to share miracles with everyone."

Lucio grimaced but kept his mouth shut.

The king patted his wife's hand. "If the Goddess's Voice can heal you, my dear, and if these two please you, they may stay as long as you wish them to."

The queen clapped delightedly, but paused: her shoulders began to quake, and she struggled with a loud, heavy cough. Wincing, she slumped against her wall of pillows. A lady in pink scuttled to the bed to press a washcloth to the queen's cheek.

"Go on," said the king, waving a hand at us. "A song of healing, please."

Lucio opened his mouth to speak, but then seemed to have second thoughts, and instead licked his lips. He turned to me, stooping down so as to whisper in my ear.

"You'll have to perform without accompaniment and without music," he muttered. "What do you have memorized?"

Dozens of litanies, and of course, the little cheerfulness

spells we sang over crowd after crowd. A song of healing, though—one in particular was stuck in my head, from the time I woke up to when I laid my head down again.

My song.

The smile on Veronica's face. The light in her eyes. The warmth in my chest. Her gait, healthy and confident once more.

A voice echoed through my mind, a voice that was a stranger's—and yet utterly familiar. I gasped at its volume as it shouted at me, commanded me: *Sing it!*

Lucio touched my arm. "What?"

If he knew this song was my own, he'd forbid me from singing it. But the queen, with the child in her womb and the sweat on her brow and her horrid cough—it wasn't fair for me to withhold my song from her, no matter what Lucio said.

"I know what to sing," I whispered.

"What's the title?"

"*Song of Restoration.*"

His pale forehead scrunched together. "Who's the composer?"

"Unknown," I said, the lie slipping easily off my tongue despite the dryness in my throat.

Lucio grimaced, dropping his hands to his sides with a thump. "How am I to conduct you, then?"

"You don't have to."

His pressed lips, the concern in his eyes, the way his

fingers twitched, I found it all quite endearing in that moment. In all things, he always wanted to give his very best. It was the same reason it took him draft after draft to write a song—he wanted everything to be perfect.

And this song would be.

"All right," he said, nodding. "I know you'll do wonderfully."

The comfort of his praise filled me and gave me the strength to step closer to the queen, to prepare to sing for a monarch. I pressed one hand against my stomach to help me concentrate on my breath. With the other hand, I guided myself—for it was my song.

As my composition spilled from my lips, my hand danced through the air as if I were painting. For long, steady phrases, it cut a straight line before me. My fingers curled into a fist for the soothing, grounding low notes at the quiet parts of the song.

At my core—right where my breath came from—I wondered if the song would only be that: a song, not a spell. If the magic I'd created before was only an accident or a misunderstanding.

But my stomach clenched and my neck broke out in gooseflesh, and I felt that same, faint assurance that Caé was with me now. I'd felt it when I sang for crowds, when I sang for Veronica, and barely at all when I sang for the governor. That night, it had seemed like Caé had Her back to me.

Now, with my eyes squeezed shut, I could feel Her standing beside my left shoulder. Her breath rose and fell to the rhythm of the song. I wanted to open my eyes, to catch Her standing there, to know for certain that She was truly there and truly approved of me, of this song, of this composition—but I knew that if I looked, She'd not be there. Not to the eye.

I arrived at the *Let it be so,* and my heart glowed and lifted. Turning back to those old, familiar words was like cresting the hill that led to my home with Mother and Father: one-room and simple, but pure and beautiful.

My mouth hung open in an O, letting the final note reverberate and rest in the air for a moment longer. When I sealed my lips and opened my eyes, I met the gaze of the king and queen. They were not majestic, impassive, and stately, but rather, overflowing with tears. The king had a shaking hand pressed to his lips, tears dropping onto the gems of the rings he wore.

And the queen! Her breaths were faster and steadier; her teary eyes were bright and attentive; and with a flick of her hand, she threw back the white bedcovers and raced barefoot toward me.

The Queen of Basso threw her arms around me, her cheek against my head, her perfumed hair falling over my face as a curtain.

"A miracle!" she exclaimed, passing a hand through my curls. Her voice was airy and, I realized, accented; the *r* flipped and the vowels carried out delicately, like a singer. "Blessed be the Goddess!"

"Blessed be the Goddess," echoed the lady's maid, the king, and Lucio. He was beaming with pride.

The queen lifted her hair from my face and turned me toward the king.

"Massimo," she said, "we must keep them here with us. I can breathe again, I feel whole again—we must do whatever we can to keep the Composer and the Singer as our guests. Especially when the baby comes."

Her dark eyes sparkled as she gripped my shoulders. "We will pay you both," she said, turning back to me, "and we will erect a new monastery, if the Church requires compensation, as well."

She left my side, grabbing Lucio's arm. "Can you write a new composition for us tonight, Maestro? Could you write one every night?"

I thought of Caé's call for us to go and restore the world being torn asunder by war, of our charge to always be on the move, to see and experience and to share magic.

"Your Majesty," said Lucio in a soft, uncertain voice, "we are not to linger in any place for too long. The Goddess wants us to spread her miracles. She calls on us to restore the world."

The king rose from his place beside the bed, striding to Maestro Lucio. Sweat shone against my composer's pale forehead.

"That letter from Governor Mosso?" said the king. "He suggested you serve as court composer."

I gasped.

Lucio was so young, and had always served as the student of another composer, as one step below another teacher in the Church. Even though he was celebrated for being able to write holy music at so young an age, he had never been recognized like *this*. Acknowledged by a king.

Lucio kept his head bowed, as if he was not worthy to look upon the king in this moment. "While I am pleased to serve you, Majesty, we must first serve Caé."

The king lifted his chin imperiously and glared down at Lucio. I took a step closer to my friend, grasping his hand. My stomach squeezed tight—Governor Mosso had reacted so poorly to Lucio's protests. The king would be no better.

"Composer," he said, "who was it that gave my family this kingdom?"

Lucio's throat bobbed as he swallowed. "The Goddess, Sire."

"Exactly. Her charge to my family was to look over Her people and carry out Her will. I am Her proxy here in this kingdom. I am king by divine right! Therefore, by serving me and my family, you serve the Goddess."

I glanced back and forth between the two men, my heart as a rolling drum. In my mind's eye, I could see the faces of the faithful we had helped. The well we repaired in a tiny Bassan village. The fire my voice was strong enough to put out at the border—and how the townsfolk there had wept and thanked us. The generosity of the people of Passaggio.

We had seen much of the world, its mountains and

valleys and forests, but that was not why we had traveled for these two long years. It was because Caé wanted us to share our miracles with the whole world.

"Your Majesty," I said in a small, fragile voice, "we cannot stay in one place for too long. We have a holy mission."

The king's gaze turned upon me, but it was softer than it had been with Lucio. I felt Lucio's hand tighten on my arm.

Just as the king was about to speak, however, his wife stepped close to him, a small smile on her lips.

"I understand," she said softly. "I do not wish to rob the Church of her treasures." The queen rested a hand against her round stomach. "What about a year?" Her beautiful dark eyes glittered with tears. "I want to know that my child will be blessed. That she will *live*. And that...that I may live to see her, too. Would that not benefit Basso and her people?"

On our travels, we had given many blessings to newborns and to expectant mothers. Birth was a miracle, not only because life was created, but because surviving such an ordeal was something to celebrate. Just as many times, we had been there to sing funeral hymns after a young mother and newborn passed away.

Not even being a queen could guarantee her life would be saved. Or the baby's.

Lucio and I exchanged a quick look. The Choirmaster had given us instructions on Caé's behalf; instructions to journey the world, spreading hope and healing. But perhaps we had been called here, too. Keeping a woman and her child alive; blessing them with good health—that *did* seem like something Caé would like us to do.

On the other hand, in a year's time, we could help many, from peasants in the Bassan mountains to nobles on the plains of Acuto. All of them were Caé's people—and all of them needed hope.

Lucio gently brushed the Goddess Eye hanging from his ear, his reminder to listen for Her guidance, and I nodded. *That* was what we should do. Listen before we acted.

"Your Majesties," said Lucio softly, his hand on my shoulder as if to shield me from something, "I ask that you give us a week to pray to the Goddess about this. If She gives us a sign of Her favor, then we will stay in your court for a year."

The king's face reddened, but his wife nodded, reaching out to sweep Lucio's hands into hers and kiss them. "Thank you, Maestro. I will continue to pray, also."

King Massimo stood tall, canting his head in acknowledgment to Lucio and to me.

"Sing for us the anthem of Basso," he said.

I didn't understand. I glanced at Lucio, startled, and he gave my shoulder a tight squeeze in response.

It was a proud, mighty song, but I sang it at a whisper:

"Over the snow-capped peak of Brio,
Caé's voice rings strong and true:
'Reign forever, Blessed Basso;
I have shared my crown with you—'"

The king nodded, enough of a cue for me to end the song. Beside him, the queen clapped for me, her smile just as brilliant and hopeful as before.

"There," said the king. "On behalf of the Mother Goddess, who shares Her crown with me," he said, "I gladly give you and your composer a place in my court. The palace is your new home."

I wanted to add *For a week,* but King Massimo had snapped his fingers at a page standing in the doorway. "Let it be so. Prepare the accommodations for the Voice and the composer."

The page bowed and ran out the door like such business was terribly urgent.

His Majesty inclined his head to us. "You're dismissed."

He turned away from us, speaking to the queen in a low voice, his hands cradling hers.

The door clicked shut. Except for a few guards down the corridor, Lucio and I were all alone. We pressed our backs to the wall and let out a deep sigh.

"Caé Almighty," he whispered to the ceiling for help.

I lightly nudged him with my elbow. "He wanted you to be the court composer! Could you imagine!"

He slowly shook his head. "I—I don't know. I could never have dreamed of something so grand. Caé gave me a different mission. But what if . . . what if being here is Her mission, too?"

I wasn't certain. It seemed strange, us staying in one place for a year while the other eleven Voices continued our mission as intended. And what would the Choirmaster say? She had planned our journey and expected us to be in Acuto in a few months' time. We would send a letter back to Cadenza Citadel to assure her of our safety.

"Would the Choirmaster approve of us staying here?" I murmured.

"She would if Caé does. And maybe She does." The faintest smile crossed Lucio's lips. "Whatever's happening, this court composer position, your healing the queen, our ending up here...there must be some purpose for it. Even if it seems confusing." He smoothed back his silvery-blond hair and smiled down at me. "We'll pray over this for a week. We'll know what we must do—if the Goddess is displeased, She'll give us a sign."

"And then?"

He pressed his lips together. "We'll leave. We'll continue our journey."

I nodded slowly. Lucio was right, after all. Caé's plans for us were so strange, so unknowable. The teachers in the monastery told me it was Her plan that my parents were imprisoned. That it was part of Her plan, too, when our king died and the nations warred over their claims to the throne; when the Choirmaster became regent and our journey across the world started. Perhaps Caé *wanted* us to be here.

It seemed so different from all that She had told us before. The joy and the heaviness of Her presence beside me as I sang for Her people.

But I allowed for the possibility of this strange, new plan that had led us into the palace.

Just for a week.

VERSE EIGHT

As the king had ordered, Lucio and I each received a room of our own. We were just across the hall from each other, so on that first day, I spent most of my time with him, praying and asking for guidance. We sang litanies together. He wrote prayers to Her in new compositions. As he did, I sat at the window, watching the sun set as I whispered to my Goddess Eye.

"Should we stay here?" I asked Her. But I couldn't hear anything.

There was a small scratching sound at the door to Lucio's room.

Lucio lifted his head from the desk he hunched over. He frowned, setting down his quill and striding over to the door.

The page Rodolfo was waiting on the other side. He bowed to Lucio. "Good evening, Maestro. His Majesty is holding a ball to celebrate you and Her Holiness. He asks that you perform something for the court... and that you be dressed appropriately."

I frowned, rising from my window seat. In the doorway,

behind Rodolfo, stood a crowd of people, holding wooden boxes and bundles of brightly colored cloth.

"Those are for us?" I asked.

Rodolfo smiled. "Yes, Your Holiness."

I stood at Lucio's side, tugging on his sleeve.

"Should we go to such a ball?" I whispered in his ear.

He shrugged. "I don't see why not. We'll both be serving our purpose for the Goddess—me with my music and you with your singing."

I supposed that could be right. I didn't know what to expect—I'd been to celebrations in towns across both Cadenza and Basso, but never to something as grand as a ball.

I retreated to my room, flanked by a horde of women in gowns of every color. Together they were brilliant as a sunrise, each clothed in purples or reds or yellows, with their hair worn loose in big, frizzy curls on the sides of their heads. Some wore pearls or Goddess Eyes as decorations in their beautiful unbound hair.

They made quick work of me, removing the hood I used to keep my hair hidden away while in the modest Bassan villages. Then they gave me clothing, every stitch of it new—fresh stockings, bright blue with red ribbons; a whole trunk of clean chemises; even a new set of stays, which they laced me into without my even having to ask.

My head spun as they whirled around me, giggling and chattering and asking me more questions than I could answer. They hung large pearls from my ears. They gave me a velvet skirt that was the same deep blue as the lakes of Cadenza. To match, they chose a bodice that fit me the best, with large sleeves puffing out around my shoulders as theirs did.

A lady with a bright smile and red, red lips placed me in front of a tall looking glass. Mirrors were expensive, and the one we had in the carriage was small and warped—but this one was clear and smooth, and I could see myself for what felt like the first time since we'd left the monastery.

I was taller. My face was a little thinner; my eyes a bit more tired. I felt so young, so foolish, always, but for a brief moment, I felt a little like a grown-up. The rouge on my cheeks, the shape of the deep-blue dress on me, how well it seemed to suit me. Even if the earrings and the way they'd done my hair made me feel a bit silly, I felt almost as one of them.

My parents wouldn't have been able to recognize me. Their little girl had changed so much—she was practically someone new altogether.

Had they changed, too?

Were they still waiting for me?

Were they even alive?

"Here," said the lady nearest me. "A gift from His Majesty."

She lifted a short pearl necklace out of a box and wrapped it around my throat. Another maid untied the Goddess Eye string from around my neck and set it on a nearby table before I could speak.

The lady clapped her hands against my bare shoulders, grinning at my reflection. "Oh, you look as though you could have lived here your whole life, Your Holiness!"

She was right. I didn't look at all like a peasant girl from Cadenza.

Cadenza. Warm meals with my family. Singing in the comfort of our tiny, leaky-roofed home. Lying in beds of flowers.

My heart shattered. I didn't want to lose that part of myself—any of it.

"Come along, Blessed Voice!" urged one of the ladies-in-waiting.

The flood of them began to hurry out the door, but I lingered one last moment, sweeping up the Goddess Eye from the table and tying it around my neck where it belonged. Mother and Father had given me the Eye for my seventh birthday—my last with them.

I tucked the little bead under the collar of my gown, resting right against my heart.

Lucio and I stood outside a set of elaborate double doors, carved with notes and staves and curlicues and birds. Behind it, I could hear soft music, sprightly and without any words, all hautboys and strings and horns.

"Elissa, another scale, please," said Lucio, plucking a note on his lute to show me where to start. I obeyed and continued to warm up my voice with the old notes and words that Caé had used to breathe life into us.

"Does your voice feel ready?" he asked.

I nodded, and he handed me a sheet of paper, dotted all over with notes. *For His Majesty King Massimo* was the title.

"With any luck, it's a song for cheerfulness," Lucio explained.

I looked over the music and could hear it in my head, lifting and lilting and playful. But it was missing something. If I changed that note, if I turned that final phrase into a cadenza, leading into a new, stronger part of the melody... The song morphed in my head, turning into something lighter and chirping as birdsong.

"Focus, please."

A blush burned my cheeks. Lucio always caught me with my head in the clouds. I exhaled loudly, as if to breathe out the silly thoughts—those that said I could make songs of my own.

The doors to the ballroom opened a fraction, allowing an attendant to slip through. He smiled at us meekly. "Maestro, my lady—it's time."

I took one last glance at the sheet music and then held it against my chest.

"Do you have it?" Lucio whispered.

I nodded. My heart beat against my throat.

Lucio held his lute at his side and wrapped an arm around my shoulders in the briefest hug. He looked different, too, with his hair down in loose waves. His handsome sapphire suit matched mine, with great clouds of lace at his sleeves and a primly tied cravat. Such brightness suited him much better than the cold, dark colors of the Bassan countryside.

"You'll be excellent," he said to me. "You always are."

The doors opened, and side by side, we walked into the ballroom, a vast long room lined with pure, smooth mirrors all along one wall. Candles flickered on gilded candelabras decorated with crystals. Tables covered in white cloth bore pyramids of pastries and towers of sugar-coated fruits. It was beautiful—but it was far, far too much. I imagined the families who had helped us along our journey, the folk who had shared what little they had to help us feel welcome. There was enough food in this room to feed a whole town's worth of people.

In the middle of the ballroom, courtiers gathered around the king, all their eyes turned to us. His Majesty was in a new suit, gold from his cravat to his breeches, with tall scarlet heels on his shoes. The queen was at his side, her hand against his arm, joy brightening her eyes as we approached. Her outfit matched the king's: gold satin, but with voluminous sleeves like mine, and roses tucked into her black curls. The nobles around them whispered excitedly as we approached.

"My friends," said the king with a smile, "I'm happy to present Maestro Lucio Arioso, our guest. And, with any luck, our new court composer!"

He gestured to Lucio with an open hand. As the crowd clapped, Lucio and I exchanged one quick, uncertain glance before he bowed to the king. *Not forever. Just for a week.*

"And the Voice of the Goddess, who has healed our dearest Queen Flora," the king said, nodding to me.

"*Brava!*" cried Queen Flora amid the applause. I wobbled on my new high-heeled shoes as I attempted a curtsy before them.

Lucio smiled at the king and held his lute in front of himself. His pale cheeks had turned bright pink, and his fingers quivered against the neck of the lute. I didn't think I'd ever seen him so nervous before.

"Your Majesties," he said, "we'd like to thank you for your warm welcome with a song of celebration. An original composition by me. One we hope will bring felicity and good health to the whole palace." He turned back to me, lightly strumming the opening chord of his song. He lifted his eyebrows, as if to say, *Are you ready?*

I nodded, keeping my eyes on him alone. I couldn't think about the dozens of people, about the king and queen, about the needling voice in my head telling me that something was awry. When I was just singing with Lucio, I didn't have anything to be afraid of.

He strummed the mirthful opening of the song, and I joined in. My voice hopped like a stone skipping across water, soared and swooped. Lucio bobbed his head in time to the music and grinned back at me.

His cheerfulness filled me, and I smiled more and more brightly with each verse, crescendoing a melody as golden and warm as sunshine. The candles in the room flared to the beat of our song. It made me want to dance, or laugh, or do all at once. In fact, in time with the rhythm of my heart, I could hear faint footsteps tapping, like someone was dancing along to our song. Someone unseen—someone always with me.

With a flourish, Lucio played the final chord, tossing back his head and laughing. I couldn't help myself; I reached out and hugged his side, mindful of the precious lute.

The room erupted in applause, a grand smile on the faces of everyone in the room, most especially the king and queen.

"Bravi, bravi!" the king cried, and he bowed to each of us—Lucio and I exchanged a shocked look. "Now please, enjoy this party. We intend to celebrate you until sunrise!"

At this, suddenly, the nobles flooded us. Ladies in violet and crimson touched Lucio's arms and beamed at him.

"Are you truly from Cadenza?" one asked.

"Y-yes, my lady," he replied.

Her companion giggled. "He really is, see? He has the most charming accent!"

"Did you make up that song all on your own?" asked a fellow in blue.

Lucio beamed. "Yes. I started it this morning."

The man's eyes widened. "Remarkable! What talent!"

"Look at this," cooed a lady in green, reaching out and touching the Goddess Eye hanging from his ear. "I've never seen one worn such as this before. Is it a custom in Cadenza?"

Lucio's blush deepened. He tucked his hair behind his ear. "For some, yes—it's so I remember to listen to Caé—"

"Do you play the harpsichord, Maestro?" asked a man in pink.

"I—I do, yes—"

A blond girl clapped eagerly and then grabbed Lucio by the arm. "Play something for us, please, Maestro!"

The men and women around us jabbered in agreement.

"Well, I—all right," he said, and then was swept away by the nobles before I could even say goodbye.

More courtiers gathered around me to ask questions of their own, to tug on my dress or pet my hair or ask me to sing something else for them. They were parted when Queen Flora approached me. They quieted and sank low for her.

She held out her hand for mine. "Come," she said. "Let's get you something to eat."

I happily let her pull me out of the maelstrom of strangers.

Queen Flora squeezed my hand as she led me to one of the many tables. "You sing so beautifully. Thank you, again, for healing me."

The frayed, fissured part of me that felt so unsteady, so uncertain, felt a little less raw. This was what I was made for—that kind of song. "I'm so glad you're feeling better, Majesty."

She chose two pastries stacked atop each other, smothered in chocolate, and handed them to me upon a golden plate. They looked just like the ones my father would give me to reward me for keeping my gift hidden. I saw them before me, drenched in Cadenzan sunshine and hot with the smell of sugar; I heard my father's voice, telling me I deserved them, that I had been a good child today.

"May I ask you something, Caé Elissa?"

I blinked, waking up from the memory. "Of course, Your Majesty."

She leaned against the wall beside me and looked out at the crowd before us. "You must have traveled for a long while. You serve Her well, but do you ever miss your home?"

The question startled me. This was the war within me, always. I missed my family. I missed Cadenza. I even missed the monastery, which was my home for three years. I sometimes hated this mission of ours, pulling me from familiar lands, and I sometimes hated the Church itself, because it had ripped me from the arms of my parents—these were my deepest and ugliest secrets. But I loved Caé. And I trusted her. Yet those wounds within me, those little flames of hate—they didn't go away.

"I miss Cadenza very much," I admitted. "I miss my family so much it aches."

When she didn't reply, my stomach fell. Lucio would have

scolded me—I should not have spoken so frankly and so personally to a queen. I opened my mouth to apologize, but she began brushing tears from her cheeks.

"I miss my home, too," she murmured. She turned her lovely dark eyes to me, a small smile on her lips even as she cried. "My sister. My palace. Goddess above, even the *food*."

"Me, too!" I yearned for the smells of melted cheese, warm chicken, fresh bread, pastries with fruits and nuts— everything that we'd share together around our little table. Father baked the most wonderful bread, with herbs and ricotta. I dreamed constantly of eating with them again. "You have a sister, Majesty? What is she like?"

She laughed. "Fierce. Fearless. Mina has always been a warrior, even when we were children playing make-believe. She doesn't bend or break to anything." The queen's eyes were soft with memory. "I wish I were like that, sometimes."

She turned to me, pressing a light kiss to my forehead. "Thank you. It's nice to hear that someone so holy could feel pain like I do. It makes me think that the Goddess might understand how I feel." Queen Flora smoothed back my hair, just like my mother used to do. My heart twinged like a plucked string. "You bring us much comfort. I thank you for being here."

She left me by the table, but even after she had gone, the words echoed around in my head, tied to words of my own: *This is what I was made for. To bring comfort.*

I nibbled on the pastry, flaky and buttery and filled with

chocolate cream, and watched the nobles dance to Lucio's music. Bowing and skirting around one another, never touching.

I imagined a life where this was all I did. Where I sang for these people, the same people, every night.

I couldn't picture it. Every night I spent singing in a ball-room such as this, I could be singing songs of hope, of comfort, of provision, to hundreds more.

But I had brought some joy to the queen tonight. That had to count for something, surely?

I drifted around the ballroom, the air fragrant with sugar, strawberries and cream, chocolate, cinnamon, and even fresh oranges. The nobles drank from crystal goblets and laughed at one another's jokes. In a corner, they gathered around a table, watching intently: a man set down cards, and another set coins atop them, and when a card was pulled, everyone erupted into cheers and laughter as the first man triumphantly swept up the pile of money. A lady ran past me, giggling as she hid under a table. Another girl followed after her, her arms in front of her and a blind-fold tied around her eyes.

Following the trill of the harpsichord, I found Lucio, sur-rounded by men and women who laughed and smiled and kept themselves pressed close to him. A girl offered him a sparkling drink, and he took it, continuing to play the bass line of the song with his left hand as he tipped back the drink. Even this was enough to garner their applause.

I was glad to see him happy. Glad to see him not at work, for once. And the people around him seemed to really like him; and for that I was proud—he was talented and smart. The courtiers here understood that and loved him for it. Now he was as a flower blooming under the sunshine of their attention. I'd never seen him smile so brightly before.

From behind me, someone tapped my shoulder. It was a lady in a scarlet gown, clasping her hands together as if she were praying. "Won't you come dance with us, Singer?"

I looked back at Lucio for permission, but he was distracted as a boy offered him a plate of grapes.

I could dance. I could enjoy this party. There was nothing wrong with such enjoyment.

Yet a song was starting to play in my head, somewhere over the faint, one-handed playing of the harpsichord. A joyful, gliding melody, shining silver and playful, almost teasing me.

Come sing me, it urged. *Come write me down.*

I looked back once more. A girl was leading Lucio by the hand toward the table with cards and coins.

He would not notice if I left. He would not know I was in my room, writing songs.

The thought, forbidden as it was, thrilled me.

"Thank you," I told the lady in red. "But not tonight."

Ducking past dancers and weaving through the laughing crowds of women and men, I finally reached the double doors. Then, with the song chiming loud as church bells in my ears, I dashed back to my room, my heart and the melody flying within me. I flung the bedroom door closed behind me and darted to my desk.

The thrill and novelty of being among Bassan courtiers had made a *dozen* new melodies start to form in my mind, I found. Like catching fireflies, I had to be quick in writing them down before they flew away. The notes dotted the lines—birds jetting across a pale sky—and it felt as if my hand was not my hand at all but some animal, twitching and moving about with its own ideas. No, more than that—it felt like my whole *arm* was moved by another person.

Writing music was not my place, Lucio had said.

Music was what I was born to make, said Veronica.

My hand flashed across the page, unable to move fast enough to write down all the melodies. I penned them until my eyelids grew heavy.

VERSE NINE

In the morning, I sought out Lucio, ready to begin the day with prayers and songs. We still needed guidance from Caé as to whether we would be staying here.

He was waiting outside his bedroom door, wearing a dark, heavy coat. His eyes were shadowed with sleeplessness, but he grinned at the sight of me. "Good morning."

I nodded in greeting, my back pressed against my door, as if to keep my sheet music locked and hidden away within. "Good morning—are you going outside?"

His eyes brightened. "Yes, actually. I made some friends at the ball last night. They say there is a royal hunt today. They asked me to come along."

My heart fell, just an inch. I didn't want him to leave me. And I wasn't certain he should be spending an entire day on a hunting trip with nobles instead of writing new compositions.

His shiny new boots clicked across the marble as he crossed toward me. "I hope you'll join us," he said. "I think you'd quite like these Bassans. And you could see more of the beauty of these mountains!"

I clasped my hands over my heart, excited despite myself. "You want me to come along?"

He nodded, his eyes crinkling with a smile. "I'll find someone to get you a coat."

I caught his sleeve as he started to turn. "Do you think She'd mind?"

Lucio's brow furrowed. "Would who mind?"

"The Goddess." I swallowed. "We're supposed to be in contemplation about what to do next. And preparing more music to help people. Maybe She wouldn't want us to spend the day on sport."

His smile faltered. "I don't think the Goddess wants us to spend every hour of our lives studying. Why would She make such a beautiful world if we couldn't spend a little time enjoying it?"

I hadn't thought of it that way. Sometimes his lessons made me uncertain of myself or of my knowledge of Her, but this seemed right. And besides, to see Lucio so happy, and for him to invite me into this happiness of his...it was such a rare gift that I would be foolish to turn it down. He was far too serious these days.

So, bundled in furs and velvet, we joined a large group of courtiers heading out into the wintry morning. Sunlight shimmered off the snow. Some nobles sat astride horses, while others huddled in golden sleighs—and many were already off, zipping across the snow-covered lawn to the misty forest on the horizon. All around, I could see the peaks of mountains, white and blue and so beautiful. I stood on my toes and wondered if perhaps I could even see Cadenza from here, the height was so great.

Lucio approached me, arm in arm with a boy and a girl about his age. "Elissa," he said, "these are my friends, Leporello and Zerlina."

The boy, Leporello, swept his feathered hat off his dark hair in a bow. "I'm honored to meet a Voice of the Goddess."

Zerlina, the girl, bent in a curtsy. She wore a black mask to shield the top half of her face from the cold, a strange trend I had seen among the wealthier folks in Basso. It was practical, I supposed, but rather startling.

"It's lovely to meet you, Your Holiness," she said sweetly.

"Let's not trouble ourselves with titles," said Lucio, patting her arm. "Today, I'll just be Lucio, and she'll just be Elissa."

I nodded eagerly at this, at the thought that for a few hours, I could just be an ordinary girl.

Zerlina grinned and slipped her arm out from Lucio's. "Well, if *that's* the case, I want to sit next to Elissa in the sledge. There's much gossip to share!"

She shepherded the four of us to a large sleigh led by a trio of horses. We sat across from one another, two by two, huddled in close, with fur blankets on our laps. Lucio and Leporello sat with their backs to the driver, Zerlina and I with our backs to the track.

"I've never ridden in a sleigh before," I murmured, my heart racing in a strange blend of fear and excitement.

Lucio grinned at me, gripping the painted-gold edge of the sleigh with his gloved hand. "Me, neither."

Zerlina removed a pale hand from her silver-furred muff to give my hand a squeeze. Behind her mask, her gray eyes twinkled. "Hold on tight, then!"

With the crack of the reins and the jingling of the horses' harness, the sleigh *whoosh*ed across the snow, onward toward the forest. My curls tickled my cheeks in the wind; Lucio laughed and pressed his hat against his head to keep it from flying away.

"So what comes next?" I asked Zerlina over the rushing wind and the jingling bells. "Are—are *we* going to be hunting anything?"

"Caé, no!" she replied with a giggle. "Not in this weather! Only the king and his inner circle will try for quarry. The gentry have a little party, with a bonfire and hot cider and food and music. That's all!"

I straightened in my seat. "Music?"

Zerlina nodded. "The king *adores* music. He has twenty-four string players that serenade him all day long! There should be a group of flautists and horn players that will join us, I'm certain."

The king's love for music was just as strong as my own—but quite different, too. When I heard music, I felt a deep, inexplicable love within me, something tying me to the earth itself. When I heard music, when I sang, I thought only of Caé. King Massimo loved songs, too—but because they entertained him. They made him happy.

Lucio was smiling brightly as he talked to his friend about dancing, about card games, about costumed balls.

Was it so bad? To want to be happy?

❧

The king took off on his horse into the woods, flanked by lords and ladies and a pack of barking dogs. Meanwhile, the rest of our group gathered together under the pines, some sitting on velvet chairs brought by servants, others huddled together in the glinting sledges. As Zerlina had said, a group of musicians appeared, playing the flute and recorder and horn and hautboy in a beautiful, smooth-sounding quartet.

I stayed close to Lucio and his friends—there were more of them now, all of us standing by a crackling bonfire—and kept my hands warm with a mug of cider. With the thundering of hooves, the last of the king's group disappeared into the wood.

"What are they hunting?" I asked.

The courtiers around us chuckled.

"A stag, Elissa," Lucio told me.

"Do you not hunt in Cadenza?" Leporello asked Lucio.

Lucio's cheeks reddened. "Not for sport, no."

I frowned at Zerlina. "It's not for food?"

She laughed noisily, and those who overheard me joined in.

"You are so charming!" she cooed, smiling kindly. "You silly thing, do you think the king hunts his own food?"

I supposed not. It seemed sillier, though, that this was a game to His Majesty, chasing and killing an animal with no purpose. Not far from here, his people were dying for food.

"Where is the queen?" I asked. The more unsettled I felt, the more I thought of her, who also felt like a stranger in this land.

"She's back at the palace," Lucio answered among the tittering of the nobles. "She's in no condition for travel, with the child near due."

A noblewoman near me pinched my cheek. "Oh, Lucio, she's darling!"

I meekly thanked her, but couldn't help thinking of the queen, left behind at the palace while merriment carried on without her.

The courtiers asked Lucio about our travels, and he regaled them with stories of the towns we'd passed through, the mountains we'd climbed, the beauty of Cadenza, the moments when we'd narrowly escaped trouble. They watched and listened to him with rapt attention. He smiled so brightly.

After a while, Leporello waved his hand at the group of musicians playing their wind instruments, silencing them.

"I'm bored with this music," he said with a dramatic sigh. He squeezed Lucio's arm through the thick fur of his coat. "Did you bring your lute, Maestro?"

Lucio's cheeks flushed pink. "N-no. I didn't think you'd want—"

"Then our Elissa should sing for us!" Zerlina declared loudly.

The circle of nobles around me applauded and gasped, bright-eyed with excitement as they gazed back at me. I fidgeted with the Goddess Eye against my heart.

"I don't think Elissa should perform magic without the supervision of the king," Lucio said above the chattering crowd.

Relief breezed through me. I smiled at Lucio in thanks.

Though some courtiers sulked, Leporello nodded to me encouragingly. "It doesn't have to be magical," he said. "You can sing some ordinary songs, can't you? Say you'll sing!"

"Yes, yes, you must sing!" cried Zerlina, and the others shouted their agreement, clapping and whistling and encouraging me so much I felt a blush rising in my cheeks. I could see Lucio mumble something, but over the din, I couldn't hear what. He was frowning.

He *had* said we could bring some joy to these people. Perhaps it wasn't as important as healing or comforting, but I supposed there wouldn't be harm in singing a plain, magic-less song.

As I stood up, they applauded even louder, sitting on the edges of their seats, their eyes round and eager.

I didn't often sing *a cappella*. Lucio was always there to play the lute or the harpsichord alongside me. Back in the monastery, there was the organ. Even in my cottage, when Mother and Father and I sang together in secret, Mother played along with the warm, humming music of our family's old hurdy-gurdy.

I closed my eyes and remembered walking through the stone halls of the monastery. I thought of my favorite corners, dark and peaceful, every inch of the place bearing some sign of the Goddess I loved; of how my voice would swoop and soar and bounce so beautifully against the stones. In those moments, I pretended that it was just Caé and me—like I was giving Her a private concert.

I imagined the same thing now.

I sang a song in the Cadenzan dialect instead of our common tongue, a bright, jumping song about a boy and a girl falling in love. In my mind's eye, Caé was watching me sing, leaning forward in Her throne, grinning, Her hands against Her heart. In my mind's eye, Mother and Father were there, too. No shackles on their wrists. No tears in their eyes. Just proudly smiling at me.

The final note rang through me and through the cold air around me, spinning and twirling like a snowflake. When I opened my eyes, I found all the nobles around me with smiles on their faces. They jumped to their feet, clapping and cheering.

"Give us another song!" begged one girl.

"Sing the anthem of Basso!" suggested a boy.

"Sing us a folk song!" urged another.

The glorious feeling of sharing my music, of sharing in the joy of music, of being loved—it all made my heart feel as if it were glowing. I could see myself doing this every day, singing every day, singing songs for no real reason but because they made me happy.

Looking into the bonfire before me, I remembered a different kind of happiness.

The grateful smile from Veronica as I offered her a warm cup of tea. As I healed her foot.

The joyful tears of the villagers in Passaggio. The hope that brightened their eyes, to think that they'd finally receive provisions.

And the Queen of Basso, her shoulders loosening, a smile on her face, as the sickness left her body.

This happiness I brought the courtiers was good, but my songs were capable of something even greater.

I kept my head low and avoided the gazes of the nobles as they continued to call out to me, asking for more music. Some even grabbed at my sleeves as I passed by, tugging on me like tides. I swam through the crowd till I arrived at Lucio's side. As I clung to his arm, I was startled to find his face so cold, so emotionless.

"What's wrong?" he asked me in a smooth, quiet voice. "Don't you like performing?"

The chill in his voice made me shiver. I hid my face from the others behind the curtain of my hair.

"I want to go back to the palace," I whispered.

Lucio nodded. "I think that's wise. You should rest your voice."

Guilt gripped me as I slipped away from the crowd toward one of the sledges. Lucio was quick to sate the crowd's need for entertainment by suggesting that the musicians play a dance. In moments, they were back to laughing, to spinning, to smiling.

Riding in the sledge, I watched the courtiers and Lucio grow smaller and smaller on the horizon. With nothing around me but snowy fields and mountain air, I felt small and alone.

But the jingling bells on the horses' harnesses reminded me of music, of the comfort that Caé's music gave me.

A sneaky, exciting thought slithered through my mind.

Alone at the palace, I could rest my voice, yes.

But I could also write down the songs flitting about my imagination, beautiful and bright as butterflies.

VERSE TEN

After a night full of composing, I woke up on a hard, uncomfortable pillow. My neck throbbed with pain, and as I untwisted myself from my strange sleeping position, I found myself not in my bed but at a desk. Sheets of paper were beneath me, and by a miracle, I hadn't knocked over my inkwell in my sleep.

Memory flooded me, delicious and sunny. I grinned down at the sheet music, at the new songs I'd written.

They were lovely. Joyful, careless songs that made me feel like I was a bird, flying high, high above green fields.

I gazed at the vase at the edge of my desk as I thought. It was filled with the same pink Giacomo flowers that had been in the queen's room. I reached out, stroking their feather-soft petals.

An idea was blooming in my mind—dangerous and silly.

I glanced back down at the first song I'd written, the bright, buoyant one.

In a small voice, I sang it. The high, chirping notes, the way the melody zipped up and down, the trills that mimicked the song of a thrush.

On my final note, something tickled the back of my neck, like someone was whispering just behind me.

I whirled around, my hand against my neck, my eyes wide and frightened. Back on my desk, the ceramic vase of flowers wobbled. Once more, I whipped my head around, and caught the vase seconds before it would tip over. Only one flower fell out.

It hit the floor. And then it hopped.

I shrieked, leaping out of my chair. I gawked, certain that I'd imagined the flower moving on its own—

It hopped again.

"What on Earth?" I whispered, my hand fisted against my thrumming heart.

The flower trembled and rustled, and then, in a blink, it twisted: growing, blossoming.

Into a bird.

My mouth hung open. I rubbed my eyes. I pinched my arm—I was dreaming; I *must* be dreaming!

Yet there it was, hopping about. A perfect little bird, bright pink and spotted with bits of yellow. It had two little black eyes and cocked its head at me. When it opened its beak, it chirped three notes at me, the notes of the songbirds in Cadenza: C-A-E, C-A-E.

I plopped onto my bed, gaping at the little bird. *Caé.*

Her magic was capable of a great many things. But I'd never seen it make life before. The last time such a thing had happened was—was the *beginning.* When She had created all of mankind from a song.

The bird flapped up and pecked at my sheet music, the music that had birthed it.

I stared at my trembling fingers. Touched a hand to my throat.

Lucio had cautioned me against playing around with the power of a goddess. And now, with Her magic in my voice, I had brought something to life. I had done the impossible.

It was too much power. Too fearsome. If I could make life from practically nothing, what else could I do? The first song I had written healed Veronica *and* the queen. If my second song could make a flower come to life...

Dread was ice water in my stomach as I gazed at the little bird. Was Veronica wrong about this gift of mine? Could the Goddess possibly approve of this? Had I gone too far—would She be displeased with me?

The bird chirped its three-note song again, then took flight, working its tiny wings until it sat on my shoulder. With a trembling hand, I touched its little head. It cooed and nuzzled my finger with its beak.

It didn't seem sinful to me. It was a miracle. Small and beautiful.

But why was it given to *me*? Why was She giving *me* these songs? Why not Lucio?

Lucio. He'd know why all this was happening. He knew the Goddess and Her magic better than anyone.

I turned, sharply, to go to him. The bird took flight,

settling itself on my headboard with a disgruntled little shake of its feathers.

"Sorry," I whispered. "Stay here. I must show you to Lucio!"

I dashed into the hall and closed the door fast behind me to keep the new flower-bird contained. As soon as I'd reached the door across from mine, I beat my fist against it.

"Lucio?" I called. "Lucio, wake up, I have to show you something!"

There was no answer. I called for him again and waited a minute, but I quickly lost patience. I jiggled the doorknob until it opened. I peeked in through the crack of the door. He wasn't in his bed, or at his desk, or at the window seat, or near the large oak wardrobe. I hadn't seen him since the hunting trip the day before—with a stab of fear, I wondered if he had returned at all.

"Your Holiness?"

The voice behind me made me yelp in surprise. When I spun around, I found the young page from before, Rodolfo, his cheeks red as apples. He hastily bent into a low bow.

"Forgive me for startling you, Your Holiness—"

"It's no trouble," I said tightly. "How can I help you?"

"The king asks that you sing a new song for him and the queen this morning. Your ladies-in-waiting are on their way. You and Maestro Lucio are expected in the king's bedroom in an hour."

Another song.

I grimaced. "Have you...have you seen Maestro Lucio, Rodolfo?"

His red hair flopped over his forehead as he looked up at me. "He was dancing in the ballroom with a group of courtiers until late last night, Your Holiness."

I could picture it so well. The men and women surrounding him, smiling at him, clapping for him. Perhaps he was still there.

"Right," I mumbled. "Well, um, tell the king we will be with him soon."

Rodolfo bowed and scurried off to deliver my message. With no one watching, I ripped the uncomfortable heels off my feet and sprinted to the ballroom in my stockings. I skidded to a halt outside the double doors. The sounds within were faint; laughter and clinking glasses and harpsichord music.

And a voice I recognized.

I flung open the doors and rushed in, immediately finding Lucio sitting at the harpsichord, surrounded by a small group of friends. Zerlina lay fast asleep on the floor. Leporello smiled at Lucio from across the harpsichord. Another girl placed a kiss on Lucio's cheek, leaving a red circle of lip paint.

"Lucio?"

He looked toward me, his brows raised, his eyes wide and ringed with dark circles. "Elissa? What is it?"

I wanted to tell him about the bird, about the song I'd written, but to speak of such strange miracles in front of his friends seemed...unwise. And other business awaited us now.

"I—the king has asked for us," I said. "He wants a new song from you in an hour."

At once, Lucio shot up from the harpsichord bench, swaying in place. He gripped the harpsichord for support.

"No, don't leave!" said a very sleepy-looking boy in blue.

"Play us another song, Maestro!" begged a girl. "Just one more!"

Lucio smiled. "Unfortunately, His Majesty has called upon me. I must go."

The sleepy courtiers grumbled in protest, but Lucio simply grabbed his lute from where it was propped lazily by the window and made for the door. I raced to catch up to him.

"Were you in there all night?" I asked him.

"I suppose so." He grinned at me over his shoulder. "I don't think I caught a wink of sleep, but it was the most fun I've ever had! They love my music."

His hair, unbound and frizzy, was tangled and had a strange purplish stain on one side, like he'd slept in a puddle of juice.

"I—I don't think you should spend all night merrymaking," I said softly. "You need your rest."

"I'm just doing my job," he said, striding on. "That's why we're here. To bring pleasure to the court."

I frowned. "That's not why we're—"

"It's what the king wants me to do. He wants me to act as the court composer."

"But—but we may not stay. We're only here for a week."

"If the Goddess objects. And She hasn't." He shrugged, stopping in front of his door and laying a hand on the door-knob. "Maybe She even wants us to stay."

My stomach curled tight into a ball with worry. "Well, even if She does, you don't need to stay at those parties all night. She just wants you to—"

"Right now, She wants me to compose a new song for the king." He stopped in front of his door, nodding at me. "I'll see you in an hour."

As he opened his door, I remembered my song, the miracle, the bird.

"Wait!" I cried, but he had already slammed the door shut behind him.

I didn't like seeing him so tired, or so untidy—it was very unlike him. On the other hand, he seemed very happy, being among people his own age. People who were interested in him. He smiled so much now.

I chewed on my thumbnail. The monastery would not have approved of his behavior. They would have called him irresponsible for staying up all night playing profane music instead of sleeping or studying. And in this moment I felt sure they would have been unhappy with him for wanting to be the court composer of Basso.

But he *wasn't* the court composer—not yet. It was just for a week. Or until the Goddess gave us a sign.

This wasn't the first time Lucio had enjoyed himself a bit too much at a party. When he had the chance, he liked to stay up very late. He liked to dance with strangers. He liked to laugh; he liked to jest. But he was always responsible, always mature, and these past two years he had grown more and more careful.

I trusted him.

I returned to my bedroom, where the little pink bird remained sitting on my windowsill. It chirped its three notes and pecked at the glass of the window, over and over.

For a moment, I imagined telling Lucio that my song had made a bird out of a flower. Showing him the power of the music Caé had inspired me to compose. But I knew that he'd hate that I *had* composed. He'd say I was misusing Her power. And perhaps I was. These songs of mine, as delightful as they were to listen to and write, they bore a great deal of holy power. Power that I should not have been playing with.

I crossed to the window, unlatched it, and opened it. The bird flew off, a soft pink blur like a cherry blossom floating in the wind.

This must be the end of it.

≀

The days at the palace passed in the same way, one after the other; a beautiful whirlwind, like a trilling, repeating melody. In the mornings, Lucio and I gave concerts for the king and queen. They always sat at their small breakfast table, holding hands and weeping with joy for every song we gave them—a new one every morning; always a new song. Even though Lucio spent his nights in the ballroom, playing games and singing and dancing and enjoying new friends, he was ever able to produce something for the king in the nick of time.

At lunch, the royal couple insisted that we eat with them at their table, not stand among the courtiers watching and whispering to one another, a strange audience to a strange affair.

The afternoons we could spend as we liked. I rarely saw Lucio; he retreated to the ballroom, the orangeries, the galleries, or any number of other places, playing songs for his friends to charm them and lift their spirits.

Without his supervision, I retreated to my room, sitting at a desk with paper and pen.

I had tried not to write songs. I had. But finishing a song made my heart gallop every time. I'd smile at my creation and feel a strange, pulling sensation in my chest, like someone was tugging on a string attached to me. And it was connected directly to Caé, I knew.

It was a lovely, heady feeling, but at the same time, gazing down at my creations with pride, I always regretted making them. Her music was to be shared, but this? This never could be.

Composing was Lucio's role. But the more he composed,

the more he played for the king and the nobles, the wearier his eyes became. Like the weight of making so much music so quickly was pulling him down. He used to compose one piece a week, at the most. And I was certain that the parties every night did nothing to make his writing easier.

On the sixth night, we sang the same song he'd written our first day here.

My final note echoed against the rounded walls, and when it came back to me, it sent a chill through me. Caé was close, Her breath against my cheek.

Tonight, the audience clapped, but no one wept with joy. No one shouted praises to Caé. The smile on the king's face was less pronounced.

His Majesty crossed the marble floor and took my hand, presenting me to the crowd with a flourish.

"How happy is our kingdom to have a Singer amongst us!" he exclaimed.

"Hear, hear!" shouted the queen, and the others joined in.

I grinned at Lucio, but he kept his face solemn and still. He gripped the neck of his lute and bowed stiffly toward the audience. When he lifted his head, his eyes were ringed with red.

With a wave of the king's hand, the men and women playing harpsichords and strings continued their own music, magicless as it was, and courtiers swept across the floor to stand in neat lines and prepare to dance.

His Majesty swept Lucio and me to the fringe of the

crowd, a few paces away from the musicians. His reddish brows pressed together. "What happened?"

The warm, delighted fire in my chest cooled to ice. "Your Majesty, is something wrong?"

He looked at my composer. Lucio kept his head bowed and his gaze lowered even more than normal.

"The song," said the king. "Why didn't it make me feel as wonderful as the other ones have?"

The white silk of Lucio's cravat bobbed as he swallowed. "The more a song is sung, the less power it has, Majesty," he explained.

The king blinked. "Then write a new one. That is your job, isn't it, Composer?"

Lucio nodded furiously and swept into a bow. "Yes, Sire. Right away."

"I look forward to your newest composition in the morning." The king turned on his ruby-red heels but looked over his shoulder at me. "Well done, nonetheless, Voice of the Goddess."

I dipped in a curtsy until he strode away, sitting at his wife's side to watch the dancers.

Spinning on my heel, I clutched at the lemon-yellow brocade of Lucio's sleeve. "Are you all right?"

He batted my hand away, reaching up to the Goddess Eye hanging from his ear. He rolled it back and forth between his fingers. "I'm fine."

It was not much of an answer. I chewed on my lip and

inched nearer to him, worried. "I thought it was a lovely composition, even the second time."

Lucio squeezed his eyes shut and tucked his lute under his arm.

"Luciooooooo!" cried a girl with her brown hair in large, fashionable frizzes on the sides of her head. "Play us your song again, we beg you!"

Around her, young men and women clapped in agreement, waving at him.

"Come play faro with us!" called one.

"You must try this chocolate tart, Lucio!"

"Show us how you dance in Cadenza!"

The shine in his eyes began to return. He straightened his back, a smile dawning on his lips. He took one step toward his new friends.

I caught him by the arm. "Lucio—shouldn't you compose?"

He pried my hand off his sleeve. "The Goddess will give me a song at just the right time, I'm certain. She has so far."

Once more, he turned from me, walked from me. But I couldn't let him. I tugged on the back of his coat.

"Lucio, please listen to me," I said.

When he whirled back, his eyes burned at me. His nostrils flared.

The voices of fear and worry within me grew louder and louder.

"You look so *tired*," I told him, the words coming in a rush. "The king makes you write all those songs. And there are so many distractions here. All we do is perform for the king and his courtiers. We haven't healed anybody since the queen. It's good to make friends, of course it is, and there's so much here that's lovely, but there are other people we should be helping. Maybe... maybe we ought to leave."

"Have you gotten a sign yet, Elissa?"

I couldn't say. I stood there, dumb.

"Then there's no reason to act unless Caé commands us to." Lucio tipped his head back toward his friends. "If you'll excuse me."

He strode over to a card table. The brown-haired girl wrapped an arm around his shoulders, and a boy bowed in his presence.

Bowing. Playing. Laughing.

That *wasn't* our purpose.

But Caé hadn't given us a command. Maybe this uncertainty of mine was my own doubt, my own sin, trying to push and pull Caé in the direction I wanted Her to go. If She chose the Bassan king, then his authority was also Hers, and his wishes must also be Hers.

I left to pray alone. I sang and whispered and waited for a sign until I fell asleep.

VERSE ELEVEN

A drumbeat pounded from the foot of my bed.

I gasped and tumbled onto the stone floor, the world tilting. I looked about, trying to understand what was happening. There was no drummer, only the door to my chamber—trembling as it was beat against.

"Elissa!" cried Lucio. "Elissa, wake up!"

I still wore the dress from last night, but had somehow lost my shoes. Upon opening the door, I found that Lucio had slept even less than I had. The whites of his eyes were dotted with red; his white-golden hair frizzed and refused to stay in its queue. He wore no coat, just a chemise half tucked into a pair of red breeches.

Before I could question him, he took me by the shoulders. "I need you to bless me," he said, his voice broken and hoarse.

"What?"

"Sing a blessing over me." His voice was thin. His eyes shone like rain-slicked glass. "The king wants new music in an hour. And my mind, it's—it's been harder and harder to compose these days." Lucio exhaled shakily through his nose and clutched my shoulders harder. "I need you to ask Caé to give me inspiration."

I nodded, my heart thumping against my ribs. I'd never seen him like this. So unrestrained. So clearly upset. "Which blessing should I—?"

"Any of them," he croaked.

"All right," I said. I pulled on the string of my Goddess Eye, holding the bead tight more for comfort than for guidance. *Caé, I prayed, he is clearly distressed. Give him all that he needs, please.*

The song I sang was one that was sung in the monastery in the mornings, meant to help our minds wake up for the day. We sang it over the Composers to help urge them on in their studies. I hoped it would work now.

But as I sang it, the simple melody like a child climbing slowly up a set of stairs, Lucio shook his head like a wet dog.

"No," he grumbled, "no, that's not working."

He'd hardly given the blessing a chance. Still, I cleared my throat and tried a different song. The Goddess's Choir sang this one at the graduation ceremony for the Composers who had completed their apprenticeships. With our voices, we helped inspire them, encourage them, and build their confidence in the new power of their music.

Lucio gripped my arm tighter still. "It's not working," he said. He shook his head, his chest heaving. "I can't—I can't hear any music!" He staggered past me into my bedchamber, dropping onto the end of the bed and holding his head in his hands. His shoulders quaked.

"Oh, Maestro," I said, my hand light against his shoulder. "Your other compositions are so lovely, surely—"

"I can't use my other compositions," he whimpered. "The king, he—he will send us away! He'll banish us! He'll hate us forever!"

"He won't," I said. "And you said we don't need to fear him. Caé protects us."

"She gave him power over Basso. If we displease him, we displease Her."

I sat down beside him on the white sheets. I felt strangely motherly, comforting him like this—that, and seeing him so small and weak and helpless, made my insides clench.

"Sometimes I find that the pressure to think of a song makes it harder to come up with one in the first place," I offered quietly.

He said nothing but slowly raised his head. He glanced first at me, and then at my desk. As if struck by lightning, he leapt to his feet, somehow fully recovered, and lifted the pages from my desktop.

My stomach fell. I hid behind the bedpost. "Maestro, I can explain—"

He coolly sifted through the pages, one after another. "You remember what I told you. You remember I warned you about stepping outside your role. I must take a portion of the offerings you've earned as punishment for this."

Every cent was precious. Every coin offered to me brought me a minute closer to my parents' freedom.

To lose even a farthing made me hate the music I'd written.

"Maestro," I said, my voice fraying as tears rose, "please, I'll tear it up. I'll never write again. I swear it."

"You said that last time. And you've disobeyed me." The sheets of music made a rushing sound as he flapped them under my nose. "And this is not your property to tear up as you please. It belongs to the Goddess."

I nodded frantically, my hands clasped tight. "Yes, yes, do whatever you like with it, just please, don't cut my salary!"

He shuffled the papers neatly and tucked them under his arm, standing tall and smoothing back his hair. "What's done is done. I want you to sing a song of penance to warm up your voice, and then, in an hour, you will sing one of these songs for Their Majesties. What you made selfishly, let it be given away to our generous patrons."

Our patrons.

Our week was up, and his decision was made—he wanted us to stay here. To work for the king for a year.

"Lucio, we—we can't stay under their employ." My voice was small and pathetic and bore little strength.

He rubbed his temples like I was giving him a headache.

"Caé's eye, why *not*? She gave us no sign! She does not object to us being here. And would it be so bad? To call someplace a home after wandering for years?"

"What if we *have* a sign?" I pointed to him, to the music. "The quiet in your mind, the way She's not giving you music as She usually does—what if *that's* the sign of Her disapproval?"

Blood flooded Lucio's cheeks. "And that is why She gives Her music to you and not to me? Because She means to censure me? Is *that* what you're saying, Elissa?"

I didn't have an answer. My hands trembled so greatly that I clung tight to my skirt to still them. I didn't know why Caé gave me Her songs. I didn't even know the extent of the power they could wield. With them, I had made life out of a simple flower.

But seeing Lucio angry made me feel so small. I didn't want to vex him; I didn't want to hurt him; I just wanted his wisdom. I wanted answers.

"No. Perhaps...perhaps those songs I composed are even dangerous," I said shakily. "It's like you've said; I'm not trained in composition like you are. I shouldn't sing them. I don't understand them. We shouldn't even perform them for Their Majesties. Do you understand why She would give me these compositions? Why, Lucio?"

"You seem to be blessed by the Goddess in all things," said Lucio acidly, tucking in his chemise and strolling toward the door. "I believe She will look mercifully upon you and let

Her music go on to please the king." He stepped through the doorway and turned to look at me over his shoulder. Anger still simmered in his eyes, barely contained. I hated it. "Sing your prayers, Elissa. I will see you in the performance hall shortly."

Lucio shut the door behind him with a slam. I pressed my hand against the doorknob, my pulse pounding so heavily that I could feel it in my palm.

}

The antechamber to the king's room was dimmer than normal. Most days, sunshine reflected against the white snow, resplendent as a beacon, and the many windows made the chamber clear and bright. Today, gray clouds hovered in the sky, gathering like a group of gossipers. A young man in black even had to light some of the lamps, despite the early hour.

Lucio had changed into a scarlet coat with a white lace cravat and a matching bow for his hair. The soft, comforting blue of the Goddess Eye earring stood out against the shimmering red fabric of his coat. At the sight of me, he bowed.

"Good morning," he said, as though we'd not seen each other earlier.

"Good morning." My voice came out *pianissimo*.

An attendant rapped a large staff against the polished floor. We pivoted toward the double doors; servants opened them and let us enter.

The king's bedroom was as extravagant as all the other chambers in this palace. A painted ceiling with Caé smiling lovingly over Mount Brio. Painted gold walls. A massive bed surrounded in gold and red curtains. A little golden fence separated the bed from the rest of the room. Only the king's trusted courtiers could pass through, where they would dress him in the morning. Lucio said that the nobles lined up to hand him a piece of clothing one at a time, and that even giving the king his glove or a shoe was a great honor.

It all sounded a bit silly to me, if I was being honest.

King Massimo was dressed in violet today, matching his wife again as they sat at a small round table with a tea set. A little mountain of pastries stood on a silver tray for them, and the king was already chewing on one when we entered.

"Good morning, Singer!" said Queen Flora. "Good morning, Composer!"

We greeted them with a bow.

The king wiped his hands on a silk napkin and then leaned back in his chair with a deep, tired sigh. "Now then, Composer," he said, "I dearly hope you've written up something new this time. I have become used to sleeping well, thanks to you, but last night..."

Lucio inclined his head. "Forgive me, Sire. I hope to make amends today." He turned and offered me a sheet of music— as though I'd never seen it before. As though it hadn't come from my own mind.

Maestro Lucio lifted the tails of his coat and set himself on his chair, his lute balanced on his knee. The paper fluttered in my hands.

He played the notes, *do-mi-sol,* as if I hadn't written the key signature myself. As if I didn't know the music to come.

A film of tears formed over my eyes as I watched him. He nodded to me once; nodded to me as he did before any one of our hundreds, thousands of performances.

My song. My voice. Wasn't this what Caé wanted? Wasn't this what *I* wanted?

Lucio cleared his throat. I jumped, startled, and shakily sang the first note.

One step, then another.

The words were so simple; the old, familiar *solfège* that created the world. They provided me with a sort of refuge in that moment. I used to think that I knew music, that I understood music, that I loved music. Singing this song made me uncertain.

And then, I began to feel a lightness, from the soles of my shoes to the crown of my head. A feeling so light and so marvelous that I remembered what a glory music was, how *enjoyable* it was for me to master a difficult, rapid phrase of notes, to sustain a note and then to resolve it, to cry a note so loud it hurt and then diminish it, whisper it.

I *loved* music. I loved it, separate from myself, from Lucio, from my past, from my parents. Reaching the final four notes, the majestic, triumphant *Let it be so!* of this song, I realized what the power of the melody was, what power the Goddess had imbued it with—joy.

The queen held her hand against her chest, a rapturous smile on her face. The king grinned, his hands clasped. Even Lucio held his head high, a smile dimpling his cheek.

The first person to clap was an attendant standing by a candelabra. His partner jumped up and down, crying out and demanding another song.

The king and queen laughed and rose to their feet, clapping raucously. Bowing to their praise, I felt a new warmth flooding my cheeks and resting in my belly. *That melody was mine, and it was strong enough to make a king laugh.*

"*Bravi!*" said the king, approaching and clapping Lucio on the back. "I knew last night was only a wobble. This song is better than all your others put together!"

Lucio's smile dropped for a fraction of a second. "I am most grateful, Your Majesty."

The queen kissed my hands. "And bless the Goddess for so mighty a voice!"

King Massimo snapped his fingers at a page standing by the door. At this signal, the page approached, holding out a mahogany box to us. The king opened the golden latch and procured two velvet pouches, filled to bursting with gold coins. He dropped one into Lucio's hands. And one into mine.

All the breath left my lungs.

"Your salary," explained the king, a proud grin lighting up

his face. "Paid in advance for your year in our service. We are glad to show our generosity to our most faithful friends."

Money. So much money; more than I'd ever carried or even seen. More than anyone could ever offer me in a simple donation.

Years ago—after men in black uniforms came to our house, took Mother and Father away, and told me I would be going to the monastery to serve Caé—I was permitted to see my parents one final time: at their trial. The price on their heads, the price for their heresy, was a number burned into my mind as a brand. Four hundred silver pieces.

For so long, I'd wondered if I could ever sing enough to earn four hundred coins.

It was over now.

They were free.

I held my quivering hand against my forehead. I had more than enough money—I could hire a coach and a mercenary and have them brought to this palace. They could be here in a month. I could clothe them in fine velvet and give them sugared food. We could stay here and be happy under the king's protection. Be together again.

But in that perfect vision of my life, my songs would only remain in this palace. I wouldn't be helping the poor and the devastated. I wouldn't help end the suffering caused by this war. I'd only sit about and sing to make a king and queen smile, day after day after day.

It would be a comfortable life. But I remembered the

words that the pilgrim, Veronica, had said to me: *When you tell the Goddess you'd like more responsibility, She'll give it to you.*

Traveling. Miracles. Sacrifice. Poverty.

That was what my responsibility looked like. I knew this, unshakably, down to my bones.

"Thank you, Majesty," said Lucio, bowing his head. "We are happy to stay in the court of Caé's chosen king."

"No," I said.

Every eye in the room turned upon me. Lucio went pale as a sheet.

The king raised a brow at me and gave a soft, bewildered chuckle. "What did you say, Singer?"

I wanted my mother and father to be free. I wanted to do what was right. I wanted Lucio to be happy. I wanted Caé to be happy.

With trembling hands, I tucked the bag of coins back into its box. "You've been so welcoming to us, Your Majesties. But our command from the Goddess was to travel. As lovely as this palace is, I choose to obey Her."

King Massimo's smile had faded away. The queen wilted in her chair, her lip quivering.

"Sire," said Lucio with wide, frantic eyes, "Sire, she does not speak for me. The Goddess has brought us here; I'm certain She wants us to be here—for the queen's sake! I intend to stay, just as She asks of me."

The words were a knife twist to my gut. The future I'd

planned for just a moment, where we carried on as before, Lucio and me and Melody and the carriage, composing and singing miracles…it could not be. He did not care what I chose. He would not follow where I went.

The king pointed to Lucio and looked at me. "You see? The Goddess is in agreement with me. She expects a happy, humble servant to sing Her miracles to us. That is Her will!"

A soft tapping sounded from behind me, like rain striking the window. An attendant shyly opened the double doors, his face pallid and afraid.

King Massimo turned on the boy, his teeth clenched. "What could be so important that you'd interrupt my meeting with a Composer and a Singer?"

The boy shuffled into the room with his head kept low. "F-forgive me, Sire," he said. "I bring news from the group you sent to Passaggio."

"The mountain town I sent provisions to?" The king's footsteps echoed as drumbeats through the hall. "What could this possibly be concerning?"

The young herald glanced at Lucio and me. "Do you wish for me to tell you now, Sire?"

The king batted a hand at the air. "Yes, yes, out with it!"

The boy nodded, hastily swept the tricorne hat off his head, and worked it back and forth between his hands. "When we arrived at Passaggio, Sire," he said, "we—we found all of her inhabitants dead."

Icy hands gripped my heart.

The king's rage was doused in an instant. "What?"

"We came to deliver the provisions," the young man said, his voice quivering, "but they—they were all dead. They were so thin. Lying in the snow."

King Massimo furrowed his brow. "Well—well, what happened? Was it a surprise attack from Acuto, what?"

The page's mouth opened to say something, but it took several seconds before he could speak. "They looked starved, sir. But…but we found some food still there. Enough to last the entire village a good week or so, I reckon, but…it was all untouched. They looked like they'd not eaten in days."

Like they'd not been hungry at all.

The golden hues of the bedroom swirled in my vision, and I soon found myself on my hands and knees on the wooden floor. Faces blinked behind my eyelids. The mayor. The people who'd given me the food off their plates. The people who wept to hear my songs.

I'd killed them. My song had killed the whole village.

VERSE TWELVE

"Caé," I cried out, my voice like a bow grinding across violin strings. "I killed them, I killed them!"

Lucio knelt on the floor beside me, pushing my pale curls from my cheeks and looking me in the eyes. "Hush," he whispered, and the sweetness in his voice nearly made me forget this morning and the coldness in his eyes.

His gaze flitted back and forth from the king to me. A small, cynical voice, ever growing, said to me, *He does not wish to comfort you. He wishes to silence you.*

"Unnatural," murmured the king, his footsteps pounding a steady rhythm as he paced. "Ghastly. The girl's been reduced to hysterics. This must be an attack by the Acutians—perhaps they poisoned the wells, or the food itself."

I shook my head, Lucio's face appearing as a smudge of white and gold paint through the blur of my tears. "No," I said, and then louder still, "No, Sire, it was not the Acutians!"

Lucio's hand gripped my chin. Panic glimmered in his eyes. "Elissa, please," he whispered. "Please, he's the king— do not anger him! He doesn't need to know."

But I didn't care. The truth was a startled bird, flapping wildly in the cage of my chest. I must set it free. With both hands, I pushed Lucio aside, sending him falling against the cold floor.

"What's this?" the king asked me. His jaw was clenched, and his eyes were storm clouds.

"I sang a song to the people of Passaggio," I said. "It was supposed to alleviate their hunger, Sire, until provisions came. But—" My voice had lost its strength. My lip shook, and I bit it hard to keep sobs bursting from me. "It did not rest well with me, Majesty. I know that it is my song that caused the Passaggians to starve."

He folded his arms and held his fingertips against his chin. "You did this, by Caé's magic?"

I nodded, continuing to rake my teeth against the flesh of my lip. Slowly, I knelt to the floor before him, my head inclined. "I did not want to hurt anybody," I whispered. "But it is by my voice they are dead."

My mind was wickedly clever at coming up with the images of the Passaggians' faces in death. Blank eyes. Open mouths. Sunken faces. Thin bodies, covered in a blanket of snow.

"And who composed the song?" asked the king. "Maestro Lucio?"

My throat pinched. "Yes, Sire. But only at the behest of Governor Mosso! He asked that we—"

"Come here, Composer," the king interjected. It was not a shouted command—it was a calm, thoughtful request. I could tell by the pattern of his speech that he had a plan brewing.

A hand covered in golden rings entered my line of vision, palm out. I delicately placed my hand in the king's, and he lifted me to my feet. By the time I rose, Lucio was standing at my side, his face as white as the lace at his cuffs.

"How far away were you from Passaggio when she sang the song over their village?" asked His Majesty.

"A—about half a day's journey, Sire. We were higher up, at the governor's mansion. Caé Elissa sang to the village below." He spoke softly, his voice quaking just as mine did.

The king gazed at the floor and drummed the pads of his fingers against his thin lips. When he lifted his stare, he looked first to his wife.

"Page," he said, "escort the queen out, and bring back General Giusto at once."

The boy in black swept a bow and offered his arm to the queen, who watched the scene with a furrowed brow. On her way out, the queen touched a hand to the king's shoulder.

"Be gentle with her," she said.

As soon as the door thumped shut behind the two, the king strode to a desk at the far end of the room. He unrolled a scroll of parchment, took a pen, and flitted the red quill across the page at a rapid pace.

"Lucio," I whispered, my voice high and pinched, "our music, it—it *killed* people—"

He squeezed my hand tight, shaking his head. "There's nothing to be done about that now."

I bunched the soft dark green fabric of my skirts in my fists. "I thought you said Caé's power couldn't be used for evil."

Lucio said nothing.

"Why would She allow this evil to happen?" I whispered, blinking back tears. "Is it my fault? Yours, for your notes? Do you truly believe Caé *wanted* this to—"

"I don't know." He took a shaky breath. Tears beaded on his eyelashes, but still he did not look at me. "We'll be all right. She ordained this. All of this." But his voice was so faint. So weak. So uncertain.

A woman walked in, dressed in a blue coat and breeches like the guards at the gate. She bowed to the king and carried a scroll in her hands.

"General Giusto," said the king to her, "I believe I've found an end to this war."

The general's brows bunched together. "Sire?"

He swept his hand toward Lucio and me. "A Singer and a Composer," he said. "They represent a sort of power man alone cannot achieve. In the battle to claim Caé's homeland, what better to use than Her own power, Her own Voice?"

Like me, the general frowned. She bowed her dark head. "Pardon me, Sire—I don't quite understand."

The king marched up to me, and I gasped as he thumped his hands upon my bare shoulders. "With only her voice, with the power of a song, this child starved an entire village of people. She was not even *in* the village—she sang her song from the mountains." With movements as stiff as a wooden toy's, he shifted in place toward Lucio. "What was the intention of the composition you sang for Governor Mosso, Maestro Lucio?"

"To eliminate the hunger of the people of Passaggio, Majesty."

Turning back to the general, he pointed to the two of us. "You see? Perhaps with the right spell, sung the right way, sung from high up—perhaps we could fell the Acutian army."

Lucio was silent, even though the king's eyes were aglow with hope and excitement. He clutched Lucio's shoulder, making him flinch.

"This is the reason, Composer," he said, beaming. "This is why Caé has brought you to us. To write the song that will defeat our enemies."

The word *No!* rumbled through me, vibrating as a resounding gong. But I kept my mouth clamped shut and my hands balled tight.

I reached for Lucio's sleeve, silently pleading with him to listen to me, but he jerked back his hand and swept into a low bow. "I am Caé's servant."

My heart lifted for a moment—he was resisting, he was listening to Caé's desire for peace, not the king's thirst for victory.

But the king smiled. "Then you are my servant." His Majesty pivoted back to the general. "We will need a proper vantage point to have her sing over the Acutian army."

With a flick of the king's hand, a servant cleared away the tea tray and the breakfast from the small table between two chairs. The king sat; the general stood, laying a map down. She pointed to a spot. "We believe they've retreated to Mount Maestoso. We'd need to travel someplace higher." She circled a gray blotch on the paper. "The peak of Mount Brio would do well. There's a clear path carved up the side."

"Excellent," said the king. He pointed to Lucio and me. "Both of you, prepare for a journey that will last a fortnight." Then he gestured us away, a dismissal. In a way, he was a conductor, too; waving us about instead of speaking his instructions.

Lucio walked past me, but I stayed still, watching the king and the general discuss their war.

They wanted to end this war. They wanted to end it with my voice. With the song that had killed innocent people.

I thought of the queen, perfectly lovely, a woman from Acuto, and a woman just like those I'd met in Basso and in Cadenza. The Acutians were the enemies of Basso, yes. But they did not deserve to die so cruelly. They did not deserve to die at all.

Lucio's hand curled around my arm, trying to guide me out of the room. I pressed my weight hard through my shoes. "Sire," I called, my voice echoing *fortissimo* in the hall, "I will not use my voice this way!"

The light and the eagerness that had brightened the king's eyes quickly passed away. "That is not your decision to make."

Lucio tugged harder on my arm, pulling me toward the door.

I pushed against his chest. "Let me go! Your Majesty, it was never my wish that my voice do harm to others! It is not the way things are meant to be. It is not how Caé wants to use my voice—"

"You serve me," said the king through his teeth. He held up a hand. "Who has given you a home? Who has fed you, clothed you, paid you?"

I shook my head, spilling tears to the floor. "The Goddess did not call me to be your weapon, Majesty."

He stood up, pointing, his face red as carmine. "*Be silent! It is not you who commands me, girl!* You should be on your *knees* thanking me for my mercy. You killed *my* people. The Goddess did not give you that voice to speak thus to a king, a sovereign by divine right. If you wish to keep your life, you'll sing." He snapped his fingers at Lucio. "Talk some sense into her. She will come with us to the mountain, willingly or not."

Even though I struggled and ground my shoes against

the floorboards, Lucio practically dragged me out of the room, through the antechamber, and into the corridor. He slammed me hard against the stone wall. I gasped. Fear coiled in my stomach.

"The king will kill you," he whispered, shaking me. I imagined King Massimo on his horse, hunting me down with his pack of dogs. "Do you *wish* to die, Elissa?" He held me fast against the wall. "Everything I do, every *thought* I have is for your safety. I do not know what I must do for you to obey!"

"I cannot obey!" I strove against him as best as I could, but I was smaller, and younger, and unused to such roughness. The way he'd hurt me so, the very fact of it, left me trembling like I was in an earthquake. "I cannot obey, not when I am asked to do something monstrous!"

"He is asking you to end a war, Elissa! That is no monstrous thing. We came here on a journey of peace and goodwill." He shook his head. "The king is right! Everything, every step along the way, it was Caé—She brought us here. She brought us to *this court*. She means for you to bring the war to a close!"

"And I must do so by starving people?" I spat. Tears rolled into my mouth, cold and salted. "There is nothing peaceful about bringing more death. I did not want to sing that wretched song the first time! I cannot, and never shall again, end the life of another man." I looked into his eyes, and despite everything, found a fraction of comfort in the sorrow there. Deep down, he could feel this was not right. "You know Caé as I do. She would not want this. She...She lives for creation, not destruction. We are all Her children. She taught us that."

Lucio bent his head. "All my life I've wanted to be useful. To have a purpose. To make Her proud. She brought us here, Elissa. She's used my music. People love my music. This is what She wants to use *us* for. She ordained all of this. She *knew* that we'd come this far—"

"Perhaps She wanted us to make a choice," I said. "To make the right choice." My heart struck my ribs so hard it ached. The Goddess bead against my chest vibrated, and I thought of Her, I thought of home, I thought of the monastery; I thought of Cadenza. "We could go back to Cadenza, Lucio. We could forget all of this."

He shut his eyes and shook his head. "What would we do? We would be enemies of Basso."

"Do you remember what you promised Maestro Tenuto?" My throat ached, like each word I spoke was sharp-edged. Our time at the monastery seemed lifetimes ago. I was a child still, but I was even more of a child then. And Lucio was different then. I clutched his hand. "You promised to protect me."

He clenched his eyes shut, as if the sound of my voice hurt him. "That's what I'm trying to do! I told you so! That's all I've ever done; I just want to keep you safe "

"You could come with me," I said. "You could see your mother and your father and your brother again, and I could see my parents in the valley again—"

"Elissa," he said, his voice cold and sharp, "there is no place for you in Cadenza. Nowhere but the monastery. And there, the king would surely find you."

My eyes narrowed. "Why would I have no place? When I earn enough, my family—"

"They died. They died a year ago."

I left my body for a strange, brief second.

I could see myself from above: the top of my head, Lucio's hands tight against my arms. A second passed, and then the pain of the words registered: a low, steady note crescendo-ing fast.

"You're wrong," I whispered. "They can't be."

"They died a year ago," he said again, more forcefully. "I got the letter. I did not tell you. It would have disheartened you."

His eyes were hard as jade. I curled my hands into fists. My chest sealed tight.

My parents could not be dead. It wasn't possible. Such a world was not possible. "You're—you're lying."

"You have to believe me—if you run away, if you go back to Cadenza, there will be nothing for you but war-torn fields. The king will find you there easily. And he'll execute you."

My pulse crashed in my ears. Lucio's face danced in my vision. His words were separate, disjointed, a language I did not speak.

Sing for the king. Kill. Live.

Run. Pursue peace. Die.

"You cannot give up your life for this," he whispered. "You know I'm right: Caé brought us here to end this war."

No. Not like this. Tears affixed themselves to my lashes as I looked up to him again. A voice repeated itself in my head, in time with the beat of my heart.

Listen to your own voice. Listen to your own voice.

"Lucio," I breathed, "Lucio, my brother, please come with me."

He took a shuddering breath and then shook his head. "No. No, I won't go with you. Caé wants me to stay here."

"Do you really believe so?"

Fear shimmered in his eyes. But he said nothing.

"You *know* Her," I pressed. "You know She isn't like this. Cruel and violent."

"I know that She is unknowable," he said, his shaking voice betraying the sternness of his words. "And I know sometimes sacrifices must be made in the name of peace."

He'd made his decision. No amount of pleading was going to change that: I knew that deep to my core. I could only pray he would listen to his own voice, the one that was filling him with fear and doubt.

Listen to your own voice.

Listen to your own song.

I couldn't stay here.

A song was playing in my head, an old Cadenzan lullaby, but with an edge to it. Sharp notes, unresolved scales.

I parted my lips and began to sing it to Lucio and to the guards at the ends of the corridor, the same simple non-sense words that had formed the universe. Lucio's forehead wrinkled. He opened his mouth; gripped me tighter—

And then his hands went limp.

I sang more softly. His eyelids shut. His knees buckled. There was a thump and a clang as the soldiers at either end of the corridor fell, their halberds resting on their sides. Lucio collapsed against the round stones of the floor, his chest rising and falling deeply.

Standing in the hall, surrounded by the echo of my own voice, I pressed my hand to my Goddess Eye. She was above me, painted on the ceiling, smiling and serene. I hoped She could see my anguish now, and that it pained Her just as much.

"Merciful Caé, let them wake up soon," I whispered. "Don't let the falls have hurt them."

I did not have the chance to see for myself—for I ran down the hall, as fast as I could, then down the stairs and toward the mammoth front doors. I sang the lullaby again and again: to the guards in the great atrium, to the courtiers strolling the snowy grounds, to the guards in front of the glittering, sunshine-bright gate.

Then, running, I escaped through a little postern door in the outer walls. I stumbled out, racing across the cobbled road and into the snowy wilderness of Basso.

Movement Three

VERSE THIRTEEN

The pretty red heeled shoes supplied by His Majesty's court were very little help when it came to climbing down snow-covered rocks. The gown I wore was equally useless to me—the green velvet fabric pooling around my arms and dragging along the icy stones was beautiful, but not the slightest bit warm, and I cursed the way the dress left my shoulders bare and stinging in the cold. I plucked the pins out of my hair and let my curls tumble down over my shoulders for an extra measure of warmth.

I only lasted a few minutes rubbing my hands against my bare arms before I knew I needed the help of song to survive this bitter cold. This was all I could think of—how my toes had lost feeling in my shoes, how my teeth clattered together, how my skin had frozen so much it felt warm again.

Softly, my voice quivering like the rest of me, I sang out the quick, jumping song used to heat our teapot. As I pressed my hands tight against the flesh of my arms, they warmed up, as if my hands were gentle candle flames. It was not much heat—but it was something.

I sang the spell over and over as I clambered down the

slope of the mountain, and by the time I reached the bottom, the sun was low in the sky. My stomach burned. My legs shook as I leaned, panting, against a tall pine. My chest rose and fell like a bellows.

On the mountaintop, the Bassan palace glowed orange in the sunset. An antlike dot left from the palace gates—a carriage with four horses.

They were searching for me. I was sure of it.

"Caé help me," I whispered, and then ran deeper into the shelter of a dense pine forest.

I did not know where I was going. My mind was too muddled, and only one thing mattered—leaving the palace behind. Leaving behind all thought of death.

Passaggio. The armies.

My parents.

What good could I do to all that I'd harmed, now that I was powerless, hopeless, and lost in some Bassan forest?

I held my breath to stave off those thoughts. I couldn't think about it now.

Once more, I sang the warming spell, but after so many times, my hands bore no more warmth than if I'd rubbed them together. Fading sunlight streamed through the dark branches all around me, yellow on black bark. Pine needles crunched beneath my feet.

Caé, please, please, give me a song, I pleaded. Every time I blinked, my eyes closed more and more slowly. *Give me a song or I'll die.*

I trudged on. Night came. The world was muted, just the black of trees and the white of moonlight. Far off, a wolf gave a mournful cry.

E-flat, I thought.

There were patches within the forest where the trees had protected the earth from snow. I curled up beneath a tree, hiding my stockinged legs beneath my skirts. My stiff, frozen fingers did a pathetic job of trying to massage my feet. Something sticky clung to my stockings. Blood.

Tilting my head back against the hard tree trunk, I looked up, and between the crossed fingers of tree branches above, stars poked out through the darkness.

When we die, we become stars, said Father, once upon a time.

I shut my eyes and wept.

Stars were cold and distant. Untouchable. Unreachable. I stood on Father's shoulders as a child, reaching up to heaven, crying petulantly that I could not touch them.

Were the dead watching me now? The citizens of Passag gio? My parents?

Would I join them soon?

Fear and cold made my body stiff, and breathing became more and more burdensome. My mind was empty of music, and I thought, *This is the worst way to die—to die without song.*

Somewhere, so far away it felt as if a dream, a bird called out to another. I opened my eyes, unsure of my own senses.

But there was the cry again—three notes.

C. A. E.

A Cadenzan songbird. Here, singing in the middle of the night in Basso.

I rubbed my eyes and stared openmouthed at the boughs of pine above. Was it the bird I had made? Any Cadenzan songbird here at all would have been a miracle—it must have been a sign. It must have been *Her*.

"Is that really you?" I whispered. "Please, please sing again, if it's you!"

C. A. E.

I gripped the tree and pulled myself to my feet, nodding to the trees like they were the Goddess Herself. "Please show me what to do, Caé. Please, help me live through this night."

C. A. E.—the song came from behind me somewhere. I followed the call.

After only a few steps, I smelled smoke. I followed the scent and then, as distant and beautiful as sunrise itself, I could see a fire glowing somewhere deep in the woods.

Even though I ached from head to toe, I sprinted closer to that fire, my mouth watering as if I could somehow consume the flames and become nourished. I ran into the halo of its golden light, and before I could hold out my hands to warm myself, something wrapped tight around my neck, pressing the necklace of pearls and the string of my Goddess Eye hard against my throat.

I gagged, clawing at the thing choking me—an arm. A knife poked against my stays.

On the other side of the fire stood a man with a short beard and piercing blue eyes, glowing as little flames. His brow furrowed. "Easy, Ubalde," he said, holding a gloved hand toward me. "It's just a girl. Easy now."

The man behind me shifted, his hand tight on my arm. The knife had not moved, so neither did I.

His companion rounded the fire and tilted his head, crouching down so he could meet my gaze.

"What in the world brings you here, my lady?" he asked.

"I'm cold," I whispered.

"I can see that." His eyes narrowed. "You've no coat. Are you mad or something?"

I didn't know what to say. More than anything, I was weary, and I wanted nothing more than to lie beside the crackling, sweet-smelling fire.

"Look at these, Danilo," said Ubalde. His knife no longer prodded at my stomach, but instead grazed the lobe of my right ear. The king had given me a large pearl for each. "Must be a courtier."

"A courtier lost in the woods," muttered Danilo. "You must be truly unfortunate. Or truly fortunate." He folded his arms. "You mustn't be here to steal from us, then?"

"No, sir," I peeped. Fear brought the cold from around me right into my veins. "I—I saw a fire, and I wanted warmth. I didn't think."

"Your accent—where are you from?"

I squirmed, trying to shift away from the blade. Every breath was a reminder of the knife now pointing against my throat. "Cadenza, sir."

Danilo's mouth fell open, and soon he was laughing, slapping his knee. "Caé's eye, *Cadenza?* What brings you to this frozen heap of garbage?"

I didn't know how to answer. It could either be advantageous or dangerous for me to state my station. Before I could speak, he approached me, tipping my chin to see me better.

"A little blond Cadenzan girl at court," he muttered. Then his eyes grew wide. "You're the Singer!" He waved a hand at his partner. "Ubalde, you fool, you're about to stab a Singer!"

The man behind me withdrew his knife. I stepped forward, gasping for air, and kept my hands in front of me, curled into fists. What I'd do with them, I had no idea.

Danilo held his gloved hands in front of him. "Forgive us, my lady," he said. "We would never wish to do harm to someone as venerated as yourself." He swept an arm toward the fire, where two wooden stools sat on either side. "Please have a seat. You are our honored guest."

I stood there, waiting for him to change his mind, or for the man behind me to jump at me again, but neither man moved. I cautiously shuffled forward and sat on a stool, extending my hands toward the flames.

Danilo and Ubalde—a broad man with a long, drooping moustache—murmured to each other and watched me.

My heart was lost, fluttering inside my stomach. I stretched my hands to the flames and carefully slid one stockinged foot out of its shoe. Red patches stained the yellow fabric along my heel and toes. I didn't even feel any pain.

"Miss Singer," said Danilo, his boots crunching in the snow as he approached, "we have some food left over, if you'd like something to eat."

I nodded in spite of myself. "Thank you very much."

Danilo nodded to his partner. He took the cue and walked to their carriage, dark gray with spots of dirt on the wheels and along the bottom. Danilo took a seat across from me, and Ubalde returned with a block of cheese, some bread, and a blanket. I nearly wept as he placed them in my arms.

After wrapping myself tight in the blanket—though it smelled of tobacco and mold—and eating the bread and cheese as fast as I could, I sat there, dazed and happy, watching the dancing flames.

"Why are you so far from the palace, Singer?" asked Danilo.

I rubbed at my eyes. With my belly full again and the warmth of the fire beating against my face, all I wanted to do was curl up and sleep. "I, um, no longer felt my purpose was being served with the king."

Danilo's russet eyebrows raised and he guffawed. "Must

be some great purpose, if the king wasn't good enough for you!"

"I don't mean quite like that," I mumbled, but did not know how to properly articulate how I felt. I did not wish to share with them all I'd seen at the court, nor tell them of the violence my singing had caused. Thinking of such things was the beginning of a dark path my mind could get lost on. *Sunken faces, bony fingers, the dead lying in the snow, all by my voice—*

"Your purpose is singing, isn't it?"

I nodded to Danilo. His friend slid his knife along a stray tree branch, peeling back shavings in long ribbons.

Danilo smiled. "Then you must sing for us!"

My throat and my chest both ached from the singing I'd done all day and the way I'd run and climbed since this morning. Still, I owed a song to these men. That was what my power was, after all: a gift.

I opened my mouth and sang a high note, cascading quickly down, then jumping up again. The melody whirled and twirled and danced, expressing joy in ways that the simple *solfège* couldn't. Ubalde turned his gray eyes from his carving and watched me, slack-jawed. An even broader smile spread across Danilo's rosy face.

When I'd reached the benediction of the song, the men were standing and applauding before I'd even finished the final word. People applauded for my songs each time I performed, but the glowing feeling in my chest never seemed to fade. I smiled and sheepishly bowed my head, as if I could hide myself from their praise.

"Goddess be, I feel amazing!" said Ubalde, his voice a deep bass.

"That's quite a gift you have there," Danilo said, striding to my side and giving me a pat between the shoulders.

"Thank you, sirs," I said. "And thank you again for your hospitality."

Ubalde held his knife aloft like he was giving a toast. "Sing another one!"

I rubbed my throat, tickling and rawer by the second. "Thank you, but I ought to save my voice."

"Nonsense," said Danilo, his hand cupping around my shoulder. He leaned close, so I could smell the stench of his breath. "We gave you food and warmth. And you blessed us with such happiness. It's what the Goddess would want, sharing more with your generous hosts!"

I chewed on my lip. *What the Goddess would want*—that was just what Lucio would say.

Minute by minute, I trusted less in what Lucio said.

Delicate and awkward as a newborn fawn, I wobbled to my feet, the blanket still draped around me as a cloak. "I won't encroach on your generosity any further, gentlemen." I unwound the scratchy gray blanket and held it out to Danilo. "I should go. Thank you, again, for all you've done for me."

Danilo scoffed. "Do you have some appointment you'll be late for? Come, now, sing us another song."

Certain facts began to arise more prominently in my mind: I was in the woods. In the dark. In the cold. With two strange men. Two strange men who were walking closer and closer to me, with sudden anger burning in their eyes.

Shirking politeness, I ran.

Not four steps later, one of them grabbed me around the middle. I screamed so loudly I could hear my heart pumping in my ears. One of the men clapped a large hand over my mouth. I tried to bite his palm, but in the next moment, he pressed a knife to my throat.

"Don't hurt her," said Danilo, his voice farther behind me. His footsteps grew faint as he walked to the carriage and then returned, standing before me with a length of rope.

Tears beaded in my eyes, and my chest burned as I held back a terrified whimper. Danilo wound the thick, scratchy rope fast around my wrists. His hand pushed down on the top of my head, and I knelt, my skirt growing damp and cold in the snow. The frigid tip of the knife grazed the nape of my neck, and the ribbon of the pearl necklace slipped loose. Danilo caught it and stuffed it in his pocket.

Something else slipped from my neck. I caught it in my bound hands. My Goddess Eye necklace.

"How much do you think we could make per song?" asked Ubalde.

Danilo touched my ankle, and I flinched, kicking to keep him away. He gripped my leg and clucked his tongue disapprovingly. "Listen, dear," he said, "we'd like you as a business partner. We will treat you like a princess if you don't squirm and fuss about like an animal." He huffed and finished tying the knot around my ankles. He started talking to his partner about numbers, about coins, about how many songs I'd sing a day, and I thought, *I am going to die. I am going to be trapped here. I am going to be hurt. They could kill me. I will never see Cadenza again.*

"Please," I said, but the word was completely stifled, utterly unintelligible as Ubalde covered my mouth with his hand. They mumbled to each other, clearly with no intention of setting me free or letting me speak.

But they'd let me sing.

From underneath his hand, I hummed the lullaby I'd sung to Lucio this morning. Low and calming, dancing up to a prolonged high note.

Danilo's eyes widened and he batted a hand at his partner. Ubalde removed his hand from my lips.

With the moment I'd gained, I said, "If I sing for you, will you please let me go?"

Ubalde's body pulsed with a laugh.

Danilo's smirk was like a gash that had been carved into his face, worsened by the sinister yellow glow of the fire. "I'm not a fool. You could use some dangerous magic on me." He took a curved knife and hooked it underneath my jaw.

I gasped and cringed, my eyes squeezing tight as if I could block out this whole nightmare. He was right. With a twisting of my stomach, I thought of Passaggio, of all the cruel things my songs could accomplish—but I was already drowning in fear, drowning in hopelessness.

My voice was my only escape.

"I can sing the song of riches!" I cried.

The two men shared a hungry look.

"The song of riches?" Ubalde repeated.

"Yes!" I started to nod but flinched at the cold knife against my throat. "It brings good luck and good fortune—it...it works almost immediately. You can find gold in your pockets!"

The knife drooped slightly.

"Let's hear it, then," said Ubalde.

"And no tricks." Danilo's smoky breath was hot and damp against my cheek, sending a shiver through me. "Now *sing*."

Though my whole body quaked, I dared to look into Danilo's eyes. This spell was for him, after all. And for his friend.

I continued the lullaby; a comforting, sweet song, all while a knife was to my throat and my hands and feet were bound. Danilo's eyes grew cloudy, and his satisfied smirk dropped into something silly, moony, and droopy. His eyes wrenched shut in a large yawn.

Something behind me thumped, and then Ubalde snored loudly. Danilo, too, lay down and curled up on the snowy forest floor like it was a feather bed.

I crawled across the rough, frozen earth and snatched the knife. Carefully bending myself, I wedged the blade between my ankles and sawed at the ropes. They snapped loose, and then I held the knife between my feet and cut my wrists free.

My head was spinning. My whole body ached. And I had no idea how long this sleeping spell would last.

I moved quickly, animalistically, barely thinking at all. I swept up the blanket from where it had been tossed aside.

There, by the fire, glowed something small and blue.

My Goddess Eye. The last piece of my parents I had.

But I couldn't carry it. The blanket, the knife. My hands were full.

I needed to stay alive.

I left it there in the dirt.

Verse Fourteen

The forest grew darker and darker the more I ran.

Westward, I chanted. *Just go west. Go home to Cadenza.*

I could only hope it was west. The night was black around me. When my ears started to pop and the forest floor began to slope, I started to have hope that I was finally leaving the mountainous lands of Basso.

But in my dizziness, in my weariness, I knew I could be stumbling in the wrong direction. I could be going north, toward Acuto. A strange land full of strangers—and more war.

The very thought made me finally stop in my tracks and look around. I had no compass, no map. I tried in vain to search the sky for the North Star, but the thick boughs of the fragrant evergreens hid it from me.

I was completely lost.

I crumpled onto the forest floor, leaning against a tree and shaking with cold and with sobs. As I wrapped the woolen blanket around me, I didn't even mind the musty smell.

With my eyes closed, I pretended I was in the arms of my

parents. I pressed the blanket against my cheek, damp with tears.

I wanted home. I wanted rest. I wanted Mother's kiss on my forehead and Father's hands brushing my hair. I wanted the aching in my body to end. I wanted to hear their voices again, singing to me.

I thought, too, of my second home, of the monastery in Cadenza Citadel. The Singers, my second family, helping me sing difficult enchantments and helping me endure the heartbreak of the loss of my parents. Their voices, strong and warm and familiar.

Lucio. My brother. Giving me flowers after a big concert. Writing songs, beautiful songs, and saying he'd written them with my voice in mind. Those rare, sunlit moments when he laughed at something I said. When I sang and he *smiled*.

Curled up tight against the tree, I sang another song. A song that would, I prayed, heal my sore, bleeding feet and my groaning bones. The same song that had healed the queen and that mysterious pilgrim, Veronica.

I tipped my head against the bark of the tree and sang the melody through numb, cracked lips. My voice was no stronger than a breeze. My heart was so very tired.

But when I sang, I didn't feel alone.

Desperately, I searched for that feeling of comfort, of Caé's presence beside me. Again and again I rasped my song, until it felt as if I'd replaced the rhythm of my breath with the notes. Every exhale, every sigh, was another phrase of the song. But I couldn't feel Her. Couldn't find Her. There was nothing but a heavy darkness enveloping me.

{

Barley. Carrots. Parsley. Bay leaves. Thyme.

The fragrance made my mouth water. But I kept obedient and stayed in my seat, as my parents would have expected. Father used to make this soup for me on the coldest Cadenzan nights—though compared to the winter of Basso, those cold nights would have seemed balmy.

I was at home. By the hearth, a lady spooned soup into a bright blue bowl. She carried it to me and set it atop the swirling grain of the old oak table, the one where I'd carved an *E* before Mother had noticed.

With a clink, she placed another plate before me—a thick slice of the cheesy bread that Father used to make—and a flagon of steaming cider.

"Go ahead," said the woman.

The voice was so familiar it startled me. I gaped up at Veronica.

I must have been making some ridiculous expression, because her eyes crinkled, and she laughed. "Hello, friend."

She was dressed differently now. A sapphire-colored skirt to her ankles, a simple apron, a plain chemise with a yellow vest covered in embroidered flowers. Her dark hair was braided over her shoulder, with a blue ribbon woven throughout.

It was how we dressed in Cadenza.

"I'm sure you have plenty of questions," she said, "but you should eat something first."

Veronica sat in the chair across from me, folding her arms and resting her chin on her arms as a child would.

Far, far in the back of my mind, I remembered something. A warning, in Lucio's voice.

I fiddled with the cloth napkin in my lap. "Maestro Lucio said he didn't know you, madam."

She let out a soft huff of a laugh. "Oh, he knows me. He's been a bit stubborn lately. But I know him well."

"Where did you meet him?" I murmured.

"In the monastery at Cadenza Citadel. He was about twelve."

Ah—that seemed very possible. People came and went through the monastery all the time, asking for blessings or giving up offerings to the Goddess. And if it had been five years since he met her, perhaps he'd simply forgotten.

A little more at ease, I pulled the plate of bread closer, gnawing on the crust. Cheese and garlic, parsley and butter. My shoulders loosened. Warmth flooded me. It was just as delicious and comforting as I'd remembered. I gobbled up the bread and sipped the soup and drank the cider till my belly and my heart were full. I let the flavor of the soup sit in my mouth for a moment; let it give me courage, like it was my parents' presence, distilled.

I missed them. My missing them hurt me, every fiber of me.

I remembered. The song I'd sung over Passaggio. All her inhabitants, dead. The king, asking me to destroy the Acutian army. How I'd refused his command, left Lucio behind, and wound up wandering in the woods. Without direction. Without my Goddess Eye.

"I did something horrible," I said, not to Veronica, but to my mother and father, wherever they were, safe in Cadenza, *alive* in Cadenza. "Governor Mosso wanted me to sing for him. He wanted me to sing a spell that got rid of the hunger of the people of Passaggio." I blinked back tears and drank more soup, like it was a very important task. "My song, it… it killed them, and it was all my fault. All because of me."

Veronica walked around the table to stand beside me, touching the hem of her apron to my cheeks and underneath my nose, all of which were now damp with tears. Her brow was crumpled—and tears shone in her eyes, too. "I'm so sorry."

An invisible hand squeezed my throat and my chest. More tears rose, and I could hear Lucio saying, *The Voice of the Goddess does not cry,* and it made my lip tremble even more.

After taking several gulps of air, I shut my eyes tight and imagined Mother and Father. I needed to tell them all of it.

"I did not want to hurt any more people," I said, "so I ran from the king's palace. I ran and ran and I thought I'd die in the woods."

Words were flowing from me like a burst dam. "I just

don't understand. I thought Caé wanted me to help people. But Lucio and the king...they said Her plan was to use my voice like a weapon. What if I was wrong, and I was supposed to help end the war, as the king wanted? She—She must be punishing me now. I was disobedient."

As I quaked, as my voice grew higher and thinner, Veronica laid an olive hand against my arm.

"I'm certain that's not true," said Veronica. She knelt beside my chair, her hands in her lap, her eyes attentive and warm. "You did the right thing. The king wanted to use you for evil, and you resisted. He wanted to use your music for destruction. And that isn't what Caé wants." Her gaze flitted toward the hearth. "Seeing people squabble over Her land, shedding blood to try to win Her favor...it disgusts Her. She wants peace."

I wiped my arm across my eyes. "How—how can you know for certain what She wants?"

Veronica flinched, her dark brows pressing together, as if I'd hurt her personally. "I thought you know Her well. You are Her Singer, after all."

Confusion and pain were a storm building fast in my chest. I bowed my head, my shoulders quaking so violently that my curls trembled as they drooped against my shoulders. "No one seems to know who She is. Caé the Wrathful. Caé the Merciful. Caé the Loving. Caé the Mysterious. Caé the Good." I covered my tearstained face with my hands. "I don't know who She is anymore."

Veronica's hand touched my wrist. I lifted my head.

She was smiling. Tears streaked her cheeks, yes, but she was smiling, peaceful and patient. Her eyes were the deep blue of a summer sky. "What do they call you?"

I frowned. "Elissa—Caé Elissa."

Veronica shook her head, a playful, secretive smile spreading across her rosy lips. "No. You have a title. Now, what is it?"

If this was a riddle, I couldn't solve it. "A Singer," I said. "The Voice of the Goddess."

"*That* is who you are," she said. She smiled grandly.

"I don't understand."

She laughed, squeezing my hands. "It's not just a title. It's not just a name. It's who you are. You are the Voice of the Goddess. You are Caé's voice." She touched her fingertips to her throat. "Every word you speak, every word that is spoken by Her Choir, *those* are the words of the Goddess Herself. How can you know who Caé is?" Her hand pressed against my cheek, and the touch sent lightning bolts through my body. "You *are* Caé."

Cold spread through me at the very sound of the blasphemy. "No, no, that's wrong—I'm just a girl, I—I'm *Elissa!*"

"You're both," she said. "The voice inside you that directs you, that gives you conviction, that told you it was wrong to sing for the king, even when it was simpler to do as he said—that is the voice of Caé. It's a gift given to you by Her.

And with your music, you share that Voice with the rest of Her world."

I pushed back from her, my heart pulsing from my throat to my fingertips. "I'm not," I repeated, a hoarse whisper this time. "I just sing, and She gives miracles. You—you're lying!"

You sound like Lucio, said that voice; that wretched, supposedly holy voice.

A small, sad smile pushed dimples into her cheeks. "The Goddess made the world through a song. She made mankind from the debris of stars. Why would it be so impossible for Her to speak through you?"

"I'm just a girl!" I cried. "I'm no one important!"

She clenched my hand. "You are utterly important. All that I said about you being Her voice—it's true. And She chose to come to you because you are so young, Elissa. You have not been made hard and bitter by the world; not yet. All of Her singers have parts of Her…but most of all, *you* bear Her need for hope." Her finger playfully swiped down the bridge of my nose. "She needs someone like you. Someone who desperately wants to see goodness in this world. At the end of everything, you will see that goodness will triumph."

I couldn't understand how she knew all this. How she spoke so confidently. Or how she could imagine my war-torn world having any goodness to it.

"If She wanted goodness to triumph, She could have ended the war," I whispered.

Veronica nodded. "She *will* be the one who ends it. Just not in the way you think."

"Then *how*?"

"She gave you and eleven others a very powerful gift. You are all twelve pieces of Her. Joined together, you are strong enough to stop any army."

I pictured the twelve of us on a mountaintop, facing the armies of Basso and Acuto. Using our voices as a weapon. As the King of Basso had wanted. As I had done to the people of Passaggio.

The memory twisted like a knife. "I don't want us to use our music to hurt anyone."

"She doesn't want that, either. That's why you'll sing a different kind of song."

I tucked my hair behind my ear to look at her. "What kind of song?"

Veronica's lips drew into a smirk. She didn't say anything, just lifted her eyebrows. Something about her eyes reminded me of how my mother used to look at me when I was keeping a secret from her.

But I *did* have a secret.

My eyes grew round. "Do you think She'd want to use a song that *I* wrote?"

"Do you remember what I said about asking the Goddess for responsibility?"

A lump formed in my throat and dread pooled in my stomach. "That She'd give me more."

"Exactly. The other Voices cannot compose as you can."

Brightness, *hope*, filled me from head to toe. "Really?"

She grinned. "Yes. She made that gift for you especially. You are very smart and very resourceful, Elissa. If you wanted to, you could be the one to write the song to bring peace to the three lands."

The lightness in me dimmed somewhat. "If I wanted to?"

Veronica stood up, clearing the bowl and the plate from the table. As she walked to a washbasin, she said, "This isn't a command of the Goddess. This is a choice for you to make. If you'd like, you could go home. You could rest. You've been traveling so long. You must be very tired."

Home. A land with spring again. The place where I'd spent my childhood. The fields beyond Cadenza Citadel. The tolling of the monastery's bells. The glassy waters of Lake Placido, only an hour away from my family's cottage. Familiar faces and smells and feelings.

But no. It wouldn't have been familiar. It would be torn apart by war, just as the rest of the world. Even if my parents were there, even if they were alive and waiting for me in prison, the only way I could see them again in a peaceful land was if I stopped this war.

If all this was true, it would give me, and this gift of songs in my head, some greater purpose. I would be a part of the song that Caé was writing. And someday, perhaps, if this plan worked, if we sang together and ended the war, I could go home to Cadenza. Maybe I would find Lucio there.

The chair groaned as I rose from the table and walked toward her. "What if I chose to write the song for Her? To sing it?"

"That would be the harder path. You'd need to find the other Singers; they are in Acuto. You'd need to tell them about this song of yours. It is only in unison that you'd be able to combat the destruction of this war. You would need to stand on a mountaintop, over the whole world, and sing your song over the two armies before they met on the field of battle." Veronica looked at me over her shoulder. "The journey would be a difficult one. Could you endure that?"

I had endured so much. Dangerous men. A slippery mountain. The wrath of a king. The bitter cold. The loss of my parents—and of my dearest friend.

But I remembered the songbird that had sung Caé's name to me, even in the middle of a cold, desolate forest.

"I'm afraid," I said. "But I feel as if…as if perhaps I'm strong enough to overcome all of this. She gave me my songs." My voice was louder now; growing and stronger by the second. "She gave me my voice. I lost Her Eye, but I feel like She's still watching me. Like She hasn't abandoned me."

Veronica turned to face me, her hands on my shoulders. Her face was clearer than I remembered it being, as if my memory had been a fogged-over mirror. She had a smile just like my mother. She had eyes like my father, warm and brown and full of love.

And yet—

One eye was blue from end to end.

"I will *never* abandon you," said Caé. Her voice was the same as the one I heard in my head, familiar and sweet and strong.

"It's you," I breathed.

Her eyes scrunched up with Her smile. "Say hello to the other Voices for me. And when you see Lucio again, I have a message for him."

I nodded, my heart crashing against my ribs, my thoughts muddled and confused and delighted all at once. And most of all, rejoicing as I imagined seeing Lucio again, in some blessed, peaceful time.

"I want you to tell him to look to the sky, and then I want you to tell him that I find his voice to be lovely."

She smoothed back my hair and pressed a kiss to my brow. "Caé Elissa, my voice, my hope, my love: you will do great things."

VERSE FIFTEEN

When I awoke, the world was blindingly bright.

I rubbed my eyes and bit by bit, my surroundings came into view: sparkling snow all around me. Tall, emerald-green trees. Sunlight, warm and encouraging, spilling through the gaps of the trees above.

Something glittered in the snow beside me. A silver knife. Memories flooded me all at once, bitter and sweet. The reason I had run here—the men I had run from—the king who wanted to capture me. And the dream I'd just had.

There was a pit in my stomach, but not from hunger. I felt strangely full. I ached because the dream had been so *real.* I had heard of other Voices or even people outside the Church having such dreams, but I'd never experienced such a miracle myself. I hadn't expected it to leave me with such longing. I wanted to live in that dream, with the Goddess caring for me, never having to wake up and feel the cold biting at my face.

This part of the journey wasn't meant for comfort or ease. I had asked Caé for more responsibility, and She was giving it to me.

I glanced back at the knife. Caé had spoken to me. Caé had told me what I had so dearly wanted to hear. That I was not made for violence; my voice was not made for war, but for peace.

With the scratchy, musty blanket draped over my shoulders, I pulled myself to my feet and trudged forward, leaving the knife, the cruelty, behind.

I would go to Acuto.

If I could figure out which way led me there.

Standing there in the snow, I looked about, as if there would be some great signpost declaring *Elissa, Acuto is this way!*

Instead, I found a Giacomo flower, blooming in the middle of the frozen ground. Bold and bright pink.

My heart lifted within me.

I dove for the flower, a signpost of its own, saying *I will never abandon you.*

The flower of my homeland. The flower that bore my father's name.

I wondered if it was a sign of something else, too. Thinking of Father made me remember that awful thing Lucio had said—that they had died—and I was crushed with regret that I hadn't asked Caé about their fate.

I longed to know, but I dreaded the answer. And whether they were in a cell or in a grave, a war still raged on. I could not return to Cadenza until my mission was accomplished. So I needed to move forward.

Staring at the Giacomo flower, I remembered the pink

blossom that, by Caé's music, by *my* music, I'd turned into a bird.

I frowned in thought and pulled myself to my feet. As I put weight on them again, I noticed that they were no longer sore and damp with blood. I wiggled my toes within their yellow socks. They felt completely normal. Healed.

By my *Song of Restoration*.

Lucio was wrong about my compositions. They worked. They were meant to exist. This gift of mine wasn't some aberration or form of disobedience. I wasn't acting outside the role I had been given. I was stepping into the role I was always meant for.

A knot formed in my throat.

There'd been something else Caé had wanted from me. Something big and daunting.

She wanted a song that would end the war.

I exhaled and leaned back against the nearest tree. I hadn't a clue what sort of song that would be. If I wrote down one wrong note, if I wrote a *piano* where I should have written a *forte*, would the whole thing be ruined?

A cold breeze pulled on my curls and batted at the flower in my hand.

One step at a time.

I scowled at the blossom. If I sang the song to make it a bird, it wouldn't do me much good just flying about and singing. With more traveling ahead of me, an unforeseeable amount of it, what I wanted most was the old carriage, or some grand horse that could carry me off to my next destination instead of leaving me to stumble about in the woods.

Perhaps that wasn't such a silly idea after all.

I held the flower in front of my eyes. Making a bird was one thing, but something else?

A steed. I pictured it in my mind, trotting through forest and then galloping across plains. A rhythm of hoofbeats like Melody's. The flick of its ears, its long, graceful mane.

A strange song formed in my head bit by bit, cascading like water. Four notes again and again, like hooves clattering against the earth. Then the song changed, firm and piercing and directed. A creature that knew its path. A horse that would take me wherever I needed to go.

A tiny voice inside said, *This is impossible. You've never made such a song before. This is useless.*

But I sang.

My voice came out trembling and small, a cloud of mist rising from my mouth. But with each note, my voice grew in volume and strength. A flock of birds overhead fled from their nests to another tree, startled by my rising song. I continued, the repetitive, jumping start changing to the second movement, where the song was smooth and clear and narrow. In my mind, I knew where the song would lead, that I'd sing one note, and an even higher note—

My overstrained voice cracked.

All of the power and excitement rushing through me vanished. I leaned back against the tree, touching a cold hand to my throat.

In the monastery, there had been complicated songs, songs that could repair broken bridges or convince storm clouds to blow away. We practiced them again and again. The Choirmaster would guide us through them but then stop us the second a wrong note was sung, or had been held too long, or wasn't sung softly enough.

"Again," she'd say, and we would start over—until another mistake was made. Usually by me.

One day, after stopping and starting and restarting a spell a dozen times, Choirmaster Aria shut the lid of the harpsichord with a deep sigh.

"Take a break," she said, rising from the bench and shaking her head. She turned to me with a disappointed frown. "Caé Elissa, have you adequately studied this spell?"

I had nodded sheepishly.

The Choirmaster looked to heaven and then retreated into the hallway, mumbling prayers under her breath.

I had felt so *blocked*. I kept forgetting that the high note in measure twenty was to be held for three beats and not four—and the arpeggio on the next page was even more complicated, with too many notes, too many nuances, and no place to breathe.

Tears had welled up in my eyes. I was incapable of singing correctly, I felt, and incapable of pleasing Choirmaster Aria.

One of the three tenors, a Singer named Ercole, had leaned close to me, their dark brown hands covering mine. "It's all right to make a mistake," they had said in a honey-sweet voice. Their gentle smile encouraged me to do the same. "Make as many mistakes as you need to. Each one is a step closer to perfecting the spell. And when you sing that phrase right, the victory will be even sweeter because of how you fought for it."

The words had comforted me then, and as I stood in that Bassan forest, they encouraged me now. Because I knew, finally, that when Ercole spoke, Caé's voice, Caé's truth, gilded their every word.

I attempted the song once more, and failed again, unable to sing through the longest phrase without gasping for air. And the highest note was so high I couldn't quite reach it.

Each mistake is a step closer.

With my eyes firmly on the Giacomo flower between my fingers, I sang. Not as a task, this time, but for the wonder of it. I marveled at the high notes and let my voice slip and slide and dance about as it needed to. I pushed through the longest phrases and landed delicately on the highest notes. The end of the song was in sight.

"Let it be so," I sang, and all of a sudden, my voice was cut off by another gust of wind, this one knocking the flower out of my grasp.

I cried out and chased after the flower, but as the wind carried it, the petals pried themselves from the long green stem. They scattered about like pink snowflakes, swirling and whirling and eddying in the air.

The petals drifted to the earth, four of them in four corners.

Suddenly, they morphed, blossoming into more branches from the ground, taller and taller, in strange abstract forms. Curving, ovular, rectangular blobs of paint on a palette. A blink, and the blurs of color formed together into a more familiar shape:

A horse.

It tossed its head, shaking out a long pink-and-yellow mane. Its body was the color of the Giacomo flower, blushy as the bird in the castle, with yellow dappled throughout, almost as if a child had painted it.

"Impossible," I whispered.

It took a few cautious steps close to me, tipping its head so that I could look it in its deep-brown eye. Or so that it could look at me. My hand quivered as I reached out and touched its snout. Its hair was short and coarse as Melody's had been.

It snorted at me. I leapt back in alarm.

The pink horse turned, walking a few steps around me. For a moment I feared this miracle of mine might suddenly run away, but then it bent down, kneeling in the snow. The horse gave a pointed snort.

I'd created this horse to take me to Acuto. It was ready to do just that.

Riding Blossom was surprisingly comfortable, as if being carried in a sedan chair instead of upon the back of an animal. And as I'd created her to be, she seemed to know exactly where she was going, carefully weaving through trees and rushing onward with surprising determination.

For more than a day, I'd been all on my own. Once, I yearned for solitude, cherishing those moments sitting at a desk by myself, enjoying the stillness of a hidden corner in the monastery, relishing a silent prayer as Lucio drove the carriage. But last night, the loneliness had nearly choked me. So as I rode on this strange and beautiful horse, this gift from Caé, I was thankful for her company.

Time passed to the beat of the crunching snow beneath Blossom's hooves. Sunlight glowed amber through the gaps of the trees, glimmering against the snow and then—suddenly, finally—against a long, wide road. It was vast, dusted with sparkling snow.

Blossom slowed as she approached the road. She stopped in her tracks, suddenly bending down as before. I gasped in surprise and flopped off her back and into the soft cushion of snow.

"I suppose you're tired of me," I said, pushing myself back onto my feet. "Though I can't say I blame you." My palms stung from touching the snow, and I hastily brushed them against the velvet of my skirt. I brushed pine needles and ice crystals from the soft pink of Blossom's mane, too. "Thank you for taking me this far."

Blossom whinnied and nudged her head toward the path before us.

And I understood. It wasn't a path at all.

It was a frozen river. Under the thin layer of snow, ice gleamed at me, the bright blue of Caé's eye. And there was no bridge in sight—none for a long stretch, most likely. Basso and Acuto wanted little to do with each other, and many of the bridges from before the war were now dismantled or destroyed. This was why Lucio and I had to travel through the mountains to reach Basso from our homeland: a long, winding path necessitated by two countries that wished to avoid each other.

Caé's mission to me rang in my bones as an echo. If I didn't listen for it, I'd forget it; I'd forget why I was doing this and where I was going. It seemed mad to want to cross this frozen river, but to reach Acuto, to reach the end of this war, that was precisely what I had to do.

You are very resourceful, Elissa, She had told me in my dream.

I huffed a breath, making my hair flutter before my eyes. "Well," I said to the sky, orange and dotted with pale clouds, "you did tell me this would be difficult."

A breeze tugged on my hair and on the branches above me, making a collection of icicles chime like laughter.

With my hand shielding my eyes, I looked once more toward the sunset. I couldn't spend too long here, debating what to do or how I'd cross this river. It would be a dozen times harder under the cover of night.

I ground my teeth and stared down the icy path before me. I wondered if I could write a song to make a bridge—but no, such a thing was too complicated. The songs Composers wrote could not form something from nothing, but only harness nature; in the same way, I had turned a flower into a horse, but not made something from *nothing*.

We have nothing to be afraid of, Lucio used to tell me. *The Goddess brought us this far.*

He had been wrong about a great many things, but not this. She would not have promised me a future, She would not have laid great plans for me, if She did not intend for me to survive my journey.

I shuffled onto the riverbank and carefully set one foot upon the ice, still wearing my garish, useless, scuffed-up courtly shoe. Step by step, I walked farther onto the river. With the snow beneath my feet, I didn't slip, but my heart was beating so violently and my stomach was turning so wildly that I felt I could fall over at any moment. If I did, would the ice break? Would I plunge through and be trapped underneath, to drown beneath that frozen glass?

No. I had to go on.

Blossom remained standing on the Bassan side of the

riverbank, her pink-and-yellow mane floating peacefully in the breeze. She didn't seem to be afraid for me. Perhaps there was nothing to fear at all.

A crack sounded to my right.

I whipped my head toward the sound. A small fracture had formed several paces from me. Frantic, I glanced back at Blossom, as if *she* could help me somehow. But I was only halfway across the river.

More snapping sounded. The cracks grew, spreading like a spiderweb toward me.

I ran.

I couldn't think; I bolted forward, my mind and the world a blur of white.

In my rush, I slipped, falling hard on my knees. Ice fractured beneath my palms, and below me, below the splintering ice, the river whispered and churned.

With fear running hot in my blood, I could only think of one thing: music. I wanted music more than anything; I wanted it to wrap me up like a blanket and fix everything.

Fix.

A song sprang into my head faster than the next breath. As fast as I could, in my exhausted voice, I sang the notes of my *Song of Restoration*.

The soft rush of wind blew over the river. Beneath my palms, white-hot with pain against the ice, the cracks began to shrink, like wounds being healed.

Slipping and sliding and frantic, I scrambled onto the

snowy Acutian shore, falling onto my knees. I gaped at the river behind me.

It had completely closed up again. The ice was once more a smooth, unbroken sheet of glass across the river. *Restored.*

I sobbed with relief. I couldn't believe it. I couldn't believe that a song that *I* wrote could be so powerful—that it could *save* me.

And yet Caé had promised me it would. She knew there was power in my music.

With utmost confidence and calm, Blossom crossed the frozen river next. Her hoofprints on the river left little circles in the snow, deep blue against sparkling white. They reminded me of notes skipping across a sheet of music. When she finally crossed onto the shore, I threw my arms around her neck and felt as if I could breathe again.

We were alive. Caé hadn't abandoned us. She had kept her promise, yet again.

VERSE SIXTEEN

Side by side, we walked on. It was strange—I was in a country I'd never seen before, a country upon which I'd never set foot, yet it felt no different from Basso. Snow still dusted the earth. Tall black trees trembled in the wind. These two kingdoms acted as opposites, but I had difficulty telling them apart.

After a while, as we followed an old, faded path, we found the first signs of life. Tiny villages were nestled here and there amid the snowy hills, and as we traveled, each welcomed us.

One candlemaker and his family let me stay in their house for a week during a snowstorm. Only one of them could speak my tongue, but even so, they gave me a bed to sleep in and dinners of potatoes and saffron rice and chicken. Even though they resisted, before I left I paid them with one of my pearl earrings left over from my days in the Bassan court, which I was all too happy to leave behind.

Being with such people reminded me again and again of Passaggio. Of the kindness I'd been shown there—and how I would never return such kindness with cruelty again.

Day by day, I wished more and more to share my gift of music with the people who showed me such kindness. Like the farrier who gave Blossom horseshoes and provided me with a saddle, and who would take no payment at all. I longed to sing him something—a song of health, or joy, or restfulness—but now I kept my magic a secret from strangers. Ever since my escape from those two men in the woods, I was warier, wiser.

The land changed as we journeyed, a smooth crescendo from still, snowy forests to plains of silver ice to fields where bright green grass poked up from the last patches of snow. The air was not so frigid anymore, not so thin.

Before long, I felt quite encumbered by my heavy velvet dress from the court of Basso, always kept carefully hidden under the cloak of my gray blanket. I traded it to a seamstress for a plain new frock, and when she was finished, I marveled at the outfit she'd made me. A bodice of linen, simple and gray, with slim, sensible sleeves to my wrists. A red scarf to wear on my hair. And—this I loved most—a skirt, worn with thankfully few petticoats and the same color as a poppy. I looked like any other Acutian girl—which was exactly how I needed to look. I traded her my second earring, too, for a pair of simple shoes.

As eager as I was to carry out my mission, to see my fellow Voices again, to be a part of this song designed by Caé, I had to admit to myself that I was quite enjoying the journey through Acuto. The world became beautiful and warm:

I rode past rolling fields of grass and rapeseed, bright green and golden yellow. Farmers tended their crops well, and everywhere leafy vegetables were piled atop overflowing carts. Instead of jagged, unforgiving cliffs there were now softly sloping hills, dotted with olive orchards, with farms keeping goats and cows and horses, with vast fields of wheat. The breeze carried the bouquet of scents to me, and I found it strange how I was drawn to this place, how I wished I could live here. To me, Basso was death. Cadenza was infancy. And Acuto...Acuto promised growth and abundance.

The farther we went, the more the heat beat down upon everyone. Women combatted this with straw hats and linen dresses. When I saw the men, I thought of Lucio, for he would have greatly favored their fashion: long hair kept in nets, vests and breeches of rose red and buttercup yellow, earrings and silver finger rings.

The road became paved, and one morning I reached a long marble bridge over a vast, sparkling lake. At the end of the bridge was an island with what looked like a white forest at its center, but I could see it for what it was: the towers of a monastery, stacked high above a town.

After I rode into the town, past the shouting fishmongers and the guards at the gate, I could see that hundreds were crammed onto this little island. In truth, it was more a city than a town. To my right, a tavern, full to bursting with noisy guests laughing at their tables. (I craned my neck to smell the warm bread, the herbed potatoes, the roasted vegetables.) To my left, two boys sitting outside a bookshop, sharing their bench, sharing a book, sharing a kiss. Over there, a red-haired girl selling tonics and lotions; over here, a woman selling freshwater mussels from two damp baskets. Above, gulls cawed and soared through a bright blue sky.

And still the stone road twisted upward, the shops following, dozens of them lining it all the way up to the monastery. The farther we climbed, the nearer we came, the more I could hear a faint but familiar sound: *music.* Strumming guitars, laughter.

A blue-roofed turret appeared above me, then domed towers. The monastery was made of white stone that seemed to have been carved from the rock of the island itself.

Somewhere in my heart, an invisible string tugged *tight,* pulling me forward. I gasped at the sharp feeling. When I sang, when I was near Caé Herself, feeling Her presence even when I could not see Her, I felt something similar.

Someone dear to me was close.

I touched my chest. A note rang in my head. An A.

Whenever I heard a single note, I always felt the inexplicable need to harmonize with it—to complete it. I hummed the C-sharp; I felt it buzz in my chest. Shutting my eyes, I felt as if I were a monastery myself: stone halls and high ceilings, sound bouncing all throughout me.

Other sounds echoed through my head.

Fast footsteps clicking against stone floors. The whisper of light fabric. Wind whistling through an open window. And music, the same guitar music I had just heard with my ears, drifting in with the air.

A woman asking, "Elissa will be here soon?"

And another voice, a voice that stirred my heart like a hand pressed tight to my chest, said, "In only a few moments."

Musetta.

Her voice was in my head somehow; I couldn't explain it. When I opened my eyes, I saw nothing but the road, the monastery, and the bright-pink horse. How had I heard her?

I blinked, then leaned forward on the horse, my fingers curling in her mane. "Musetta," I said, as though she were standing a few feet from me, "Musetta, can you hear me?"

There was no sound but the thumping of the horse's hooves against the stone street. I scrunched my brow and tried to remember how I'd heard the voice in the first place.

A note.

My eyes on the monastery, I hummed a C.

A voice rejoined with E. And then the strange woman again: "Musetta, are you all right?"

"Shh!" Musetta's voice carried through my head. "Elissa?"

My heart leapt; I squeezed the horse's mane tighter and pushed my legs against her sides. "Let's go!" I urged her, and she slowly accelerandoed to a canter, careful of the winding, narrow way. She carried me to the top of the citadel, slowing only once we approached the outer gate of the monastery.

Without being asked, the horse carefully knelt on the cobblestones, letting me leap off. I wobbled in place, growing accustomed to standing again, and then hurried onto the monastery's grounds. To my right was a courtyard, the source of the guitar music.

It was common practice at my monastery to gather together and offer hymns to Caé in thanks or in supplication. That was always a staid, reverent affair—*this* was a party.

A woman sang, her voice careless and loose and frayed at the edges. But it was not an ugly sound, not by any means. It was a well-loved blanket, familiar and cozy and, in this case, colored beautifully. Her singing was like laughter. Three men played guitars, accompanying her. I stood on my toes and stared at her, a tall woman with her hair hidden beneath a black veil. As I suspected, she was grinning—you could always *hear* a smile in the voice of a singer.

Couples danced together in the courtyard, twirling in circles around each other. With their hands high above their heads, they held some sort of small instrument that made a rapid clicking sound to the beat of the music. Their skirts and trousers of red, white, and yellow made them look like flickering flames.

There was so much I still didn't know about music. This was a whole other world I'd not yet seen. Music with Mother and Father had been sweet and quiet and secret; in Cadenza Citadel, it had been solemn, powerful, and important, accompanied only by an organ or a quartet of woodwinds. Bassans favored lutes and harpsichords; violins and pretty, orderly dances. This was loud and big and *delightful*. A man shook an instrument that looked like a plate surrounded by bells, making a jingling, clinking sound. Those who didn't have instruments joined in with clapping, stomping, or even shouts, as if to encourage the dancers.

There was no power to this kind of music, no miracles—but it felt like magic to me, all the same.

Lucio would have loved music such as this.

Then there was another shout: my name.

I whipped my head toward the sound, where a gray-haired woman stood in the doorway of the monastery. My heart pushed against my chest as if it wanted to fly to her.

Musetta.

Not ten seconds later, she flew forward and threw her arms around me, covering my head with kisses.

"I heard your voice!" I whispered. "I can't explain it, but I heard you—"

"And you heard the Goddess, didn't you?" She drew back, her warm brown hands trembling against my cheeks, her dark eyes glimmering. "It's the same with me. I cannot explain it, but I heard someone speaking to me, telling me I was Her voice, telling me how beloved I was—and I knew at the core of my being that it was *Caé* speaking to me..."

I nodded feverishly. "I met Her. I *met* Caé. In a dream, and in person! She—She was disguised." I shook my head, tears rolling suddenly onto my chin. "She's fearsome and beautiful and so familiar."

Another woman with deep-brown skin, her hair wound in a harmonious braid of black and silver, appeared beside us, resting a hand on her hip. She pointed to the horse. "Musetta told me to expect you, but not...*that*." Musetta's friend pressed her palm to the horse's neck; her eyes widened, and she drew her hand back. She glanced at Musetta and then at me.

"You can see that she's pink?" I asked. No one else had, not in all our travels. It was as if Caé Herself had protected us from the dangers of strangers' curiosity.

"Of course," the woman said.

Before I could explain Blossom, Musetta caught my attention again by saying, "Elissa—you truly *met* Caé?"

My curls bounced as I nodded profusely. "Twice. She came to me in the form of a pilgrim, and She asked me for food and shelter, and I sang for Her, and I healed Her foot, and *then* She came to me in a dream, She said she cared for me and She told me..."

Amid the wondrous things I'd seen and heard, a cold, important truth returned to the forefront of my mind. *My composition and the twelve Voices must bring this war to an end.* Our fight was just beginning.

Musetta clutched the black-haired woman's hand. "Come

inside, Elissa. I know you have much to tell us." She cocked
her head at her friend. "But forgive me; in all this excitement, I forgot to reacquaint you both." ·

The other lady stuck out a hand, which produced its own
music as the bright metal bracelets on her wrists clanged
about. "Caé Hanna," she said as I grasped her hand. "We've
met once or twice, I'm sure. I was a Composer at the monastery in Cadenza Citadel. They assigned me to travel with
Musetta." Hanna smiled at the woman at her side.

Musetta bumped her hip against Hanna's. "She's also my
wife, which *I* would have introduced firstly—"

"I was getting to that!" Hanna replied with a laugh.

My eyes grew wide. "Oh! Congratulations!"

There were so many composers back at the monastery, I
was certain I'd seen Hanna in passing before—but I felt quite
foolish not having seen her with Musetta, not having noticed
the two of them together, not perceiving any sign at all that
they were in love. Such a thing was plain now. When Hanna
looked at Musetta, something in her gaze reminded me of
Caé's: the harmony, the magic, the truth, the purity, the love.

It was not common for those who lived in monasteries
to marry. Marriage and love were not forbidden, of course,
but a great many people declared their fealty to Caé and
Caé alone. Some said they were following Caé's example
in remaining unmarried their whole lives. I remembered a
tall, skinny composer with long black hair giving me such

a speech, praising my lack of interest in boys or girls. But early on, I had seen two Singers—a tenor, Tamino, and a bass, Guglielmo—deeply in love with each other, and I decided that, clearly, Caé would find nothing to frown upon in such love. If I had the chance again, I decided, I would one day ask Her if She minded whether or not I sought love.

"I will try to find someone to take care of our interesting friend here," said Hanna, waving a hand at the horse. "She must be a gift from the Goddess, too?"

I demurred. "Well, yes. With Caé's help, I came up with a song that turned a blossom into, well...Blossom."

Hanna's mouth fell open. "You—*you* wrote a song? *That made a horse?*"

My stomach clenched, and somewhere in the back of my head, I could hear Lucio scolding me with the same words. My shoulders lifted as I took a deep breath. "Caé once told me that if we ask Her for more responsibility, She'll give it to us. I asked Her for more. And She gave me a gift."

Musetta's eyes filled with wonder. Hanna covered her mouth with her fingertips. Would they shame me as Lucio had?

"I know it's not thought to be my place," I whispered. "I know it's not what I—"

Musetta's hands gripped my arms tight. She shook her head at me, but she smiled. "No, no," she said, brushing a curl out of my eye. "I'm not upset, Elissa. Only...astounded, I suppose. I've never heard of such a thing before."

"And a song that creates *life*…," marveled Hanna, delicately stroking Blossom's mane. "Rare, complicated magic—the kind the Goddess sang in the beginning."

She made us of stardust and song, an old children's song went, to the tune of the eight creating notes. And I'd seen proof of it. I'd sung proof of it.

Musetta squeezed my hands. "You—you say it was a gift. You weren't trained in composition?"

I shook my head, and she let out a soft, bewildered laugh.

"I don't understand it myself," I told her.

"'Man fathoms not the compositions of the Goddess,'" she quoted. I never liked that verse, but in her voice, I heard it differently now. It wasn't that we *should* not fathom Her plan. It was that we *could* not do so.

To our right, the group of worshippers gasped and cried out. When I looked up to see what was drawing their attention, I found them pointing at us—at the horse, at me, and at Musetta. It seemed everyone could suddenly see the miraculous strangeness of Blossom now.

"Mother Caé!" cried one of the musicians. "Is this one of Her miracles?"

As they murmured and began to approach, reaching out to touch Blossom and kneeling before Musetta, Maestra Hanna touched my shoulder.

"I'll distract them," she whispered. "You two go on inside."

The Composer stood by Blossom's side, holding her

reins, as Musetta whisked me away into the entrance of the monastery, shutting the door behind her.

"The people are lovely," she said, her voice echoing about the marble halls, "but they make it difficult to find a moment of quiet."

She led me down a corridor, pale white and shining in the sunlight. The monastery's stone floors sparkled, and the halls were lined with marble statues of Caé wearing intricately draped robes. They looked nothing like Her. Her nose was too small and demure; Her chest was too large, Her lips too thin. I smiled to myself. No one song, no one painting could capture all of Her.

Neither could one voice.

In the middle of the hall, I grabbed Musetta's arm. She halted, her eyes cool and understanding, as if she'd known I'd reach out to her.

She would speak first. I knew this deep within myself, like I was remembering something that had already happened. From the hard limestone floor, sound vibrated through my feet and rested in my chest. I was a plucked string. In the hand that clutched hers, I could feel the music humming in her body, too.

We were in harmony.

"I have started hearing voices," she whispered. "Yours. Hers. Those of the other singers. When they sing, I can feel it in my chest, like the body of a lute, carrying sound."

We opened our mouths at once, the words coming forth unbidden—"*We are Her Voice*"—and our eyes grew wide.

Musetta shut her eyes tight and clung to my arm. "Sometimes, when I sing, I can feel Her," she said; already, I was nodding.

"Yes!" I whispered. "I can just imagine Her standing at my shoulder, or touching—"

"Touching my back. I thought it was just me."

We nodded, stunned into silence at the mystery unfolding within us.

Musetta pulled me by the hand into an alcove beside a window, streaming sunlight onto the stone seat. Outside, people milled throughout a multicolored garden, some wearing plain blue robes—people who had dedicated their lives to music, even if they did not possess the gift of wielding Caé's magic—and others in brightly colored Acutian clothes like the dancers in the courtyard, visiting laypeople.

Seeing them, my heart fluttered.

Acutians were just people. People who loved Caé as I did; as the King of Basso and his wife had; as the Passaggians had.

And they were called the enemy.

It seemed so foolish to me. This war; this division of people who were the same. Who were loved by Caé in equal amount.

Musetta touched my hand, tearing my eyes from the people outside. "You have come a long way, I can tell. But you travel alone—where is the Composer you journeyed with? Young Lucio?"

His name was like a note sung too sharp. I lowered my gaze, my stomach turning. "He works as a composer for the King of Basso now."

Musetta's mouth fell open. "What? But that's—that's against our purpose! We are not to sit idle—"

"He told me it was what Caé wanted," I said. "And I believed him. I believed him when he told me using my voice for destruction was a blessed thing, too."

Though every word ached, I told Musetta about Passaggio and about the king's charge for me: that I starve the Acutian armies. The sorrow and regret I felt for all the lives so recklessly lost, for all the kind people I'd betrayed, came anew like a reopened wound. And I knew that all of these things pained the Goddess as much as they pained me.

I desperately prayed that Lucio could feel this sadness, too. And that he would do something to stop the king.

And I told her, finally, about the song.

"More and more, I know that Caé despises this war. It is fought in the name of protecting Her sacred land, but She loathes the misery it brings," I said.

Musetta nodded. "She wants harmony."

"Yes."

Her brow wrinkled as she glanced out the window. "We'll sing this song, then," she murmured. "A song to bring peace. Something like no one's ever sung before." Her brown eyes glowed with excitement. She took me by the hand and began to pull me out of the alcove. "Hanna can write it! It'll be perfect!"

Something tugged inside my middle, an anchor keeping me in the sunlit alcove and not zipping down the hall as Musetta wanted. I stood there, my feet planted firmly against the marble.

It would be so much simpler if Hanna composed it. Or Lucio, or Angelina, or Marcellina, or any of the other worthy, learned, talented Composers who'd dedicated their lives to worshipping and studying Caé.

But it wasn't what She wanted.

Musetta frowned, stepping closer into the light. "What's wrong?"

I shut my eyes, remembering Veronica sitting before me, the playful look in her eyes as she drank her tea. The truth sounded so mad. Lucio would even say it was blasphemous. But it was true. I'd heard it said from holy lips.

"The song won't be written by Hanna. The Goddess wants *me* to write it."

Musetta stroked her thumb up and down my sleeve. Her smile was wrinkled; well worn, well used. "So the Blessed Goddess wishes to bring a war to a close at the hands of a small girl from the fields of Cadenza."

The image was daunting. I pictured myself staring down two armies, two rows of cannons, all alone on some isolated mountain. But no, that wasn't right.

"I cannot do it by myself," I told her. "The King of Basso wanted me to stand atop a mountain and sing to the Acutian armies. To bring this war to an end, we need to stand atop a mountain and sing to *both* armies. Not just you and I, but all twelve of the Voices. Of *Her* voices." I touched my chest, my heart beating *fortissimo*. "When we sing, all twelve of us together, we will be speaking on Her behalf. We will be giving a direct message to the people of the world, right from the mouth of the Goddess."

"Then by Her grace, we can certainly do this." She squeezed my shoulder. "We just need a mountain and the rest of the Voices, then." She stared at the domed ceiling as she thought. "There is a peak not too far from here; two days' journey, perhaps. Mount Maestoso; it faces the Bassan border. It is very close to the Acutian palace."

The Acutian palace. The Queen of Basso had said that her sister was there. And that they'd not spoken in so long. I knew, deep and steady as a basso continuo playing underneath the other instruments, that we must go and see this queen. "We should go there," I said. "We could explain to the Acutian queen that the Goddess wishes for peace. Perhaps the queen will provide us with protection as we travel to the peak."

Musetta's smile faltered. "I...I do not know if she would approve. She is known for being ruthless and short-tempered. And her armies are also fighting to lay claim on Cadenza. Even if our song can make the fighting stop, the

Choirmaster cannot remain regent forever—*someone* will need to claim the Cadenzan throne."

Caé's words pulsed in my veins: *Do not fear. You are all a part of me. You, Elissa, are my hope.*

"The Goddess brought me here," I whispered, "through snow and danger and weakness. I don't know how She'll do it, but She will make goodness triumph, somehow." Squeezing my eyes shut, I thought of the King of Basso, of how mighty and powerful I once thought he was. Compared to Caé, resplendent, able to create life—the King of Basso was no more fearsome than a dust mote. "If we have the Goddess on our side, nothing can stop us."

Despite my words, despite the conviction that flowed through me, we clung tight to each other. The music rising in both of our bodies was quickening, like the Choirmaster had swept her hand in a sudden, fast movement, *prestissimo!*

"Even with the mountain," said Musetta, "even with the approval of the queen, we will need the Voices. We have to contact them." She snapped her fingers, a smile returning as an idea seemed to appear in the brightness of her eyes. "This morning, I *knew* you would come here, and we had not written each other."

"And I heard your voice." Her plan was unfolding in my mind, without her saying a word of it. "I could hear you running down the halls; and I heard you singing a note; and I sang—"

She did not even give me the chance to speak further; she swept up the scarlet train of her light Acutian gown and raced down the hall. I followed after her up a steep stone stair, upward and upward.

"They have me sing over the town here in the morning," she said over her shoulder. "Long ago, they used to carry the older singers up here, and they offered such a luxury to *me*, if you can imagine!" Her laugh bounced against the pale-yellow walls and down, down the steps.

After several minutes, we arrived at an old wooden door. Musetta opened it, and light flooded into the dim tower.

The sky was cerulean, the shades of Caé's robes. Below it sat the gray and blue roofs of the houses and shops, a pile of little pebbles. The lake shone like a million mirrors had been scattered about, and beyond, in the Acutian country-side, squares of brilliant jades and golds made the fields look more like patches in a quilt.

Musetta stepped onto a balcony, clung to the chest-high stone barrier, looked toward the horizon. "Caé connected the twelve of us through music. We finally know. We are all parts of a whole, the twelve of us. Twelve notes. All Her voice." She turned back to me. "You heard me sing in your mind, you said. Just one note?"

"Yes," I said, "an A. I harmonized."

Musetta nodded. "I'll sing an A again, and I want you to sing in harmony. Sing with me...out to them." She gestured over the edge of the barrier to where the emerald land met the sapphire sky. "If we are all parts of Caé's voice, the Voices will feel us; hear us, too, no matter how far."

I stood at her side, my pulse racing, a smile forming on my face. She sang, her voice rich as the depths of a forest, and I joined with my sharp, one-note birdsong.

Joy and light warmed my chest. I used to feel this effervescent, crescendoing sensation long ago, when we all sang together as one. Our voices melding together within the echoing concert hall of the monastery. When we were Twelve.

When there was peace.

This was right. This was as all was meant to be.

The sun shone brighter upon Musetta and me. Somewhere, ringing in my ear, another note joined in our song, perhaps imagined. E, sung by a baritone.

A low, sweet voice spoke in my head. I could imagine the man's face; his meek smile, his round glasses, the way he feverishly took notes in his sheet music. *Elissa!* said Alidoro, the baritone. *Musetta! How can this be?*

I glanced at Musetta; she was already looking at me, her eyes creased in the corners with a smile, even as she sang. She heard him, too.

Her lips did not move, but I heard her voice. *We are a part of a miracle even now, Alidoro. Keep singing! The others will come soon.*

Gripping tight to the stone, I grinned and closed my eyes. I could see Alidoro's face in my head, a faint afterimage. Seeing him again, hearing his song bounce around inside my head—it was as if a missing piece of me had been restored.

It is so good to see you, I said.

He beamed. *And you.*

My heart glowed. I felt a profound, tearful pride. I felt like a mother, or something more, something *higher.* I could see all of the things I loved about him; so much so that it made my chest ache. His love for studying. His kindness. His humility.

In my mind, I looked at Musetta, and felt that same overwhelming, flooding feeling of love and gratitude. She was powerful. Fearless. Relentless in the pursuit of goodness.

The three of us together, our voices blending into something perfect...I knew that I was all of these things, too. Our traits, our notes, melded into one song.

Another voice joined; a tenor, singing their own A. I recognized the warm-honey sound of their voice, and in the dark, faint space inside my brain, an old friend, Ercole, appeared. They were a little older than me, with kind eyes and a bright, contagious smile, long black hair braided into a queue. Yet again, that desperate, awestruck feeling swept over me, and I marveled at them, at all of us.

I felt lost without you, they said, *but I didn't know it before;* and the three of us, we replied, *Yes;* the refrain of some song we were only beginning to learn.

One after another; a bass joined, and then the second and third sopranos with an F-sharp and an A-flat, notes and notes and notes, until there were twelve of us, our voices mingling in our minds and in the air. *Tamino. Susanna. Bartolo. Dorabella. Tisbe. Fiodiligi. Guglielmo. Rinaldo.* Voice after voice after voice!

With all of us together, with my love for them overflowing in my heart, I spoke. For the first time, I felt like a church scholar giving a speech. I felt like an authority, not just a child.

Caé came to me in a dream, I said. I felt their understanding within me. They believed me. My words were a part of them, true as the beat of their own hearts. *She loves us so dearly. She says we are a part of Her. That each of us plays a part in the song that She's writing. Now we are to play a very important role in the finale of this movement.*

One mind, one voice; they understood the rest of my instructions, like they'd already memorized them. We spoke to one another in one voice, explaining the plan, which hummed inside us as one messy, gorgeous tangle of notes.

We will go to the Acutian palace, we said in one voice. *Together, on the mountaintop, we will sing a new song to bring peace between the nations.*

It was as if it had been etched into our minds since we were children. We knew the way onward, even the instructions for each of us as individuals, all of us a part of a bigger, more perfect song. We were so happy, so close to perfect happiness, and so *whole.* I longed to stay like this, seeing beauty in myself and in them, feeling loved and seen and welcomed. But an invisible tether pulled on all of us; pulled us elsewhere. Pulled us to our great work.

Though none of us wanted to, we let the song taper off.

The notes faded as though stolen and carried away by

the wind. One by one, the faces vanished from my mind. When I opened my eyes, the sunlight was as blinding as the beauty of the Goddess. A hand touched my shoulder. My heart lifted; for a moment, I thought it was *Her*. And it was, in a way.

Musetta stood to my right, and with her hand pressed against my shoulder, I could feel the remnants of the beautiful, chaotic, twelve-note chord buzzing inside us.

"We have the Voices," she said softly. Her eyes crinkled. "All that's left is your song."

Movement Four

VERSE SEVENTEEN

When we had told the monastery of our plan, of our calling, and of the peace that would come once we arrived at the Acutian palace, it martialed every resource for us. The stablemaster even insisted we ride to the palace in a carriage. This was done in a uniquely Acutian fashion: the horses were given gold-studded bridles and wore feathers in their manes. (As lovely as they were, they did not compare to Blossom, who was being well cared for.) The carriage was painted in glimmering, unblemished gold and had clearly not been used very much.

Maestra Hanna had given me a small wooden traveling desk to use while we rode. I needed to compose the song for the Twelve—and soon.

She offered me an encouraging smile as she handed me a stub of pencil. "It's difficult to compose when your inkwell spills across your page at the slightest bump," she said.

We wasted no time in leaving; I did not even stay the night, only long enough for a bath and a meal. As the carriage rolled down the slowly sloping path and I tapped my desk with my pencil nub, I felt the two women's eyes upon me. Lucio's angry whispers; his *Remember your place!*s rang through my head, to the point where I could barely look at them.

"I'm sorry, Maestra Hanna," I mumbled.

She raised a dark brow. "For what? Using my pencil?"

My curls jostled as I shook my head. "No. I'm sorry that I'm composing this instead of you."

Hanna exchanged a confused look with her wife. "Elissa, that was not your decision, was it?"

"No," I said, my voice *pianissimo.*

"So you have nothing to apologize for." She reached forward in the carriage, patted my hand. "I am certain that the Blessed Goddess is using this as a lesson for *all* of us Composers. We will be humbled, watching Her great work performed through a girl of your age." She squeezed my fingers warmly. "Though responsibility is a double-edged sword. While I might have enjoyed the acclaim of writing such a song, I would also feel great pressure to succeed. It is very daunting, having the fate of three nations rest on your composition. It will change our world."

I hadn't quite thought of it like that. I kept imagining that it was only the hearts and minds of two people, a king and a queen, that I would change. But no. My song would change the shape of history for every person I had ever met, every face I'd ever seen, and those I had not met or never would.

Caé had put so many lives in my hands.

The pencil quivered in my grip.

Musetta laid her hand over mine, stilling the trembling

pencil. Her skin sent a pulse of holy energy through me, a spark drifting off a warm hearth fire.

"Don't be afraid," she whispered. As she did, Caé's voice came to me.

Your compositions are a gift from me to you. Your song will succeed in ending this war. You will set things right.

I kept my gaze firmly on the lined paper before me, the pencil captured tight in my fist. Yes. I must remember Her words. And I must do my best.

But the song wasn't coming. Not yet.

I looked at the two women and then back at my page, tapping my pencil against the paper like that would help any.

Hanna cleared her throat. "We shouldn't stare," she said, and Musetta withdrew her hand. "I can never concentrate on my compositions if I know someone's watching."

My shoulders relaxed. Perhaps that was why.

When I caught her eye, Hanna winked at me. "Though writing a treble clef wouldn't be a bad place to start."

I scribbled the sign on the page with a long sigh.

"Let's have a nap, my love." Musetta kissed her wife's temple. "Elissa, I will pray that Caé gives the song to you quickly."

"Thank you."

My gaze followed the long black lines across the page, but I could make no direction of them. My mind was quiet; the hush before a sudden *fortissimo,* I could feel it. I was sitting in a *fermata,* waiting for Caé to sweep Her hand and tell me to continue.

But how long would She hold this silence? How long was I to wait until I'd hear another melody?

We left the city, the lakes, and the fields behind. The farther we drove, the more signs of destruction there were: countryside gray and black with ash. Deep pits in the parched ground where cannonballs had exploded. Sticks planted haphazardly into the earth, a single pole, a simple sign: grave markers.

I pressed my forehead to the glass, trembling from the motion of the carriage. *Please*, I prayed, *do not make us wait much longer.*

{

The music sheet was still blank.

Musetta was not worried; not yet. Hanna encouraged me and offered small pieces of wisdom about starting a song, or considering where a song would end, or what it would convey. But this was different. The song simply *would not* come to me. And when I tried to imagine peace, the very *essence* of the song, my mind, still, was blank.

The sky was silvery gray as we reached the palace of Acuto, a contrast that left the palace to shine like a soloist. It was as wide as the Bassan palace, but much taller, with high, sand-colored walls surrounding it like a military fortress. Above those walls, great arrow-shaped turrets pierced the sky.

When we drove past the outer walls, I was disappointed

by the simplicity of the grounds. Even in winter, the Bassan gardens had been lovely and ornate, with shadows where flower beds had been, and dry topiaries still cut into swirls and patterns. Here, even with temperate, inviting weather, the grounds were barren; just long drives of gravel, filled with guards. They marched in neat lines with guns on their shoulders and sabers on their hips. A group of soldiers on horses trotted toward a building, one of many tucked behind the walls of the fortress. Seeing them, and the cannons lined up in the courtyard, reminded me of the duty Caé had given me.

Would a song really be strong enough to stand against cannon fire?

Then, out the window, there was a much more welcoming sight. At the end of the drive stood a man, tall and beaming, with little circular glasses perched on his straight nose. He had been born in Cadenza, like me, but he truly looked like a fine Acutian gentleman now, dressed all in black with a white ruff at his collar and his dark hair cropped short. I recognized him by the way he touched his chest, as he always did when he sang a particularly beautiful note.

Musetta clutched my hand. I felt the hum of her note; it resonated with my own—and there was a third note to match ours. Hers, a C; mine, an A; and his, an E.

Alidoro.

As soon as the carriage rolled to a stop, Musetta and I hopped out, dashing across the gravel to the baritone.

In Cadenza, he'd always been the one to bring questions to the Choirmaster about pronunciation, or phrasing, or whether he'd sung a note too loud. He was precise, knowledgeable, and deeply afraid of singing something incorrectly. I remembered him sitting in an alcove, his long legs pressed nearly to his chest as he bent over our assigned piece of music, taking notes with a pencil.

The three of us embraced, laughing, and felt the thrill and wholeness I felt when I heard a note played perfectly. A strange, prickling feeling danced from behind my neck and down my arms, now clothed in soft, breathable Acutian fabric.

Caé was near. She was all around us.

Tears rolled down all of our cheeks.

"Sisters," Alidoro whispered, "Caé has much for us to do."

We nodded. And we did not need to say a word. His eyes upon me were full of light and wonder.

You met Her? he longed to ask.

"Yes," I said. "She wanted me to tell all of you, all of us, how much She loves us. And that we need not do anything to earn Her affection."

Alidoro blinked, then rubbed an eye behind glasses. "She is far too generous with us."

"She is." Musetta held her hand to Alidoro's shoulder. "And if it's true that we are all a part of Her . . . we, too, must be generous with the gift we've been given."

The baritone nodded. "Our time to share Her message is

coming soon. I have arranged a meeting with the queen in a few minutes. She—she didn't quite believe me when I said I *knew* you two were coming. It is not easy to explain knowing such a thing, simply by *feeling* it..." His light brown skin took an ashen tone. "I suppose it is time, then, to introduce you to Her Majesty."

Musetta frowned. "You're frightened."

He sighed and bowed his head. "I'm certain it is the war. Normally people are delighted to have Singers as guests, but...well, Her Majesty is under a great deal of stress."

"Has she asked you to sing for her?" I asked.

Alidoro kept his gaze lowered and shook his head. "Her composer has shown Sidonie and me great hospitality as we recovered from our winter travels, but the queen herself does not seem to have much interest in music."

My stomach turned. Musetta and I exchanged a quick glance.

"I pray that she'll support our cause," Musetta muttered. "Elissa, did Caé tell you how this meeting would go? How any of this would go?"

Shame felt like hot water spilling from the top of my head to my feet. "She told me very little. Just that our song would bring an end to the war..."

Musetta nodded rapidly, patting my shoulder. "Then Her word is all we need. How the victory comes will not matter. She knows all, sees all...we do not need to fear for the approval of the queen."

Alidoro squared his shoulders and smiled, like my weak prophecy was enough to lift his spirits. "What, then, is the song we're to sing? Which of our composers is going to write it? Did She tell you that as well, or has She left that a mystery?"

I wished I could hide behind Musetta and disappear altogether. Instead, she wrapped an arm around my shoulders, beaming down at me.

"Our Elissa is going to compose the song," she announced.

The baritone adjusted his glasses, shifting them back and forth as though he could not see me properly. "A Singer will compose?" He frowned. "But the Goddess puts each of us in our own roles, Composers to compose and Singers to sing—everyone a perfectly placed note."

My stomach twisted, thinking of how Lucio had said much the same. These two men knew Caé and Her words well; they had read, they had studied, they had memorized. But Caé had assured me that She hadn't made a mistake.

Musetta rubbed my shoulder. "Every note is in its proper place," she agreed softly. "And sometimes, two notes are sung at the exact same time. We call it harmony."

Alidoro wrung his hands together. "I—I suppose that's right," he murmured. "But I've studied the scriptures, Musetta. I've never read anything like this."

Musetta shook her head, still smiling. "Elissa is a Singer as well as a Composer, and the Goddess has given her these gifts for precisely this moment in history."

Hearing Musetta support me so, hearing her find truth

in my words, in my message—it gave me the same golden strength that flooded me after a spell well sung.

Alidoro's eyes grew wide. But, slowly, a mystified smile crossed his face. "There's that old hymn of Hers...'She shares Her miracles in Her smallest treasures.'" He gestured to me. "That's *you*, Elissa. This—this compositional gift of yours: it's a miracle."

I blushed, as if I were being praised for something fantastic I'd done. But this war-ending song, this miracle—I still hadn't written it.

Before I could explain this to him, a short man dressed in a black coat and breeches walked down the gravel path toward us.

Alidoro let out a loud cry. "Caé Almighty, we're going to be late, aren't we?" he asked.

The man in black offered a meek smile. "Not if you run very fast, Your Holiness."

"Right," said Alidoro, and waved his hand at us before taking off down the road toward the palace. We needed little other explanation—Musetta and I kicked up clouds of dust as we raced after our fellow Voice.

With aching sides and heaving chests, we entered the palace, raced up a white stair, and entered an antechamber of white stone. The whole palace was like this, from what I could tell: plain white walls of stone, adorned only by a tapestry or a painting depicting a battle. The painted blood in the pictures was the only bit of color in these halls.

Before us, in front of a tall set of gray doors, stood a severe-looking woman in armor.

"Alidoro Precipitato here to see Her Majesty the queen," said our friend, drooping into a deep bow.

"And the others?" asked the guard.

"Caé Musetta and Caé Elissa, Voices of the Goddess; they are invited guests of the queen, along with a composer, Caé Hanna, who's with their carriage, which I believe is—"

The guard rolled her dark eyes. "Come in," she sighed, stepping back into the door and pushing it open with her weight.

I swallowed a lump in my throat. My previous encounter with royalty had been far from successful.

But Musetta's fingers wove through mine. "Remember," she whispered, "when Her Voices are together, She is with us."

She is with us—like when I composed; like when I sang. When I could feel Her breath on my neck or Her hand on my back or imagine the warmth of Her smile.

It was difficult to feel this now.

Still, I forced a smile and treaded behind Alidoro and Musetta into the next room.

The first thing I saw was a woman. She stood beside a high-backed chair, her black hair decorated with silver ribbons and rose petals. A long strand of white Goddess Eyes wrapped around her throat and down the front of her bodice. Her gown was blue as the evening sky, with the skirt as wide and round as a wagon wheel. She appeared graceful and confident, despite the voluminousness of the strange gown. I stopped to curtsy, but Alidoro caught my elbow.

"Not her," he whispered. He pointed to our left.

A gilt desk rested a few steps from the throne, and at it was a woman jabbing a quill against a large map. Her skin was pale, nearly gray, and her blond hair was pulled back into a simple plait. She wore a black doublet with a white ruff, like Alidoro—and, with a shock, I realized *this* must be the Queen of Basso's sister. They had the same shape to their face.

But the Queen of Basso was warmth, springtime, and kindness. This woman was wintry. They were the sun and the moon, light and darkness, utterly different. I hoped she was not as severe as she looked.

"Her Majesty, Queen Mina of Acuto," shouted a page from the back of the room.

The three of us bowed to her.

"Who have you brought me, Singer?" she asked without looking up. Her voice was sharp and crisp; strings plucked *pizzicato*.

Alidoro stammered and pushed his glasses up his nose. "W-well, uh, Your Majesty, these are my fellow Voices of the Goddess, Caé Musetta and Caé Elissa."

The black-haired lady gasped delightedly and rushed toward us. She kissed Musetta's cheek and then mine. "Oh, what a blessing! I thought I was lucky just to have met Sir Alidoro, but to meet *three* Voices of Caé!"

From the desk, the queen waved a hand. "My most enthusiastic court composer, Theodora."

Maestra Theodora blushed and stepped back from us, inclining her head toward the queen.

"I've never had so many holies in one room before," the queen remarked, bitterness and fatigue in her voice. "So, what is this concerning?" She kept her head down and swept her quill across the page, circling something. "Have we forgotten to pay a tithe to the Church?"

Alidoro's hand trembled against his heart. "Oh, no, Your Majesty—we are not here concerning money!"

"My time is short, Singer." The queen rolled her neck, which must have pained her as she hunched over her desk. She set down her quill pen and stretched her hands, then sat at her full height. "Do you realize how generous I am, accepting an audience with three foreigners, when even now the Bassan army is making plans to invade our borders?"

Alidoro opened and shut his mouth.

Musetta stepped forward, her fingers lighting on Alidoro's shoulder. "Majesty, the Voices of Caé do not speak on behalf of any nation—not even Cadenza. We serve Caé firstly. We come here at Her command."

The court composer folded her hands reverently, her black eyes wide and attentive. "Tell me, what plans does Our Blessed Goddess have for Acuto? What message do you bring?"

Alidoro and Musetta glanced at me. My pulse raced as it

did before I stepped onto a stage—but this was different. It was not the eager thrill of having my voice leap and soar and perform wonders: it was pure fear, making my palms sweat and my stomach knot and my legs tremble.

"Caé has a message for you," I told the two women, my voice soft and meek. "For everyone." I wrung my hands together, concentrated on my breath. "She wants the war to end."

Theodora pursed her lips.

The queen leaned forward and pointed to the map on her desk. "You mean to say that the Choirmaster wishes to stay on the Cadenzan throne?"

"No, this isn't about the Choirmaster," I said, wrong-footed. "The Choirmaster did not ask for this war to be fought at all. Nor did the Goddess."

"It is for Her that we fight it in the first place!"

I bit down on my tongue to shut myself up, as Lucio would have commanded me to do in front of so powerful a ruler.

But Caé would have wanted me to speak.

"The Goddess despises discord and violence," I said, a little louder.

The queen set her mouth in a hard, thin line. "How do you know what the Goddess wants, child?"

For the first time in many, many years, I felt true stage fright. A fluttering in my stomach. My pulse ricocheting in my ears. Fear of the very words about to come from my mouth.

"Your Majesty," I began, "She told me these things."

Her ice-blue eyes narrowed. "Caé *spoke* to you?"

I nodded, hope and fondness and memory bringing a smile back to my face. "Yes—She was glorious. She came to me in a dream—"

"A dream?" she repeated. "The future of our three nations rests upon a little girl's *dream?*"

Musetta took a step forward, her eyes fearless and gleaming with something familiar—something like the love I'd seen in Caé's eyes. "She is not just a girl, Your Majesty. She is as much a Voice as I am. And I, too, have had visions of the Goddess, for a vision is what she had. What Elissa says is true."

Alidoro nodded, his voice small as he added, "Yes, Your Majesty—I have heard from the Blessed Goddess, too. And there have been other signs. Miracles that—"

The queen's chair screeched as she stood up. She left her desk behind and marched to the three of us, looking down her thin nose at me. "It is not the place of the Church to meddle in worldly affairs."

She whipped around, facing her court composer, who flinched. "Theodora, are you to blame for all of this? Did *you* send for these Singers?"

Theodora shook her head frantically. "No, Majesty. I had no idea they'd come!"

Queen Mina's gaze flitted to Musetta and Alidoro, cold and sharp as steel. "I do not know why the Church saw fit to send me Singers to meet its demands, but I do not like it. The Choirmaster shall not retain her power—tell her so! And when Cadenza is in Acuto's power, we will see to it that the Church does *not* make it a habit to order about her queen!"

"Majesty?"

Somehow, the soft, caressing voice of Maestra Theodora warranted the queen's attention. She narrowed her eyes at the composer. "Speak."

Despite her immense skirts, Theodora dipped her knee in a humble curtsy. "If I may—I believe that the arrival of these three Singers speaks of Caé's favor of our fair Acuto."

"And yet they say Caé is unhappy with the war," the queen spat, her eyes fixed on me. "This one, spouting nonsense she heard from a dream!"

"Caé greatly loves our queendom," Theodora piped up. "She chose your family to rule this blessed land. And I think this is but another sign of Her partiality." She extended a careful hand to us. "I believe if we show the Goddess how much we care for Her Singers, She will know how well we will care for Her land of Cadenza."

The angry red splotches that had appeared in the queen's cheeks faded away. She took a deep breath through her nose and smoothed back a curly strand of blond hair.

"What sort of hospitality do you have in mind, Theodora?"

The composer smiled at us. "Perhaps the Voices could sing a concert for us and the court tonight. I'll write a special song for the three of them. They could lift our spirits.

It would show our people that Acuto bears the favor of the Goddess."

The queen stiffly nodded. "Yes. Yes; the three of you will sing tonight." She pointed at Theodora. "Write a spell for prosperity. For valor. For victory." She strode back to her desk, scribbling something on her map. "When we face the Bassan armies, we must have Her blessing on our side!"

But Caé would not bless either army. She wanted nothing to do with any of this bloodshed. It broke Her heart; all of it. I opened my mouth to protest, but a finger lightly brushed the back of my hand. I looked at Musetta as she spoke in my mind: *Caé is giving us a chance. We will give Her message at the concert.*

The queen waved her hand at us. "You'll perform for us in the evening. Dismissed."

We bent our heads and our knees reverently. The queen's composer strode across the floor toward us, sweeping up my hands in hers.

"The whole queendom is in need of some merriment," she said to us in a low voice. "Her Majesty may not show it, but we are eternally grateful to the Goddess for the gift of your presence."

I glanced at the queen, her brows furrowed as she moved her hand across the map, about to snap the quill in half.

I thought of the Bassan king, too, who had also treated music as a weapon, as something that belonged to him and not to the Goddess. How he had wanted so much to use it for violence. How cold he had become when I said I could not stay on as his singer like some bird in a cage.

The song of my life was repeating. A dark, sharp refrain.

Caé help us, I thought. For merriment was not what we would bring.

VERSE EIGHTEEN

The grand hall certainly lived up to its name.

The room was covered in gold, from the candelabras the height of a man to the graceful arcs of the ceilings above. Almost every panel of every wall was composed of an elaborate carving, with flowers and birds and trees and an alcove in the middle. In each of these alcoves, surrounded by candles, were carvings of the Goddess. Her hands clawing at Her heart. Tears pouring out of Her one good eye. They all seemed to be variations of Her in mourning. It ached to see someone I loved in pain.

I looked for Her in the music that a quartet played on the wooden stage. A recorder. A guitar. A viola da gamba. A harpsichord. My heart pinched. I wished Lucio were sitting at that harpsichord, someone familiar in this room of dour-looking strangers. The Acutian courtiers were nothing like those Acutians I'd met in the countryside. They wore black and white; they frowned; they spoke in hushed tones; and they absolutely did not dance.

The music was measured and steady, with the harpsichord playing elaborate trills that put the delicate carvings on the wall to shame. While the music I'd heard in the monastery's courtyard had been messy and bright and fun, this was its opposite. Dark, with no humor, and no room for error.

From where we stood huddled in the corner of the hall, Maestra Hanna gave my arm a little nudge. "Perhaps this music will inspire you for your new song."

A lump, cold and heavy, lodged in my throat. I sighed and reached for my Goddess Eye, only to remember with a pang of longing that it had fallen into the snow of a Bassan forest. "I just don't understand it," I whispered. "This...this silence in my mind. Does it mean that Caé is unhappy with me?"

Hanna scoffed. "Heavens, no. Not everything is a sign of Hers." She shrugged. "We're human. We're finite. Sometimes stress or fatigue or even one's appetite can be enough to keep a song from coming. Music is so fickle. It will come to you when it feels like it." She smoothed the white fabric of the massive skirt she'd been given. "I trust that Caé will give you the music you need, when the time comes. Trying to force it will do you no good."

I balled my fists against the deep-blue silk of my gown—fabric that matched the outfits of both Musetta and Alidoro. They were a strange sort of echo of the robes we used to wear in Cadenza Citadel. What I would have given to be back there, back home, in a land I knew well, in a place whose halls were familiar... "I worry still," I murmured to Hanna. "What will happen if the song never comes?"

"It *will* come." She gave my shoulder a firm pat. "You have met Caé. You found Her trustworthy, didn't you?"

I nodded.

"Then surely there is nothing to fear. And She has good reason to trust in *you*; I know it."

I trusted Caé, yes. It was myself I was less certain of.

The concert had come to an end; the courtiers politely applauded and tapped their feet. On the wooden stage along the back wall, the musicians took their bows and then slowly paraded off.

Maestra Theodora took her place on the stage. She was resplendent in pure white, her black hair arranged to match that of all the other Acutian noblewomen. As mine was now—made into a half-circle around my face by fluffing it out around a wire frame. I wished I could wear my hair loose; I wished my stays weren't too tight; I wished I did not have to wear this ridiculous hoop under my skirts to make my hips appear wider than my arm-span.

But the court composer didn't seem to mind her orna-mented hair or her heavy skirts. She grinned and gestured into the audience. "To pay tribute to Her Majesty," she said, "I present to you a great blessing from Our Mother Caé. I am delighted to introduce you to our honored guests: three Voices of the Goddess herself!"

The crowd gasped and whispered excitedly as Theodora swept an arm out to where the three of us were huddled in the wings. Alidoro gave a quick embrace to his composer,

Sidonie. Musetta kissed her wife. Then we walked out before the crowd.

We stood on the platform, the audience obscured by the bright flames of the candles along the edge of the stage. Theodora bowed to the three of us, and after we'd returned the gesture, she descended from the stage, giving us space.

Standing in front of a window at the back of the hall was another woman in white. She no longer kept her blond hair restrained in a casual plait, but wore it in elaborate waves and braids on the sides of her head, with large white feathers tucked into the back. The queen tipped her head back expectantly.

My stomach pinched together. Bile rose in my throat.

What was I to say? What was I to do? How could I explain my mission to her, to these people? How could I *convince* them of it? I'd never felt a terror such as this before. The stage was my haven. I could put my worried thoughts to sleep and let music overtake my body; I could become a beautiful instrument.

Now my voice was more than something pretty. More, even, than a weapon.

It was our last hope for peace.

Musetta sang a note. *Do.* The golden bracelets jangled on her wrist as she reached out and took my hand. The vibrations of her note thrummed through me. Maestra Theodora had written us a nice, pleasant trio, but that was not what we had decided to sing this night.

Alidoro harmonized with Musetta: *Mi.* He smiled, tears shimmering in his eyes, and slipped his hand into mine.

Sol, sang an invisible voice within me, completing the three-part harmony.

I opened my mouth, and unbidden, the words I'd been born to say spilled forth in a loud, commanding voice.

"These are the words of the Goddess," I declared. Hot anger flared up in my cheeks, unexpected, intense. Behind my eyelids, I saw the dead of Passaggio; the burned fields and orphaned children; the grave markers dotting the world like saplings. Every word I spoke, every song I sang, it would be for them. *"I, Caé, despise war. It is through order and harmony that I made the universe. This war you carry out over my land, it is not done in my name. I hate it!"*

The crowd gasped and murmured to one another. At the back of the room, Theodora covered her mouth, her eyes wide. The queen snapped her fingers and hissed something at her composer.

"I ask for peace!" I pled, my voice raw. My heart broke at the memory of tears in the eyes of the Goddess. *"Let my Singers sing to both nations, and I will end this conflict. Let them hear me, and let peace return to all three lands!"*

"Thank you!" came the overly loud voice of Theodora as she scurried onto the stage. "Thank you very much, Blessed Voices, for visiting our fair land! Please enjoy this party— we want you to enjoy all the treasures Acuto has to offer!" She placed a hand on my arm with a wide, strange smile, her eyes flashing. "Thank you very much!" She gave me the smallest of pushes.

The crowd pattered hesitant applause. Musetta grabbed my hand and pulled me off the stage.

"Now then!" declared Theodora, her voice breaking. "Her Majesty's orchestra will play a new piece I've written to celebrate her greatness!"

I shot a confused look at Musetta as we stood by the steps of the stage. Acutian courtiers murmured to one another. New music began, light and powerless.

"What do we do now?" I whispered. "They didn't listen to us at all!"

"I don't know," murmured Alidoro. His gaze was upon the queen, who stared icily back at us, her arms folded. A small group of guards in golden armor flanked her. "I think the intended audience has received the message quite clearly." He clenched and unclenched his fists by his side. "I do not suspect that Her Majesty is pleased by our words."

Maestra Theodora's gown fluttered like moth's wings as she raced to us, her hands against her heart. "My fellow musicians—forgive me, I was a bit startled by your message. I thought you would bring us an encouraging word tonight. A prayer for victory."

Musetta's fingers laced between mine. "No, Maestra," she said. "We are here to deliver the message of the Goddess. She asks for peace for all nations."

Theodora touched her hand to her lips, her brow knitted

in thought. "I see," she murmured. She glanced anxiously over her shoulder at her sovereign, and Maestras Hanna and Sidonie appeared at our side.

"You did wonderfully," Sidonie assured Alidoro.

"We'll see," he muttered.

Even as the orchestra played, courtiers glanced at us, their eyes narrowed. Some frowned. And there was fear in some of their eyes.

But these nobles, with their fine clothes and their revelry in this sparkling palace, they knew nothing of the war that was destroying the world. Our plea for peace meant nothing to them other than an interruption to their party.

If preventing war came at the cost of making a few nobles uncomfortable, I decided, I could bear it.

"Well," said Maestra Theodora, a strange, sideways smile on her face and her voice pitched too high, "please enjoy the party, anyhow! I'm certain the Goddess has much fortune in store for Acuto!" She curtsied deeply to us before dashing to Queen Mina's side, whispering something in her ear.

"Caé's plans never fail," Musetta reassured us, as if she could feel the doubt and the worry emanating from me.

I had once been so enchanted by ballrooms such as these. Now I could only watch the ticking hand of a golden clock upon the nearby mantel. Each minute was wasting.

The queen didn't speak to us for the rest of the night. The courtiers, too, were quite cold, but for the most part, we kept to ourselves. We were waiting for some message, some sign from Caé, some clear next step. But She, too, was quiet.

The end of the party brought me no relief. The palace had provided each of us with private chambers, their walls of dark, intricately carved wood. I could not admire this. I could only lie on the large bed, too tired to remove my ridiculous costume, gazing at the bloodred canopy above me.

"We delivered your message," I whispered to Caé. "But what good is it if they don't listen?"

I held my breath so that I could hear Her if She whispered in my ear—but the room was dark and still. Like this song She wanted me to compose, She seemed to be taking Her time.

So I waited. I waited for some instruction from Her until my eyelids drooped shut.

}

Hands grabbed me tight by the shoulders.

I gasped, and instinctively began thrashing about, but whoever stood above me was far stronger than I was. They roughly lifted me off the bed. As soon as I started to scream, a gag was tied around my head, pressed tight in my mouth like a horse's bit.

In the darkness and in my shock, the world moved quickly around me.

My captor wasn't alone; one of their partners—clad in

golden armor; a soldier?—tied my wrists and then kicked open the door to my bedroom. The men carrying me whisked me through the darkened corridor, fast and determined. The fine halls passed away, and the guards carried me down sloping stairs, until the walls, the floors, the ceilings were dark gray stone, trapping water between the cracks. The air was thick, filled with the scent of sewage and rust and decay.

I was carried into a small stone cell, and then I was tumbling—thrown to the hard, cold floor. I lifted my spinning head. There was barely any light but for the tiniest square cut out of the back wall, more of a keyhole than a window.

There were footsteps. I turned to the soft sound and saw a figure in the still-open doorway. In the thin beam of dawning light from my window, she was blinding and beautiful in her white gown.

The queen.

Two guards stood behind her, one bearing a candle. They strode into the room and slammed the door behind them. Now all four of us were in the little cell, breathing the clammy air.

In the candlelight, the queen's face was sharp and glowing as white-hot iron. Her blue eyes, turned yellow by the light, blazed down at me. She ripped the gag from my mouth.

"Who sent you?" she spat.

"Caé," I whispered.

She grabbed my face in her hand, a golden strand of hair fluttering before her eyes. "This is your last chance to tell me the truth. Are there more of you? How far does this conspiracy orchestrated by the Choirmaster extend?"

As much as I could, I shook my head. My voice came out small and faint. "None but Caé sent me, Majesty."

She pushed me away from her, knocking me back on the floor. The queen nodded to one of the guards, a woman with long lashes and large, bright eyes. The other guard grasped me from behind, my hair clenched in his fist. I gasped in pain. With the small bit of clarity I had, I prayed that the other Singers and Composers had not been taken also.

Desperately, I looked at the queen, trying to see the kindness in her, trying to see the softness that I'd seen in the Queen of Basso.

"I have met your sister!" I cried out, squeaky and desperate.

My heart quickened as the queen held up a hand, freezing the guards.

"Prove it," she said.

My mouth opened and closed, each movement aching as the guard pulled tight to my scalp. "She—she is with child. And she was very kind to me." When I blinked, the world shone through glimmering tears. "You two do not look much alike, but I pray that you share in her kindness. I do not believe she wanted this war, either—like Our Mother."

Queen Mina dropped her hand to her side. Her eyes narrowed into lines.

"It is a pity that I must fight against my sister," she said quietly, "but everything I do, I do for the good of my queendom and my people." She lifted her head and glanced at the guard on her right. "And for the good of both Acuto and Cadenza, I will ensure that those who blaspheme and challenge my authority will be forever silenced. I shall rule both nations, and I shall rule them well."

I gasped. The first guard uncorked a small bottle in her hand, and her partner gripped my jaw, opening my mouth. The queen's eyes remained fixed steadily upon me, much as Lucio once watched me, eager for me to sing my first note. For the first time, I saw her smile.

I tried to cry out to Caé, to sing one of Her songs, but I was able only to let out a feeble little bleat before the guard poured the contents of the bottle down my throat.

The drink was cold and bitter, old and moldy. It stuck to my throat, dried my mouth, made me choke. I coughed and coughed.

Queen Mina bent low, looking me in the eyes. Her eyes were more like those on a painting than a real person's—they were flat; lifeless.

I touched my burning throat. *What have you done to me?* I wanted to ask. But no sound escaped my lips. Again I tried; again, my voice was nothing; a pathetic, wheezing sound, like wind through trees.

She whispered to me in a slow, slithering voice, "Those who speak against Acuto will never speak again."

My blood turned to ice. Time seemed to halt altogether.

Voice of the Goddess, they called me.

And I could sing no longer.

VERSE NINETEEN

I woke to birdsong. Three notes, again and again.

I rubbed grit from my eyes and lifted my muzzy head from the hard stone that had served as my pillow. I had wept silently, had beaten my fists against the stones, had torn the silly ribbons and wires and false hair off my head until I finally felt like myself again. But a smaller, weaker version of myself. Incomplete. Broken. And I had fallen into a fitful, aching sleep.

My hands were white as bone in the tiny stream of sunlight. Seeing my fingers against the stones, my bed, I wondered if Mother and Father slept on floors such as these, too.

If they were still alive. If they still thought of me, as I thought of them, even in my most painful moments.

For a second, suddenly, it felt like the stone floor was trembling beneath me.

After a beat, I felt it again, the ground vibrating beneath my fingers. Not like an earthquake, but like a buzzing bee. Like—

There was an organ in the monastery nearest to my village. Mother had said that when she was pregnant with me, she would press her belly against the body of that organ and let me feel the vibrations.

I cupped my ear against the stone.

A woman sang, low and soothing, the same three notes as the birds out the window: C, A, E; C, A, E.

Elissa? Musetta's voice echoed in my mind. *Elissa, are you alive? I heard your cries...I believe I am below you. Are you in a cell, too?*

I gasped and touched the floor with my mouth as if to kiss it. My heart ripped in half—how sweet it was to hear Musetta's voice, but how horrible that she would be trapped as I was. When I tried to sing back to her, that same ugly, hissing sound escaped my lips. My throat ached. Tears dripped onto the floor.

Musetta's voice carried through my head, *Please, tell me if you're alive,* but I couldn't. I couldn't. My loudest scream came out as a coarse, broken whisper.

{

Time passed. The pinhole of sunlight moved across the floor, inch by inch.

The door opened, and I dreaded the next crust of bread they'd give me. Every bite and swallow was agony.

But a slim, golden-haired figure stood in the doorway. I raced into the back corner of the room, curling tight into a ball, my arms over my head.

"I'll not touch you again, Singer," said the queen,

snapping her fingers. I dared not lift my head as soldiers appeared behind her in the doorway. "We are leaving now for Mount Maestoso."

A man's hand wrapped around my wrist. A tiny wheeze of fear left my lips; I kept my other arm around my head, protecting me.

He dragged me into a hallway, the fragments of window light blazing compared to my cell. To our right stood the queen, dressed in armor made of a strange white metal, her hair in a tight braid down her back. She held a pair of white gloves in her hand and stared unwaveringly at Alidoro and Musetta, guards holding back the arms of each. Musetta's right eye was purple and swollen; Alidoro's face was bruised. Both of them had cloths wrapped tight across their mouths, silencing them.

The queen nodded to me. "Sing."

Music thrummed in my heart, pulsed in my throat, begged to soar from within me. My eyes stung with tears as I turned to my two friends, parting my lips.

Only a rasp came out, not even enough to form a word.

Alidoro's eyes squeezed tight, like my pain was his own. Musetta struggled against the guards holding her, grunting beneath her gag.

Queen Mina narrowed her eyes at Musetta. "This, too, shall happen to you, if you sing out of turn today. Do you understand?"

Musetta glared back at the queen. Alidoro sniffed, his head bowed; tears dripped from his glasses.

The queen snapped her fingers. "Come along."

The guard assigned to me held my hands in front of me and locked them together with metal cuffs. For the second time in a month, I was bound. And then we were led up, up, and up.

Daylight dazzled me. For a chilling moment, I was back in Basso, with light bouncing against snow and ice. I could hear the crunch of Lucio's boots in the snow—and then, all too quickly, they were replaced by the clicking of heels on marble.

The guards whisked us through halls, barreling us toward two soaring doors, open and spilling golden light onto the marble. In the main atrium stood three familiar faces: Hanna, Alidoro's composer, Sidonie; and Theodora. Hanna bore two pieces of paper in her trembling hands. Theodora's round face was deep red, and her hands were curled into fists.

She marched up to the queen. "Your Majesty, what is the meaning of this? Where have the Singers been?"

The queen narrowed her blue eyes. She might have been shorter than her composer, but she was nonetheless imposing. "Cadenzans will soon be my subjects, and they're no more Goddess-blessed than we are. We cannot let them think they are above us—or that their Choirmaster should reign over us."

Theodora thrust a trembling finger at us. "They speak for the Goddess!"

"What proof do we have of this?" snapped the queen. "Three strangers approach me with their demands as to how I am to run my queendom. They are but flesh and blood! They are my future vassals, and they will be punished as any conspirator ought to be."

Theodora clenched her jaw and strode up to Alidoro, wrenching the gag from his mouth.

He gasped and twisted his head toward me. *"Sol, Do, Re, Sol, Fa—"*

Queen Mina snapped her fingers—her habit, I was learning—and a guard struck Alidoro across the face, his glasses shattering as they hit the hard floor. The baritone struggled as the guard shoved the gag back into his mouth.

Another guard stood at Theodora's shoulder; Theodora gaped, her stare darting from the guard to her queen. "You cannot do this, Majesty—!"

"Stay and watch over the Composers," the queen said, softly and, somehow, utterly tenderly. "If you wish to pay tribute to Caé and show hospitality, show it to them. They pose no threat. They have not spoken out of turn." She threw me a dark look out of the corner of her eyes. "Maestra Hanna, give me that song you wrote me."

Sidonie and Hanna exchanged a quick glance before Hanna crossed the marble floors, her long black-and-silver braid swinging like a pendulum with every step. Her hands quivered as she held out the pages to the queen. Black dots across the five staves—the holy lines that circled Caé's brow in those paintings.

The queen accepted the sheet music with a smile. "There have been rumors of songs strong enough to starve entire villages," she murmured. She gave the pages in her hand a little shake. "Maestra Hanna promises me this song should bring the Bassan army to their knees—even faster than a famine would. I have word there will presently be an engagement between our armies at the foot of the mountain; *that* is where we will destroy them."

As the queen gave a page to Alidoro and to Musetta, Hanna's eyes were fixed upon her wife. Both of their faces were wet with tears.

"Sing the song," whispered Hanna. Her gaze whipped to me for a second, and then back to Musetta; she nodded slowly, her hands folded in prayer. "Sing *the* song."

Musetta and Alidoro looked at me.

Not the song in their hands.

My song.

The song I did not have. The song I could not sing.

Theodora strode toward me, carefully clinging to my bound hands. "Thank you for coming to our queendom," she whispered, very, very softly. "I'm so sorry that we did not listen to you."

I opened my mouth to thank her, but could say nothing—only make that thin hiss.

She frowned, touching a hand to her heart. Her black curls bounced as she turned her head sharply toward the queen. "Majesty? What's wrong with her voice?"

The queen tugged her gloves onto her pale hands. "She spoke blasphemy. So she will speak no more."

Theodora's eyes grew round. She trembled, and then she crumpled onto the marble, prostrating herself as in penitent prayer, her hands clutching tight to my blue skirts. She wept. "Oh, Caé, please, forgive us this grave sin! Have mercy upon us!"

Queen Mina held her head high and flicked her wrist. "Enough. We must arrive at the mountain before it's too dark." Out of the corner of her eye, she looked down upon her composer, still shaking with sobs. "When I return, Cadenza will be mine. You can go make a pilgrimage there; go see those fields they say She created—"

Theodora spat on the queen's shining white boots. "I want no gift of yours."

The queen shook her head like a horse flicking flies from its tail. She marched on through the doorway.

Hanna reached out to us as we were dragged away. "Musetta!" she cried, just as another guard pulled on her arm. After a yelp of pain, she shouted, "I love you!"

Musetta moaned from beneath her gag, more tears rolling down her cheeks.

They shoved the three of us into a carriage, a guard sitting with us, her eyes cold and her face flat and grim.

"Study the music," she instructed Musetta and Alidoro, sitting side by side across from us.

They looked at each other, then at me, desperation in their eyes. I had nothing to give them. No words. No music. No prophecy. Instead, I shut my eyes and turned away.

Musetta's hand touched mine. Beneath her gag, she made a soft, groaning sound. No, not a groan—a note.

C.

Her voice rang in my ear. *Did Caé warn you of this?*

I shook my head. Though I grimaced as I attempted the sound, I tried to hum like she did; just a soft, short note, so that the guard would not suspect we were making anything more than the odd, pained sounds of grief.

But no. All I could do was shake my head. I could not even speak to them in my thoughts.

Alidoro pressed his shoulder to Musetta's and hummed a soft note of his own. *When they take off our gags, we must sing to Elissa first. They won't know we're singing to heal her.*

I hung my head. Even if they healed me, it would be the three of us against the armies of Basso *and* Acuto. And where were the other Voices? We needed them, and yet we did not have them. Even if the twelve of us *were* together, what would it matter? Neither nation wished to listen to us. We had no plan. No hope.

Musetta nudged my ankle with her foot. I met her gaze. *Nothing is impossible for us,* she said. *You told me that we were part of Caé Herself. She speaks to us all the time. She visits us in our dreams. She comforts us. She rescues us.* Even with a gag in her mouth and her hands bound before her, Musetta's eyes crinkled in a tearful smile. *The queen is right. We have no proof that we are part of Caé. But the twelve of us, we know it's true. We are the song She wrote, and we will not end until She decides it's time.*

In the whole world, I was one of the only ones who could rightly picture Caé's human face. She wasn't blinding then. My eyes shut, I thought of Her in the form of that pilgrim, Her kind eyes, Her firm voice, Her warm embrace.

Friend of Caé. Promise of Caé.

A good friend keeps her promises, She'd once told me.

Alidoro leaned forward. *She said She'd give you a song. She will.*

Musetta nodded. *Let's pray. It's what we were made to do.*

Alidoro bent his head, allowing a Goddess Eye to swing from the cord on his neck and into his chained hands. Musetta, too, closed her eyes and bowed her head.

The three of us still connected, I could hear their whispered prayers, their pleas.

They couldn't hear my prayer, but they didn't need to. I only hoped Caé did. *Show us that goodness will triumph,* I begged her. *You who made birdsong, who made the sky, who saved me, who gave me my music, give me just one more song to sing. Give me the song you asked of me. I beg you. Keep your promise.*

The prayers of the other two Singers whispered and rushed in my mind as I looked out the window, watching grassy fields fade away into dry, cracked ground.

VERSE TWENTY

The air at the top of Mount Maestoso was painful to breathe, like shards of glass had been swept up in the dry wind. In the blazing orange glow of sunset, the sand and the rocks looked like liquid gold.

We stood at the crest of the peak, with the queen and her guards close behind us, and hundreds of soldiers and horses below, muskets and cannons and swords at the ready.

Far, far below, beyond the lines of men, a river raged on, coursing as loudly as the whipping wind around us. Percussion, courtesy of Caé. A small wooden bridge stretched thin between Acuto and Basso. The bridge was not used; not since the war started. But it would be today.

The queen extended a spyglass and looked at a mountain on the opposite side of the river: a Bassan mountain. Dotted with tall, fluffy pines, it seemed a world away. Sweat gathered all across my skin. My throat burned.

"They're coming," murmured the queen. "Get the Singers in formation and stand back."

Three guards came, one for each of us. They removed

Musetta's and Alidoro's gags, letting them hang around their necks like necklaces of cloth.

I, though? I bore no song.

The guards marched Musetta and Alidoro to the very edge of the cliff, and kept me back, near where the queen stood. I was only here for what I represented: the promise the queen would keep, should Alidoro or Musetta disobey.

We did not want to attack. We did not want this. Caé did not want this.

The sheet music in the Singers' clasped hands rippled like birds' wings in the wind. I looked to the orange sky.

Please, Caé. The time is now. I need your song.

I shut my eyes, cleared my mind; waited for Her voice, still and small or commanding and loud, but heard nothing.

"They're coming!" cried the queen.

On the other mountaintop, stark against the evergreens, several bright figures appeared one by one on horseback. Among the dark hair and bearded faces, I saw a pale boy, his long blond hair flowing across his cheek in the cutting wind.

Memories and songs exploded in my mind; a blow to my heart.

His hands against mine, showing me how to play a lute.

Him, dragging me roughly out of the king's room.

When I wept, and he whispered to me.

When he snapped at me.

The way he'd smiled as I sang back to him a new litany he'd written.

The song I'd first written, and first hidden from him.

Song of Restoration.

It had fused together the broken ice of the River Andante. It had helped a queen. It had healed Veronica—Caé Herself.

The song was clear in my mind, playing over and over, majestic, ringing like a deafening bell.

And I understood. Finally, I understood. It would restore the nations.

"*Sing now!*" snapped the queen. Alidoro and Musetta bowed their heads over their music.

My shoes scuffed forward in the sand. I opened my mouth, and amid the dry, coarse cords of my throat, a single strangled note burst forth.

Come to me, said Caé.

I sprinted across the sandy slope toward Alidoro and Musetta, ducking guards who grabbed for me. With my broken voice and my feeble tongue, with tears in my eyes and my hands in chains, I hummed my small, simple melody for the Voices. Musetta gasped, smiling. Alidoro watched intently; I could almost imagine him back in the monastery, hunched over his music again, taking notes.

Restore the nations, whispered Caé.

Note by note, my song did not hurt as much. A miracle, unfolding within me.

Alidoro nodded along, joining in on the final four notes. "*Let it be so,*" he sang.

Something dragged me backward and wrapped around

my neck like a snake. I gasped, my hands reaching up on their own accord to fight back.

"Be *still*," hissed the queen in my ear, her armored fingers on my throat.

Alidoro and Musetta continued my song, holding tight to each other's hands. This was the first time I'd heard anyone else sing my song, and it was perfect. Their voices bore different colors from mine: Alidoro's was the deep blue of the night sky; Musetta's, a delicious dark red, like a berry. The voices wound together—and then the song was gilt by a third.

A tall figure clothed in a pale gray coat stepped forward amid the hundreds of Acutian soldiers below. When I looked at the figure, far as they were, I felt no fear in my heart, but a strange, age-old longing, like homesickness. Like I was seeing a portrait of myself from years and years ago—or from the future. They opened their mouth and sang, a clear, honey-bright tenor, with spinning, quivering vibrato.

Ercole. The tenor, only a few years older than me. Their black hair, fashioned in thin braids and tied in a queue, fluttered in the breeze. They had grown since I'd seen them last; their face was sharper, and their eyes seemed darker. They must have traveled very far to reach us here—all to sing the song of peace with us.

In the monastery, they were quiet and thoughtful; they politely refused when the Choirmaster offered them solos. Now, they sang the song—my song—with a confident smile, unafraid of the soldiers watching.

"What's this?" growled the queen.

The three singers harmonized, the distance between them nothing. Ercole facing Acuto, Alidoro and Musetta facing Basso. They continued to sing the melody, which turned and wove, starting again and again like a circle with no beginning or end, even with the *Let it be so.*

"It's not working!" the queen whispered, her fingers tighter around my throat. Her hair flicked against my cheek as she turned her head back to the women behind her. "Prepare the cannons!"

The King of Basso waved a hand toward the soldiers behind him. They lifted their muskets, aiming them at Ercole. My stomach turned, and I pushed against the queen's hold, my eyes wide.

Lucio leapt from his horse, rushed across the snow— I even missed the quick, long strides he took!—and stood with his face to the muskets of Basso.

I let out a strangled scream.

The King of Basso held up a gloved hand, staring at Lucio. At his signal, all the soldiers lowered their muskets.

"Is this all your doing, Composer?" he snapped. Somehow— despite the distance—I heard him. I heard him by Her will, I knew.

Lucio's hair drifted in the wind. "This is the will of Caé. I will not let this song of Hers be broken."

Tears stung my eyes. Lucio, a hairsbreadth from death, from musket fire.

Then, far away, a soprano's voice floated above the melody, changing the song ever so slightly, lifting it higher, lining it with silver.

Below, on the banks of the river, two silhouettes dressed in the sapphire blue of Singers appeared, hand in hand by the rushes. *Susanna and Dorabella.* Susanna sang piercingly, sang high, and Dorabella's alto voice wove deeper notes into the great spell I had been given.

"Wait," said the Bassan king. He trudged closer to the edge of the cliff, despite the gasps and cries of protest from his generals and soldiers. His Majesty looked down at the plain, his gaze transfixed.

From below came another voice, and then another. One after the other; eleven in all.

Guglielmo's thundering bass, providing a foundation for the melody.

Tamino's noble, powerful tenor, a bolt of lightning.

Tisbe, Bartolo, Rinaldo, Fiordiligi.

All of them were here. They appeared from every compass point, in every kind of dress, in every sort of attitude, with every shade of emotion. They had answered the call.

The king gaped at the Singers far below. But the song was not working completely, I could tell—there was no golden light, no feeling of restoration, of peace. And the queen still stood behind me, unmoved, gripping me hard.

The song was not finished. The song was not working. Eleven voices united, eleven pieces of Caé, of myself—

It lacked *my* voice.

Once more, I opened my mouth and sang; a groaning, gravelly sound, like an old door swinging open.

The queen threw me onto the sand on my hands and knees. My head spun. Disoriented, dry-mouthed, and tired, still I sang—just barely sang—and I listened to the tapestry of sound that I'd helped weave together.

Twelve voices, crafting a new universe out of eight simple notes.

An older, worn part of myself wondered: *How can this be? How did they come to us in time?* And the newer, clearer voice in my head said: *I created this song; I created the time it breathes in. I have made all things possible. I have kept my promise to you.*

My heart leapt in my breast.

As our voices intermingled, I felt more like myself than ever before. I was beautiful; radiant, confident, perfect—holy. And finally, something heavy rested in my chest, burning like a comforting fireplace.

Turn around, Caé Elissa.

I obeyed, looking back at the queen. Her eyes burned at me.

Caé's voice rang clear in my head, and I felt Her standing at my shoulder, as a comrade, as a friend. *I want you to sing to her.*

I nodded once. My throat no longer ached. I could sing again. She had fully healed me. I sang the song, my song, our song, Her song.

"Let it be so!" I sang. *"Let it be so!"*

The queen's eyes grew round, and her mouth fell open. She dropped to her knees, her sword tumbling out of her hand and onto the sand.

"Your Majesty?" an archer at her side cried, lowering the arrow she had nocked for me.

I began the song again, my voice braiding with the others'. Golden light poured from my mouth and from my hands, no longer bound by chains. As our song grew, crescendoed, magnified, immense relief washed over me in a warm flood. Lightning crackled in the air; thunder echoed a marvelous refrain.

"Let it be so," I sang in twelve voices, and as the final note ricocheted across the two mountains, the two nations, both armies fell to their knees. I stood gleaming as a star, as a beacon to keep the lost on their path. All could see and hear me.

"Again and again, I have asked for peace between you," I said, each of my Voices speaking as one. Many of the soldiers watching bowed their heads; many others wept. *"This war you fight in my name is an abomination. Whoever wishes to commit bloodshed does not do so in my name."*

There was a small, fragile voice from behind. I turned and saw the Queen of Acuto, pale and weak. "If—if you really are the Goddess," she gasped, "prove that this isn't just some trick of your music magic."

Rage flared in me, spreading like tremors through all of my Voices.

"If you really are Caé," she continued, kneeling there in the sand, "you would be grateful for all that we did on your beha—"

"*Be silent!*" I roared, and stretching out my hand, I stilled her voice. Her pupils shrank. She gasped, clutching her throat, but when her mouth moved, she was silent. "*Do you believe me now?*" I asked. "*Do you believe the Voices who speak on my behalf?*"

She nodded tremulously, holding out her clasped hands. Her cheeks were bright pink, shining with tears. Then the queen touched her throat, as if asking for her words back.

"*You tortured my Singer,*" I said, plain and firm. "So consider my judgment a mercy: for what you have done, you will never speak again."

I faced the King of Basso. On his hands and knees, he shook like a leaf in the wind.

"*You also wished to use my Voice for evil,*" I reminded him. "*In turn, you, too, will speak no longer.*"

All twelve Voices lifted a hand, delicate as a composer holding out a *fermata*. "*I wanted you to rule this world justly. To rule with love and sagacity. But you forget quickly. You forget how I made you to love peace.*"

The soldiers behind him considered themselves then to be nothing more than rocks and trees; only scenery in something far greater. But no. I wished more of them. And I wished for them to go home to their families. To live in my creation. To rest.

"You all must bear witness to what you've seen and heard this day," I declared. "And you all must acknowledge your part in this war. You are my dearest children, but you put justice and brotherhood too easily out of your minds. Pass down this story to your children. Let them know why the three nations live in peace. And let them know I love them."

Once more, I looked at the small king and queen with the twenty-four eyes of the Voices. "Children, when I gave you those crowns, I did so because I wanted to share my world with you. I did not wish to play the song of this world on my own—only to conduct it. I wished to watch you play it. You have fought this senseless war over what you call Caé's Land. But you forget…"

With my hands, I reached to the Bassan mountain, pulling at the earth and drawing out full-grown trees from where there were weeds before. Then I twisted my hands, sang a soft melody, and in the sandy Acutian foothills I formed a small lake where there had once been nothing. The soldiers— and the leaders they had so feared—all quaked before me.

"It is not Cadenza that is the land of the Goddess. Every inch of this world is mine."

They had forgotten how I'd hoped for this world to be. A place filled with miracles and song. Not shouting. Not fighting. Not death.

"I will choose a new ruler for Cadenza."

Both armies stirred. The Acutian queen and the Bassan king watched me with hungry, desperate eyes.

"I will choose," I continued, *"once Basso and Acuto have maintained peace between them for twelve years."*

It wasn't the answer any of them wanted. But neither side was more worthy of ruling Cadenza. It had never really belonged to them at all.

"For twelve years my Choirmaster will oversee Cadenza. And I will send my Voices back out into the world. They will share my power with everyone—without hindrance or persecution."

The King of Basso hid his face from me. His shoulders shook with tears.

"I gave you your crowns," I declared. *"I can take them away just as easily."*

I could hear the fear in his ragged breaths; I could see the sweat sparkling on the queen's brow. Their thoughts were muddled and terrified. They no longer felt invincible.

As my threat rang through the valley, I felt a tugging on my heart, in the direction of Mount Brio. It was the part of me that longed to go there. With Elissa, I followed the pull of the music inside me, the voice telling me, *One more thing.* Across the bridge, onto the cold Bassan cliffside.

There was someone she longed to see. Something she longed to say.

"Lucio Arioso," I said.

The boy with the long white-blond hair lifted his eyes to me. Tears were little beads of crystal on his pale face.

"I thought you—Elissa—I thought she was dead," he whispered, tears spilling into his mouth.

"*You were supposed to protect my Singer,*" I said. "*To love her. To teach her. Instead, you abandoned her. You made her doubt herself. Therefore, you made her doubt me.*"

He squeezed his eyes shut, bowing his head, thinking, *I deserve to die.*

"*Elissa shall decide what you deserve,*" I told him.

Shutting my eyes, I sang the last four notes of her song, our song, my song: *Let it be so!*

One by one, each Voice finished their note. Mine was the last, ringing and bright as a silver bell.

Lucio was bowed, his shoulders quaking as he sobbed. "I'm sorry," he whispered, again and again like a litany. "I'm so sorry."

He had made me doubt myself. He'd claimed to protect me. He'd told me my compositions, my gifts from the Goddess, were wicked. That my Voice was all that I was.

But I understood now. I was Caé. I was Elissa. Friend and Promise.

I was beside him, suddenly, the wet of the mountain mud going straight through my thin dress and against my knees. I remembered first entering Basso; Lucio played Cadenzan songs on his lute to help me sleep, carrying a bit of our homeland with us just to comfort me.

I lifted his chin, damp with tears.

"I forgive you," I said.

He blinked, his green eyes childlike, confused, terrified. "What?"

I kissed his forehead. "She is not just Caé the Wrathful."

Lucio was part of me, too; he also bore Caé's music. He had the stubbornness that She had. He, like Her, like me, *created*, and he found joy in that. And he wanted to know Her. He fought so desperately for Her love—and yet he did not realize that She'd always been with him!

"She wanted me to tell you something," I murmured. "She wanted you to look to the sky."

His head still in my hands, he glanced up.

A mountain swift streaked across the deep-red sky. He gasped, and his face crumpled with tears.

"Why did She ask that of you?" I whispered.

Lucio shuddered, wiping his eyes, keeping his head bowed and his gaze lowered. "For—for years, I've begged Her for a sign. I said, take the form of a swift, if...if..."

"If what, Lucio?"

He sniffed and clutched his hands against his heart. He bore a small, glorious smile. "If She still loved me."

FINALE

In Cadenza, my homeland, the air was no longer sweet. The fragrance of flowers was tinged with only the faint bitterness of ash. The birdsong had stilled. The clover and grass were dead, burned, torn up. The land bore deep wounds, bleeding as the two kingdoms had tried and failed to call her their own.

Melody and Blossom brought the carriage to a slow stop just outside a large field. It was whole, but it was ugly; the grass was sparse and yellowed, not the beautiful emerald shade I remembered.

I hopped out of the carriage. Nothing looked as it should, but the soft earth beneath my feet felt familiar. This was *home.*

But no. Not quite.

An old black fence edged the field, with iron bars in five lines like the five staves on sheet music. A place surrounded by music; surrounded by holiness.

A place I never wanted to visit.

Lucio left his post in the driver's seat and stood before me. He had changed so much, so quickly. His chemise was plain, his breeches were old—but a lovely Cadenzan blue—and his green vest was decorated in golden thread, lovingly embroidered by his mother's hands. The dark Bassan clothing had all been discarded.

When he was near me, he always had a bit of a slouch to his posture, as if he was ready to bow at any moment. When he spoke to me, his words were quiet, careful, and soft. At first, he was too afraid to talk to me at all. But on our journey back to Cadenza, we slowly remembered who we were before this journey began. Two children who loved music, their home, and each other.

"Elissa," he said. For the first few days after my *Song of Restoration*, he'd called me *Blessed Goddess, Caé Almighty, Holy Voice*—perhaps it was being here in our birthplace that made him see me as myself again. "Elissa, are you *certain* you want to do this?"

I nodded, but had no certainty within me. My heart was lodged in my throat. Tears made the world fog up around me. My lip trembled.

He fished a handkerchief out of the pocket of his vest, pressing it into my hand. I let out a meager thanks and dried my eyes. It was a futile effort. Suddenly, I was crying, and I couldn't stop. I wanted to feel safe. I wanted to feel warm. I wanted to feel *loved*. I held out my arms, and Lucio hugged me tight. I wept against him.

"I did everything She asked," I said between sobs. "I tried every day to obey!"

Lucio pulled back a fraction, and my heart dipped within my chest. I almost feared that he'd scold me. But there was sadness in his eyes.

"Of course you did. You saved Her *world*, Elissa. Why would you even think that you weren't enough?" The light of realization sprang into his eyes. His brow crumpled. "You think *that* is why your parents died? Because you were disobedient somehow?"

"That *is* why they died!" I scrubbed my sleeve against my eyes. "That day in the market, I was supposed to keep quiet, but I *sang*, and they arrested Mother and Father, and they *died* in jail! And I've done a thousand other things besides—"

"No." He bent his knees, meeting my eyes. "You've shown me how much Caé loves us. How kind She is. She wouldn't punish you so cruelly for something you did as a child."

I thought back to the words of the Church, of the old Composer who had welcomed me at the door over five years ago. "Then it was a punishment for them," I choked. Tears rolled down my cheeks. "That must be it. Why else would they be dead? *Why?*"

He shook his head. "I cannot say why. But you...you are Her voice. She told you once to listen to yourself. What does that voice say?"

I stood there, his hands against my arms, and listened close to the quiet world around me. The wind rushing through the trees. Soft as a whisper. Soft as a lullaby. I thought of my parents, how they'd held me close; how they'd taught me to sing; how they'd shielded me from every harm. They had even shielded me from the Church, when they feared I'd be taken away too young.

Love, I thought. *All that they did, it was love. Even their hiding me.*

"I—I don't think they sinned, when they hid me away," I whispered. "They just loved me. And that's not wrong."

Lucio nodded slowly, a cautious smile crossing his lips. "Then there was no punishment."

I looked past him to the cemetery, still holding on to his arm. "Will you come with me?" I asked. "You're all the family I have now, Lucio."

He laid his hand atop mine. "Of course."

Past the iron gate. Past the dying grass. Past the sticks shoved into the ground, round stones before them etched with names.

Lucio found my parents for me.

They were buried together, just one rock and one stick marking where they lay. I knelt on the dirt above them and clutched the earth with my hands.

Cadenza had suffered. Blood stained her beautiful fields. Homes had been lost; lives had been lost. And my parents were gone.

Five years had passed since I'd seen them. I wished they could see me; I *hoped* they could see me from the heavens, see how I had grown. See that their love had sustained me.

See that I had never forgotten them. See that I had never stopped singing, their very first gift to me.

I wanted to give them a song.

That ancient, mysterious voice spoke within me. I couldn't help but smile, even though my face was stained with tears.

"I can write songs," I whispered to them. "I wrote this one. And I'll sing it for you. I've gotten much better since we parted."

The voice said one more thing: it reminded me of something Caé had whispered to me in a dream.

I looked up at Lucio, who kept a respectful distance. "Would you sing my *Song of Restoration* with me?"

His eyes grew round. "It—it wouldn't be any good. My voice is, is poor, and unsanctified—"

"She told me She loves your voice," I said.

He didn't have anything to say to that. The Composer knelt beside me on the earth and cleared his throat.

"On your cue, then," he murmured.

I shut my eyes and breathed in the cool Cadenzan air. Singing the first note, slowly and carefully, I could suddenly feel the presence of other Voices. I could see their faces in my mind. Pulling on my heart, they felt the same sorrow I did.

And they were ready to sing the same song.

Once more, I sang the *Song of Restoration,* but this time, I wasn't alone.

I sang it beside the River Andante, where clover began to grow along the riverbanks.

I sang it in the heat of Acuto; flowers and grass and trees slowly blooming out of the parched earth.

I sang it in an empty, heartbroken village in the mountains of Basso. Violets and daisies and roses and forget-me-nots blossomed up through the pavement, across buildings, over the old well.

In twelve different places, small meadows grew in time with my voices: a bit of springtime coming from nothing.

In a graveyard in war-torn Cadenza, a young Composer sat beside me, singing my song, feebly and beautifully all at once. He held my left hand and sang those ancient words, the ones Mother and Father had taught me, the ones he had taught me; the ones I had taught myself.

Beneath my fingers, pink Giacomo flowers grew up from the ground. Flowers spread through the whole field, every color, small and budding, just blooming. A new song, just beginning.

 Acknowledgments

My creative world is built on such a firm foundation of love and support and cheerleading.

To my family: Mom and Dad, thank you for helping me thrive in my writing. Myles, thank you for how you make me laugh. Mr. Bingley and Cosette, I don't know what I did to deserve such great dogs, but I'm grateful. And especially to Jennifer, who taught me how to be a writer, who encouraged me even when I was twelve, and who showed me that dialogue needs quotation marks.

To Annie and Andy, for our imaginary games. To Brenna, Claire, Kristin, Emma, Bryn, Morgan, Rachel, Ana, Hannah, Ellen, Ashley, Mackenzie, Elise, Victoria, Jenny, Jennie, and Jenni, thank you for passing my stories around the lunch table and asking me for more. To Chrissy, Maggi, and Audrey, for calling me a writer and helping me grow up to love that about myself. To April, who left an encouraging note in my locker after I won a poetry slam, and then cheered with me when this book found a home. To Christina, who so generously shared her time and her music knowledge with me! And to my awesome teachers, Mrs. Bye, Dr. Holly, Mr. Hughes, Mrs. Heyse, Mr. Knerr, Dr. Gibson, and Mr. Talley, for building a young writer's confidence.

To my High Point team: Becca, Sarah, Little Sarah, Anna, Lisa, Señora, Profe Winkel, Dr. Leclercq and Dr. Leclercq, Sra. Parker, Dr. Llorens, Dr. Carrón, Dr. de Nicolas, Dr. Femenias, Dr. Headman, Dr. MacLeod, Dr. Crump, Dr. Alexander, and all the awesome staff at the library, thank you for letting my little music nerd heart shine and prosper.

To my French family, *je vous aime.* I'm so grateful for you. I miss you extraordinarily. Orphée and Alexis, Amna, Charlotte, Caroline, Corinne, Fanny, Marion (and Marceau, Colette, Lison, and Fifi). A special *merci* to Fred, Théo, and Alcides, who gave me a home in France and a place to write this book.

To my literary team, Devin, Mora, and Jordan, I am so lucky to have you fighting for me and helping my stories be the best they can be.

To my writing family: the journey to getting a book published is scary and full of so many unknowns. You were a safe place for me to find kindness and support. Thank you, Nikhi, Shelby, Alyssa, Jenna, Kalie, Susan, Emily, Zoe, Madi, Kathryn, Cass, Erin, Darielle, Ennis, Amelia, Maria, J. Elle, Taylor, Riza, Carrie, Lorelei, Allison, Ive, Vika, Isabel, Lyndall, Sarah R., Eva, Elizabeth, Kim, Ez, Abigail, Stephanie, and ALL the readers and CPs. And a special thank-you to Kelsey, who is always ready to answer an obscure history question.

To my Llamasquad: Mary, Katy, Rachel, Jania, Jacy, Alaysia, CT, Sarah Jane, Makayla, Megan, Gabriela, Rina, Cyla, Katie, Kiana, Nicole, Susan, Katherine, Lillie, Ashley, Melissa,

Marissa, Loie, Adriëlle, Trisha, Sabrina, Lenore, Erin, Dory, Lisa, Ash, Sarah, Rochele, Christine, and Rae: you are all marvels.

To Lucy, the most incredible cheerleader. Thank you for holding my hand tight and never letting go.

To God, for everything.